MISS BRAITHWAITE'S FOLLY

The wealthy and willful Miss Minerva Braithwaite had every reason to beware of Lord Dominic Claireux—for on their first meeting he shamelessly showed himself in a shocking state of undress. Soon afterward, Minerva learned of a scandalous event that threatened to make him a social outcast. And, more vexatious than anything, this unrepentant reprobate made it clear he was passionately in love with another woman.

Why the beautiful Minerva wished to wed a man with such obvious impediments was a mystery. Nevertheless, what Minerva wanted, she always found a way to get—for better or worse. . . .

About the Author

SHEILA WALSH lives with her husband in Southport, Lancashire, England, and is the mother of two daughters. She began to think seriously about writing when a local writers' club was formed. After experimenting with short stories and plays, she completed her first Regency novel, *The Golden Songbird*, which subsequently won her an award presented by the Romantic Novelists' Association in 1974.

Dear Reader:

As you know, Signet is proud to keep bringing you the best in romance and now we're happy to announce that we are now presenting you with even more of what you love!

The Regency has long been one of the most popular settings for romances and it's easy to see why. It was an age of elegance and opulence, of wickedness and wit. It was also a time of tumultuous change, the beginning of the modern age and the end of illusion, when money began to mean as much as birth, but still an age when manners often meant more than morality.

Now Signet has commissioned some of its finest authors to write some bigger romances—longer, lusher, more exquisitely sensuous than ever before—wonderful love stories that encompass even more of the flavor of this glittering and flamboyant age. We are calling them "Super Regencies" because they have been liberated from category conventions and have the room to take the Regency novel even further—to the limits of the Regency itself.

Because we want to bring you only the very best, we are publishing these books only on an occasional basis, only when we feel that we can bring you something special. The first of the Super Regencies, *Love in Disguise* by Edith Layton, was published in August to rave reviews and has won two awards. It was followed by two other outstanding titles, *The Guarded Heart* by Barbara Hazard, published in October and *Indigo Moon* by Patricia Rice, published in February. Watch for future Signet Super Regencies in upcoming months in your favorite bookstore.

Sincerely,

Hilary Ross

Hilary Ross
Associate Executive Editor

Minerva's Marquess

Sheila Walsh

A SIGNET BOOK

NEW AMERICAN LIBRARY

NAL BOOKS ARE AVAILABLE AT QUANTITY DISCOUNTS WHEN USED TO PROMOTE PRODUCTS OR SERVICES. FOR INFORMATION PLEASE WRITE TO PREMIUM MARKETING DIVISION, NEW AMERICAN LIBRARY, 1633 BROADWAY, NEW YORK, NEW YORK 10019.

SIGNET TRADEMARK REG. U.S.PAT.OFF. AND FOREIGN COUNTRIES
REGISTERED TRADEMARK—MARCA REGISTRADA
HECHO EN CHICAGO, U.S.A.

SIGNET, SIGNET CLASSIC, MENTOR, ONYX, PLUME, MERIDIAN, and NAL BOOKS are published by NAL PENGUIN INC., 1633 Broadway, New York, New York 10019

First Printing, May, 1988

1 2 3 4 5 6 7 8 9

PRINTED IN THE UNITED STATES OF AMERICA

1

AS THE traveling coach splashed and rumbled its way through the late February mizzle, Miss Minerva Braithwaite, daughter of the late Hezekiah Braithwaite of Leeds, let down the window and, with one hand clutching the brim of an exceedingly stylish bonnet, demanded in clear incisive tones: "Joshua, can you not coax at least a semblance of life out of that misbegotten pair you allowed yourself to be fobbed off with at the last change? At this rate we shall never reach Uncle Richard's before nightfall, let alone visit Claireaux, and that I am determined to do."

The muttering up front was correctly interpreted as a surly invitation to a just and impartial Maker to vent his wrath upon all impatient mistresses, and roads so full of potholes that they were like to have everyone plunged into the ditch at any minute. Said Maker was likewise called upon to bear witness to the weakening effect of being obliged to drive for such a long period on an empty stomach.

"Humgudgeon!" came the unfeeling retort. "Pa had this carriage specially built for rough driving—and as for your stomach, the Ordinary you put away not two hours ago should keep you going for a good while yet."

As she snapped the window shut, Miss Braithwaite

heard the unmistakable swish of the whip, and a moment later the coach jerked forward, depositing her unceremoniously in her seat and sending her companion, Mrs. Peach, whose short legs did not quite reach the floor, bouncing back among the squabs. The third occupant of the carriage tightened her already compressed lips on a groan and clasped her hands with ever-increasing urgency across her middle.

Mrs. Peach restored her spectacles, which had shot to the end of her nose with the sudden movement, and eyed Minerva's maid with some misgivings. "My dear," she ventured in gentle reproof, "poor Matthews is looking quite unwell. You don't think perhaps that this—" she almost said fixation, but thought better of it—"this determination of yours to visit Claireux might be set aside in view of the inclement weather, to say nothing of the lateness of the hour. In truth, we have been so long on the road that Sir Richard must by now be wondering where we are . . ." Her voice trailed away as she perceived through the gloom the pugnacious thrust of Minerva's chin.

"Matthews is frequently unwell when we travel, but you always survive, don't you, Mattie?" An encouraging smile accompanied the bracing words which were acknowledged by a fractional movement of the maid's tightly pressed lips. Minerva leaned forward to peer out of the window. "However, you may rest easy, for I believe we are almost there. I haven't been this way in years, but I am almost sure the road has just entered Claireux woods." The window was lowered again. "Joshua, look out for a pair of great stone gateposts topped by eagles." She turned back to Mrs. Peach with renewed enthusiasm. "Do you know, I used to have nightmares about those eagles when I was very small?" Her laugh rang out merrily. "How odd to think that I might very soon be calling them my own!"

Mrs. Peach felt a sudden lurch of apprehension not wholly due to the abruptness with which Joshua took the turn into the driveway between two massive pillars of stone, whose rustling ironwork gates hung open to the world. Minerva was so very much her father's daughter, and proud to be thought so, but what was allowable in a man, and a hard-headed Yorkshireman at that, could never be thought proper in a young lady. Indeed, the very shrewdness and ability to drive a hard bargain which had made Hezekiah one of the richest men in England would almost certainly, in his daughter, prove quite ruinous to the highly ambitious matrimonial expectations she entertained. It was entirely Hezekiah's fault, of course, Mrs. Peach reflected crossly—filling the girl's mind with education better suited to a man, to say nothing of giving her false notions of her rightful place in the world. That Minerva was also, if not precisely beautiful, at least strikingly handsome and, apart from a certain stubbornness, of a generous and sweet-natured disposition, only made matters worse.

Mrs. Peach sighed. Life seemed destined never to be easy. When her beloved husband, the Reverend Mortimer Peach, had passed on and Hezekiah Braithwaite had suggested that she might care to act as companion to his daughter and take up residence in his fine spacious mansion just south of Leeds, overlooking the valley which incorporated her late husband's parish, it had seemed nothing short of an act of Providence. Minerva was already dear to her, being the daughter of one of her closest girlhood friends, Emily Standish. Both she and Emily had, in the eyes of the world, married beneath them, but where hers had been an idyllic union eagerly sanctioned by parents with five daughters to bestow, poor Emily had been less fortunate.

Sir Edwin Standish had not gone so far as to disown her when she had rather surprisingly declared her love for the blunt-spoken but exceedingly wealthy mill owner, but he had never ceased to make his daughter aware of how low she had sunk, which, when one considered the number of times Hezekiah had rescued Sir Edwin from dun territory, struck even the essentially charitable Esmeralda Peach as little short of monstrous ingratitude.

Poor Emily! She had proved too frail to long withstand the constant acrimony between husband and father, and was dead within three short years, leaving Hezekiah alone with only a daughter in place of the son he had so sorely wanted. Not that he had loved the child any the less; he had simply chosen to ignore her sex and had reared her to be as clever and ambitious as himself, ruthlessly supplementing the inadequacies of a succession of governesses, none of whom pleased him, by teaching her how to keep a set of books and balance accounts. Finally, he sent her to a select seminary where Minerva received the polish necessary to help her attain that position of which marriage to him had so cruelly robbed her mama, namely a place in society.

It was upon Minerva's return from this no doubt excellent establishment that Mrs. Peach had taken up her appointed task, still blithly unaware of Hezekiah's plans for his daughter. Indeed, it had seemed at first that he was intent only upon assuring himself that in her time away, she had lost none of her business acumen, which seemed so odd when it had just cost him a prodigious amount of money having her initiated into the delicate art of leading a useless life. It was in fact Minerva herself who had blithely intimated to Mrs. Peach how, with so many members of the aristocracy finding themselves in queer street as a result of the late war against Napoleon, her papa had every expectation of securing for her a husband among their ranks; how he was at that very moment exploring various possibilities through the good offices of his lawyer and of his late wife's elder brother, Richard, who had cherished a soft spot for his young niece. That Hezekiah had passed away himself before anything of a definite nature could be accomplished had seemed yet again to Mrs. Peach like divine intervention, but she had reckoned without Minerva's determination in proceeding to carry through her father's plans.

Mrs. Peach roused herself from her introspection to find that they were driving along a winding avenue of ancient beech trees whose massive trunks supported an intimidating tangle of bare branches to form a macabre archway above them, dripping water with funereal monotony on the carriage roof.

"At last. That must be the house, over to the right," Minerva exclaimed, a note of satisfaction entering her voice as they drew nearer. "A decided air of neglect, wouldn't you say?"

Mrs. Peach peered through the misted windows and was just able to make out a rather nicely proportioned shooting lodge standing amid unkempt gardens, its stone walls webbed with the skeletal remains of last autumn's creeper, its windows staring out blank and black.

She shuddered and suggested faintly. "Perhaps there is no one in residence, dear."

"But that wouldn't make sense. The marquess must certainly be here—Uncle Richard has seen him several times since Christmas—and he would hardly choose to leave now. They have an appointment to meet tomorrow."

"Yes, indeed," Mrs. Peach sighed. "I had forgot."

Joshua had brought the carriage to a halt before a curving flight of shallow stone steps, and could be heard laboriously clambering down from his perch. A sense of urgency born of despair seized Mrs. Peach.

"My dear Minerva, are you quite certain that this is a good idea?" She braved the frowning glance that reminded her so forcibly of Hezekiah to continue, "I mean . . . it will appear so odd, our calling in this way. The marquess might decline to receive us."

"Of course he will receive us. I shall refuse to leave until he does so."

Such decisiveness quite daunted Mrs. Peach, and any further discussion on the subject was thankfully precluded by a sudden rush of cold air as Joshua flung open the carriage door, so wrapped in garments that he resembled nothing so much as a brown bear in a beaver hat, an illusion given added credence by his labored grunts as he helped his mistress and Mrs. Peach to descend. This accomplished, he left Matthews to fend for herself while he preceded the ladies to the front door where he hung upon the bell pull, cocking an ear for sounds of movement within.

"Summun's cummin', " he muttered at last.

An ancient portico sheltered them from the worst of the weather as a great number of locks and bolts in urgent need of greasing, scraped and squealed protestingly. Finally the door opened some six inches or so to show a face like a yellow wrinkled pear illumined by the flickering light of a kitchen candle.

Minerva thrust her card into the gap. "Miss Braithwaite to see the Marquess of Claireux," she said crisply.

The apparition at the door blinked rapidly several times as he peered at the card and then at the young lady, elegant in her bronze green pelisse and bonnet, flanked on the one side by a short plump lady in a voluminous cloak and some kind of serving wench, and on the other by a mammoth of a man.

"His lordship en't receiving . . ." he began, but got no further as, at a nod from Minerva, Joshua leaned on the door. The small man fluttered back in alarm, the door swung wide, and Minerva, in a manner which would have delighted her deportment teacher, Miss Pakenham, drew herself up to an imperious five feet seven inches and swept into the hall.

"Be so good as to present my card to his lordship and tell him that I will not keep him above a minute," she informed the bemused servant while her glance flicked around the dim comfortless hall illumined by a single candle sconce above the empty hearth. "Joshua, you and Matthews had better remain here." Her glance returned to the servant. "There is, presumably, a room where I may wait in more comfort?"

By now completely demoralized, the man looked

about him and finally muttered, "There's a bit of a fire in the morning room . . ."

"Good. Pray take us there at once." She smiled at him. It was like a sudden shaft of sunlight piercing the gloom, and any further objections dried in his throat as he led the way across the echoing hall and ushered her into the morning room with Mrs. Peach close on her heels. Then, forgetting to close the door, he tottered away toward the opposite end of the hall beyond the exquisitely carved dark oak staircase.

Minerva watched him disappear from view and then turned her attention to her present surroundings. The room was neither large nor impressive, and what little light there was came from the fast fading daylight augmented by a few feeble flames struggling for existence in the huge black grate. A great many large and depressing pictures, which seemed to depict the dead of night, made the dark wall coverings even gloomier. "Quite beautifully run down," she observed, sounding remarkably cheerful. "Do sit down, dear ma'am, if you can find a chair that pleases you." She cast her eyes over the furniture. "That wing chair close to the fire seems reasonably sound. It is probably the one most used by the marquess."

Mrs. Peach sank into it with gratitude, though she still looked apprehensive. "But what of you, my love?"

"Oh, I couldn't sit!" Minerva bent to take a taper from a vase in the hearth. She thrust it into the flames and crossed to light a branch of candles standing on an oval table nearby. "There, that is better. Do you know, I really believe Lord Claireux might be the very person we are looking for. I mean, we know for a start that he is not above thirty, and although he might well be tall, weedy, and chinless, or even stout and bucolic, I hope I am reasonable enough to know that one cannot have everything. In any event, he must be an improvement upon Sir Arthur Peveral." She shook her head. "Uncle Richard let me down badly there . . . robust middle age, he told me, and what did we find? Sixty, if he was a day, and a dullard into the bargain! The situation could have been quite embarrassing. So, this time I mean to see for myself before negotiations even begin!" Mrs. Peach uttered something between a whimper and a moan, which her enthusiastic companion took for assent. "Also, there is a decided atmosphere of neglect about this place which augurs well . . . one could not but notice it immediately. First impressions are so important, don't you think?"

Mrs. Peach was mercifully spared from offering her opinion by the sounds of activity beyond the door—a kind of subdued bellowing. Minerva lifted a wry eyebrow. "Stout and bucolic?" she suggested softly.

Her companion swallowed, dry-mouthed, and as the banging of a door was followed by the sound of feet thudding dully across the hall, thought comfortingly of Joshua waiting within hailing distance. A moment later, their own door was pushed wide, and for perhaps the first time in her life, Mrs. Peach saw Minerva deprived of speech.

A bare-footed giant clad in nothing but a pair of close-fitting black unmentionables appeared to fill the doorway, his dark head just skimming the lintel. His torso, amber-tinted in the candlelight, glistened with perspiration, wide shoulders tapered to a narrow waist, to a stomach as flat as a washboard, while the aforesaid unmentionables more than hinted at the muscles in his long horseman's legs. For what seemed like a lifetime he remained there, unmoving, one hand negligently resting for support against the lintel, the other trailing a white towel. Black eyes blazing beneath lowered brows examined Minerva with unhurried thoroughness from top to toe until she felt herself turning pink. Finally he leaned forward and her fine-cut sensitive nostrils detected the unmistakable aroma of brandy. Oh, dear—the marquess, for it could be no other, was clearly more than halfway disguised, which must surely account for his appearing before them in a state of undress guaranteed to put any genteel lady to the blush. She stole another look at him from beneath veiled lashes—he certainly did have a splendid physique, but that was not why her cheeks had grown warm; she was ashamed to admit even to herself that it had been from quite another cause altogether. No man had ever looked at her as he had done—as though he were mentally undressing her, slowly and quite deliberately. The mere thought of it made her hot and angry again, whether with him or with herself, she could not be sure, but she was determined that he should pay for his insolence.

"Madam," he said with deceptive calm, "I trust you have a good and valid reason for this intrusion. I am not accustomed to being summarily commanded to appear in my own morning room."

A small, indistinguishable sound from Mrs. Peach drew his frowning glance and gave Minerva valuable moments in which to collect her wits, and even to doubt the wisdom of trusting to impulse. But a kind of recklessness now held her in thrall and seemed to produce an irresistible excitement all of its own.

"I am sorry if my request appeared somewhat peremptory," she said with as much authority as she could muster. "The truth of the matter is that I found myself in the neighborhood, and must confess that I succumbed to . . . I suppose you might call it curiosity."

His face darkened alarmingly. "I warn you, ma'am, if this is meant to be some kind of joke . . ."

"No, indeed—unless, that is, you consider it amusing to be head over ears in debt. Personally, I prefer to pay my way, but then Papa always brought me up to be thrifty." She smiled sweetly at him, ignoring his thunderous expression and Mrs. Peach's faint "Minerva, I beg of you . . . " to continue, "Of course, Papa was not precisely a *gentleman* in the eyes of your world, but he was a highly successful businessman who by hard work and enterprise accumulated during his lifetime several thriving woolen mills and latterly, a flourishing iron foundry. By the way, have you noticed that your entrance gates are in a shocking state of repair —a poor way to treat such fine workmanship, if I may say so?"

"You may not say so." He draped the towel around his neck with slow deliberation and moved toward her, lithe as a wild cat in his bare feet. It took every ounce of Minerva's resolution not to retreat before the soft menace in his voice, which more than matched the expression in his eyes. "What you will *do,* however, is to leave my house this instant if you do not wish to be forcibly removed."

"By you, my lord?" Her head a little on one side, she eyed him considerably. "Would you do it, I wonder?"

What the marquess might have answered was never to be known, for with a faint sigh, Mrs. Peach slumped in her chair in a dead swoon.

"There, now see what you have done!" Minerva exclaimed, ignoring Claireux's muffled oath as she hurried to her friend's side and knelt to rescue her reticule, which had slipped to the floor. From it she extracted a small vinaigrette which she wafted under Mrs. Peach's nose, her very real concern overtaking all other considerations. "How could you frighten her so with your stupid threats . . ."

"I . . . frighten her?" The marquess plunged his fingers into his already disarranged hair, which had the curious effect of making him look like nothing so much as a truculent schoolboy. "God give me patience!"

"Pray, do not raise your voice, my lord," Minerva said coldly. "I believe she is coming around."

Indeed, Mrs. Peach was stirring and beginning to moan a little, and then to cough as the full force of the aromatic salts reached her throat. The marquess, somewhat surprisingly knelt on the other side of the chair, and Minerva, in spite of her anxiety for her friend, felt her nostrils tingle with the heightened awareness of him, and her glance was drawn irresistibly to the fine hairs of his chest, still beaded with fast-cooling perspiration. A moment only, and her attention was sharply recalled.

"Minerva? Where am I? What . . . Oh!" Mrs. Peach had opened her eyes, and had seen Minerva and then the marquess in quick succession. Apprehension threatened her already fragile nerves once more, but before Minerva could reassure her, he was saying with surprising gentleness, "Pray, do not be alarmed, ma'am. There is not the least need. Is there anything at all that I can get you . . . a little brandy, perhaps? Or Penketh might be able to manage a hot drink of some kind . . ." He sounded uncertain.

"Oh, no, really, my lord. Oh, how very foolish of me. I cannot think what came over me!" Mrs. Peach struggled to sit upright, but was urged by him to take a moment or so in order to recover herself, after which he rose and moved away. The effect of his behavior upon Minerva was to make her very much aware of her own culpability. "Mrs. Peach, dear, *dear* Mrs. Peach," she exclaimed, chafing her friend's ice-cold hands. "I have been selfish and thoughtless, and quite uncaring of your feelings . . . dragging you here very much against your wishes when a moment's consideration must have shown me that you were chilled to the bone and wanting only the comfort of my uncle's drawing room! I should not wonder if you have the greatest disgust of me!"

"Nothing of the kind, child! I know you too well to hold you in anything but the deepest affection."

Minerva's smile was wry. "I get carried away, I know it. Papa was used to say that it was my one great failing!"

"And very wrong it was of him to say so, my dear, for if nothing else, your impetuosity will prevent you from ever becoming a calculating woman." Mrs. Peach gently withdrew her hands from Minerva's and patted her cheek. "Now, if you will but give me a moment alone to compose myself, we can go on, yes?"

"Yes, of course," Minerva said huskily. She got to her feet and walked across to where the marquess stood staring out of the now-darkened window.

"Thank you, my lord," she said.

"For what, Miss Braithwaite?" He was distant—a million miles away from her.

"For not venting your dislike of me upon Mrs. Peach."

He turned to look at her then. "I may be many things, ma'am, but I am not, I hope, a monster." She moved uncomfortably as he continued in tones that grated, "However, I hope your curiosity has been sufficiently rewarded."

It seemed such a strange thing to say, but before she could pursue it further there was a disturbance in the hall where a plaintive voice could be heard demanding of the manservant where the deuce his lordship was hiding himself. "I've got a devil of a lot riding on him to win, Penketh—a devil of a lot! Ah, in here, is he?" The door was pushed wide and a young gentleman, most incongruously at odds with his surroundings, stepped in and stopped short just beyond the threshold. "There you are, Dominic," he said, not at first perceiving the ladies. "Do come along, m'dear fellow. You know, it ain't at all the thing, slopin' off in the middle of a bout in that skimble-skamble fashion! Next thing, we'll have Lowdon declarin' himself the winner by default!"

A movement beyond the marquess drew his eyes and he put up his eyeglass. "Oh, I say—clumsy of me! I had no idea . . ." He executed an elegant bow and, clearly misinterpreting the situation, cocked a laconic eyebrow at his friend, murmuring not quite *sotto voce* enough to escape Minerva's keen ears and bringing the burning color to her cheeks, "Admire your taste, dear boy, if not y'r timing!" and made as if to withdraw. "Your pardon, ma'am, I believe I intrude."

"No, you don't, Pelham," said his lordship shortly. "Miss Braithwaite is on the point of leaving."

Mrs. Peach, taking the hint, came hastily to her feet, intent only upon putting as much distance betwen her and this highly embarrassing situation as soon as possible. The Honorable Pelham Grassington, realizing that matters were not quite as he had assumed, began to apologize all over again and, by now consumed with curiosity, begged to be introduced. To this the marquess acquiesed with obvious reluctance and rigid formality, and quite suddenly it seemed to Minerva that the situation was taking on all the comic ingredients of a first-rate farce, so that she found herself obliged to suppress a strong inclination to break into hysterical laughter. Her composure was not helped by Mrs. Peach, who was sufficiently restored to respond to the introduction by inquiring kindly whether the Honorable Mr. Pelham was related to the Grassingtons of Merton.

He looked sheepish, and momentarily much less sophisticated. "Youngest of the pack, ma'am, for m' sins. Acquainted with the parents, are you?"

The question flustered her and she grew a trifle pink. "Not really . . . though I did know your mama very slightly a long time ago. I daresay she would not even remember me . . ." Her voice trailed away.

Minerva could see that the marquess found this exchange less than riveting. She interposed smoothly, "Dear ma'am, if you are ready, I believe we have imposed upon Lord Claireux's hospitality quite long enough."

The leavetaking was achieved with perfect composure on her part and a formality not untinged with relief on his—while the noncombatants looked on in some puzzlement.

The remainder of the journey passed in silence, but for an odd politeness. Mrs. Peach could think of nothing to say that would not sound reproachful, while Minerva's mind was a teeming jumble of thought, dominated whichever way she turned by Dominic, Sixth Marquess of Claireux. To acknowledge that he had not been in the least what she had expected, was to understate the case with a vengeance. To be sure, he *was* tall, almost intimidatingly so, in fact, but with a physique that Michelangelo would not have distained to take for a model, while his chin, far from receding, exhibited a thrusting tendency which verged strongly upon the pugnacious. Bucolic might be nearer the mark, though to be fair, she had caught him at a disadvantage.

Nevertheless, the somewhat nebulous image she had nurtured of a pleasant, relatively mature gentleman of impeccable breeding and impecunious circumstances who might be only too willing to offer the benefits of his name and station in life in exchange for financial security, did not fit his lordship in any particular. Furthermore, her father's will had been quite specific; she would of course conscientiously perform such wifely duties as seemed reasonable, and would bring to her chosen husband the sum of one hundred thousand pounds—a handsome dowry by any standards, plus the benefit of a generous yearly income. But she must also keep the reins of all his various business enterprises firmly in her own hands—a daunting enough proposition for any gentleman to swallow, and although she knew Lord Claireux was in dire financial straits, she felt instinctively that, quite apart from the strong likelihood of his being argumentive, demanding, and quite impossible to live with, he would object violently to the idea of his wife's holding the purse strings.

"Perhaps the visit was for the best, after all," ventured Mrs. Peach, as if reading her thoughts. "I am sure that Sir Richard will know how to handle matters diplomatically so that you do not have to meet his lordship again."

Minerva's disappointment was unexpectedly sharp and defied reason, and as the carriage turned in at the gates of Sir Richard Standish's country house, she found herself for the first time in her life questioning the wisdom of her father's plans for her.

"But I have every intention of meeting him again," she heard herself saying. "What is more, I believe Lord Claireux is exactly the man I have been looking for."

2

MINERVA FOUND sleep difficult to come by that night. Her dramatic pronouncement in the carriage had surprised her every bit as much as it had astonished Mrs. Peach. But once the words were out, she realized their essential truth—that it was an interesting, exciting idea, quite different from the rather staid life she had pictured for herself.

There had been no time to explore her feelings further just then, for Uncle Richard was waiting on the step before the carriage had come to a halt, and all had been talk and bustle as he helped them down and exclaimed over the lateness.

"There I was, imagining you up-ended in a ditch, or worse—set upon by thieving rogues!" He hugged her and smiled benevolently upon her and upon Mrs. Peach, of whom he thoroughly approved. Although it would be less than true to say that he remembered her from the days when she and Emily had been bosom bows, they had become much better acquainted of late, and he could not but feel that she would exercise a beneficial effect upon his rather headstrong niece. "However, here you are, safe and sound, and no harm done, so come along now. Gorton will see that your boxes are bestowed, and Mattie will have them unpacked in a trice, I daresay. We can dine whenever you are ready—no need to think about changing. You both look quite charming, though I have no doubt you might want to freshen up a little. But for now, come along to the fire and get warm while you tell me what has kept you."

Minerva managed to catch Mrs. Peach's eye and shook her head very slightly. "Oh, a trifling delay, Uncle Richard. Nothing of the least interest, I promise you." She glanced around the comfortable drawing room as she stripped off her gloves. "How lovely it is to be here! Your house always has such an air of welcome. Do you not find it so, Mrs. Peach?"

"Indeed, yes." Mrs. Peach tried to appear enthusiastic, but Sir Richard was not slow to note the weariness in her voice and the slight droop of her shoulders.

"But you would find it even more welcoming if you could just put your feet up for a while." She stammered the obligatory denial, but he would have none of it. "Come now, we are old enough friends not to be standing on ceremony. I suspect that you are worn to a thread with the journey, and what you would like more than anything at this moment is to retire to your room with a little light supper on a tray. Come, am I right, ma'am?" And, relieved of the necessity to dissemble, Mrs. Peach thankfully admitted as much.

So it was that Minerva, when she had seen her old friend safely and comfortably installed in her bedchamber before a blazing fire with her every need taken care of, was able to make herself presentable and sit down at last to a leisurely dinner with the uncle of whom she was so fond. His sandy hair was now lightly sprinkled with gray and his dapper figure had grown more portly with the years, but his shrewd eyes were kindly beneath shaggy brows. He was the very picture, in fact, of what he was—a contented country squire and justice of the peace, much liked by all who knew him.

"Tell you the truth, m'dear, I'm not sorry to have you to myself," he said over a tastily dressed fillet of turbot. "I rather wanted to talk to you about this business of Claireux and it ain't the kind of thing I care to air before a third party, wonderful woman though Mrs. Peach is. Fact is, I wondered if you'd had any second thoughts about his lordship's suitability?"

With only the slightest of hesitations, Minerva declared that she had not. "I seldom change my mind once it is made up," she said lightly.

"Hm." Sir Richard helped himself to some broiled mushrooms and a second portion of spinach with croutons. "These really are rather good. I must make a point of telling Cook."

His preoccupation with the food was so marked and so unlike him that she could not fail to be aware that he found her reply less than pleasing.

"I'm sorry," she said. "Did that sound horribly complacent? It wasn't meant to. I do *try* not to be dogmatic about things."

"But your father brought you up to be decisive—speak your mind and shame the devil, eh? Well, that's no bad thing so long as you remember that it can, on occasion, be politic to give way a little."

It was the gentlest of reproofs, but she felt it none the less keenly. After a moment, she said in a subdued way, "Did you have a particular reason for asking, sir?"

"About Claireux? Yes, of course. Only wanted to say that if you weren't set on pursuing him as a possible marriage partner, it might be as well to look elsewhere." He saw the inevitable question spring into her eyes. "The thing is, I've been having some rather more detailed inquiries made which have uncovered something rather unsavory. Not much of a Town Beau myself, as you well know—so I don't get to hear many of the *on-dits*. Of course, one can never be sure how much is conjecture and how much truth, but in my experience there has to be something to set folks tongues clacking."

Minerva pushed her plate aside and chose a sweetmeat with care. "I am intrigued, Uncle Richard. Whatever can the poor marquess stand accused of, I wonder?"

"Murdering a man," he replied with unaccustomed bluntness just as she was taking a bite out of a particularly delectable sugared plum. She swallowed too quickly and during the violent paroxysm of coughing which ensued, Sir Richard came to hover over her, much concerned.

"Goodness!" she gasped at last, eyes watering. "What a very silly thing to do!"

"Are you quite sure you are all right, m'dear?" he inquired anxiously as she waved him back to his chair.

"Quite sure," she affirmed. "Now, where were we? Oh, yes—did I hear you aright? Lord Claireux is suspected of murder? I must say, I would not have thought it of him! That is," she amended hastily, "it doesn't sound the sort of behavior I would associate with the gentleman you earlier described to me!"

"No, well, I'm bound to say it came as a bit of a shock to me, too. Don't know the fellow that well, of course—only met him once or twice since he's been here in Yorkshire. Can't say that I'd care to cross him, mind, but I wouldn't have taken him for a violent man, precisely. And as for talk of him sparring regularly with Gentleman Jackson—well, plenty of young bloods like to try their luck against the great pugilist, and it don't make murderers of 'em, that I ever heard."

As her uncle seemed bent on going off at a tangent, Minerva endeavored to bring him back to the point. "Did your informant know anything about his lordship's supposed victim?"

"Fellow name of Hagarth—Baron Hagarth. As far as I can make out, he was an unscrupulous, blackmailing little toad who exploited the weak and had no compunction about squeezing his victims until they either made bad worse by resorting to the Jews in an attempt to pay, or blew their brains out. Which is the situation in which the late marquess found himself."

"And which course did he take? Blow his brains

out?" If so, she thought, it could have provided his son with an excellent and quite excusable motive for murder.

But Sir Richard was shaking his head. "Poor fellow might well have done so, if a stroke hadn't carried him off first. Came out later that he'd got himself involved with some shady Stock Exchange dealing which Hagarth threatened to expose if he didn't cough up the ready. Ended up owing the man some ridiculous amount running into many thousands, every asset mortgaged to the hilt, and what with the interest mounting all the time you may imagine his dilemma when this Hagarth fellow began pressin' him—threats of exposure, ruin of family name, imprisonment, and the like! It all became too much."

So engrossed was Minerva that she leaned forward, chin on hand, elbows resting on the table in a way that would have severely displeased Miss Pakenham. "Was there nothing his son could have done earlier?"

"I doubt he knew. Been in the army for years—distinguished himself at Waterloo—and I daresay his father kept his problems from him on the few occasions when they did meet. Which I suspect made the shock all the greater when he learned that not only was his father dead, but that he'd left nothing behind him save a scandal and a pile of debts. To make matters worse, I believe he had developed a *tendre* for Winterton's eldest girl during one of his brief visits home, talk of betrothals in the air and all that, but wily Viscount Winterton withdrew his consent when he got wind of the unsavory scandal."

"Oh, no! That does seem a little unfair. It was none of the son's doing, after all."

"The young marquess shared your views. Mad as fire, according to my informant, swearing all kinds of drastic action. And there was young Lavinia Winterton breaking her heart for him, though she will probably get over it in time."

"And if she does not?" Minerva said indignantly. "I

think it is a terrible thing to do to two people in love!"

As a confirmed bachelor, Sir Richard was able to view the tragedy more philosophically. "Perhaps, but you can't really blame Winterton for seeking to guard his daughter's best interests, let alone save himself a great deal of money." He regarded his niece somewhat quizzically from beneath frowning brows. "It needs only for us to remember your father's experience with regard to my own improvident parent to demonstrate how lamentably expensive such a union can be. And Winterton does not have the financial resources of a Hezekiah Braithwaite."

Minerva was obliged to recognize the truth of this; in any case, she was more interested in what happened next.

"As you might expect, the young hothead sought out this Hagarth fellow, picked a violent quarrel with him in the presence of witnesses, accused him of causing the death of his father, and knocked him down. Hagarth then challenged him to a duel, which was all set for the following morning. But fortunately the law got to hear of it and they were obliged to call it off."

"Goodness!" Minerva cried.

"Quite. But that was not the end of it. Two mornings later the baron was found by his man, sprawled in his library with the life choked out of him, an odd-looking button clutched in his fist, and the strong box containing a great many documents, mostly of an incriminating nature, including those pertaining to Claireux, missing." Minerva's stifled exclamation belatedly recalled him to a sense of propriety. "Forgive me, m'dear—not at all the thing, sullying your pretty ears with such sordid details."

She brushed aside his apologies, though she shivered nonetheless, remembering that strong body rippling with muscle, the powerful shoulders and long slim fingers that could wrap around a man's throat with ease. "But surely," she argued, "if the marquess *had* killed the baron, he would be in custody by now and not roaming free here in Yorkshire?"

"Insufficent evidence." Sir Richard shook his head. "But it could be the case is far from closed. It only needs someone to find the strongbox, or the coat with the missing button . . ." His eyes strayed longingly toward the servant hovering with his port and cigars. "So you see, it ain't the straightforward case I once thought it, which is why I would strongly advise you to forget about Lord Claireux. A scandal, should it erupt, could have the most disastrous consequences. Not to put too fine a point on it—marry him, and you could find yourself socially ostrasized."

Common sense urged Minerva to heed her uncle's advice, yet she found herself saying stubbornly, "Well, I don't believe it will come to that. It sounds to me as though any one of a dozen poor souls had reason to kill this Hagarth creature, and while I lack your experience in these matters, it seems to me that if sufficient evidence existed, Lord Claireux would have been arrested long since. From our point of view, there can surely be no better time to hope for a favorable answer from his lordship, since he is scarcely likely to find a rich wife among his own kind."

A pained expression crossed Sir Richard's face. There were times, just occasionally, when his niece's penchant for plain speaking grated on him. His glance again traveled toward the waiting servant. Minerva took the hint and rose from her place. As he too stood up, she hurried around to kiss him on the cheek. "Poor Uncle Richard, what a trouble I am to you," she exclaimed, and he, much moved, denied it vigorously and with quite genuine affection.

"Never mind," she declared with a blithe optimism that troubled him. "It won't be for much longer. I shall retire to bed now, so you may blow your cloud and drink your port in peace." At the door she looked back. "However, I do think we should at least see Lord

Claireux tomorrow before making up our minds."

It was a simple enough decision to take under the influence of good food and wine, but when, some hours later, she still lay wide awake staring into the darkness relieved only by the faint glow of the dying coals in the hearth, she at last fell to wondering whether she was not perhaps making a mistake. And the more the thought persisted, the more restless and dissatisfied with herself she became, until finally she climbed out of bed, pulled on a dressing robe, and padded across the room to pull back the curtain.

The rain had stopped, and a fickle moon was racing in and out of the clouds, driving deep shadows across the tranquil landscape. Just like her thoughts. Uncle Richard's arguments were undoubtedly well reasoned and sound, and deserved serious consideration. After all, debt was one thing, but murder quite another—and surely, in view of what she had learned, it would be folly to proceed? So why did she have this persistent urge to rush headlong into danger? She told herself that it was her innate sense of justice which would not permit a man to be condemned without recourse to his own defense, but the truth was, she was suffering from an acute attack of ennui. Mrs. Peach was a darling, far better than she deserved, but her needs were few and easily satisfied. Even dear Uncle Richard, though she held him in great affection, was not always the most stimulating of companions, and the prospect of spending her whole life in such company occasionally depressed her beyond measure. Papa had been many things, not all of them laudable by any means, but life with him had always been a challenge—never dull. And the marquess, with all his shortcomings, might well present her with a similar challenge.

So it was on the following day, Minerva slipped a folded sheet of paper into Gorton's hand shortly before Lord Claireux was expected, and requested him to deliver it to his lordship with the utmost discretion the moment he arrived.

The marquess had not been in the best of moods when he set out that afternoon to keep his appointment with Sir Richard. The whole affair, conceived when he was in his cups, had become distasteful to him, and only a reluctance to offend the kindly, if slightly eccentric, baronet had persuaded him to go through with it. Kindliness was a virtue not much in evidence among his acquaintance of late, and he was loath to squander it lightly. The same might be said of Pelham, whose unexpected arrival heralded an ill-disguised attempt to prise him out of his self-imposed isolation. Pelham was a good and loyal friend, but his sense of timing could on occasion leave much be be desired. Thankfully, he knew nothing of the purpose of his visit to Sir Richard, and had gone off quite happily with Lowdon to shoot rabbits.

The country roads were narrow and winding, but he rode nonetheless with a kind of calculated recklessness that would have frightened the life out of most people. Drummond, however, watched his departure with equanimity. The groom had occupied a somewhat unique role in his lordship's life of late. He had been with him throughout the Peninsular campaign, and survived every hair-brained escapade he had embroiled himself in, of which there were many, and when his lordship's batman was killed just before Waterloo, Drummond had valiantly assumed the dual role.

He'd carried right on doing so when everything had gone so wrong for the marquess, as he now was, though he'd given him the chance of a better job, of course—a proper gentleman, in spite of his troubles. "I can't afford to pay you a fraction of what you're worth, Drummond," he'd said, with a rather strained smile that had made the groom want to hit out at somebody. "Besides which, there will be no stable, no cattle other than my faithful old bay, and that would mean a criminal waste of your talents. But if you wish, I will most willingly recommend you any one of half a dozen of my friends who would leap at the chance of employing you." As if he'd desert a gentleman as had been so good to him over the years! And so he'd told him. "Besides which, major, me lord, I'm just getting the hang of this valeting nonsense, an' you never know when such skills might come in handy. As for money, well, you just give me what you can when you can, and we'll get along fine!" And so they had, even through the black moods that had afflicted his lordship of late. He couldn't be blamed if he felt the need to kick against the fates now and then, for his late father, God forgive him, had dealt him a sorry hand.

The object of Drummond's reflections was at that precise moment in sight of his destination. With a final flourish, rider and mount swept around into the driveway of Standish Court and drew up amid a scattering of gravel. The marquess dismounted and tossed the reins to a waiting groom, his greatcoat swirling about him.

"Walk him up and down. This shouldn't take very long," he said.

Gorton was waiting at the door to receive the greatcoat from him, together with his hat and his leather gauntlets, and before announcing him to Sir Richard, gave a polite little cough and proffered the note given to him by Miss Minerva.

Claireux frowned as he read the brief message: "Please—do not betray to Uncle Richard that we have met," and signed in flowing script, "Minerva Braithwaite." His frown deepened to a scowl as he recognized the name of his unwelcome visitor of the previous evening. But surely . . . ? His eyes lifted to meet those of the imperturbable butler. "Miss Braithwaite is Sir Richard's niece?" he asked with deceptive quiet.

"Why, yes, my lord." Gorton was very sensitive to vibrations, and being well aware of all that might be at stake, ventured to further Miss Minerva's cause. "A most agreeble young lady, if I may be permitted to venture an opinion." He could not quite distinguish his lordship's reply, but felt that it lacked enthusiasm.

Minerva had watched Lord Claireux's spectacular arrival from her vantage point behind the muslin curtains in the upstairs saloon; had been roused to admiration as he judged the gates to an inch, shoulder capes flapping, reining in at the entrance to the manor like some towering mythical warrior. A tremor that was half fear, half excitement raced through her as she contemplated their imminent confrontation. Was she out of her mind? Mrs. Peach feared it, and Uncle Richard was fast coming to a similiar conclusion.

"Please, dear sir, if I might just be permitted to have five—maybe ten minutes alone with him?" she had coaxed earlier. And when her uncle's mouth had begun to turn down at the corners preparatory to a refusal, "Oh, do say yes! After all, what harm can it possibly do? Surely the proprieties could be well enough observed by our occupying the yellow saloon while you and Mrs. Peach wait in the drawing room next door?" Minerva grinned suddenly and disarmingly. "If he should feel disposed to strangle *me,* I assure you I am capable of screaming very loudly!"

Sir Richard endeavored to remain severe, but his twinkling eyes betrayed him. "After five minutes in your company, I doubt he would be so foolish as to attempt anything so misguided! Oh, very well, m'dear, the yellow saloon it shall be. I'll take his lordship into the library when he arrives and have a little chat with him before I bring him up to you. I only hope he won't think it deucedly odd!"

I only hope he won't turn tail upon receiving my note, thought Minerva as she waited nervously to meet the marquess once again, face to face.

3

"MISS BRAITHWAITE." The marquess was chillingly formal, and the look that accompanied his clipped greeting was not encouraging.

"My lord," Minerva answered pleasantly. "Will you not be seated?"

She led the way across the room to the pair of chairs that faced one another before the fire, very conscious of his eyes boring into her back. She had taken particular pains with her appearance, anxious to repair any damage her previous evening's escapade might have done, but the atmosphere was not encouraging, and as her uncle had performed the introductions, he had endeavored to convey some kind of message to her with his eyes. Since Lord Claireux's scrupulous politeness had betrayed no hint of recognition, she could only assume that he had declined to join his name to hers. This supposition seemed to be confirmed when she sat and found that he had remained standing in the middle of the room. He was no dandy like his friend Mr. Grassington, she decided, but his coat was well cut and he wore it with an air of swashbuckling arrogance.

In truth, the marquess did not know why he had allowed Sir Richard to talk him into this meeting at all. He had no particular desire to see Miss Braithwaite again; he certainly had no wish to ally himself to her in marriage. A marriage with so many strings attached would be abhorrent at the best of times, but in this case it would be quite unthinkable.

Nevertheless, he found himself eyeing her with no little curiosity, the light last evening having been such as to make any true assessment impossible. She was fairly tall for a woman, and her carriage as she had preceded him across the room in her slim amber gown had been impressive. In other circumstances he might even have admired her looks, which were certainly out of the commonplace, for there was great strength of character in her face, and although her nose was a trifle too pronounced, a pleasing mobility about her mouth gave evidence of humor. But that chin—decidedly he could not live with that chin! He met the cloudy blue-green eyes that were quite her most striking feature, and read the question in them.

"I am here because you expressed a wish to see me, ma'am," he said stiffly. "Though I must tell you at the outset that I can see no purpose to our meeting—unless, that is, you feel the need to apologize?"

Laughter was the last reaction he had expected, such merry laughter that it was almost impossible to regard it as offensive.

"My lord," she begged him, "do pray sit down instead of towering over me in that menacing way. I will indeed apologize, if you want me to, but that is not why I asked to see you."

Intrigued in spite of himself, he came to sit opposite her, crossing one leg negligently over the other.

"From your somewhat frosty demeanor," she began, plunging in without preamble, "I infer that you have decided we shouldn't suit?"

One eyebrow quivered. "Can you doubt it, Miss Braithwaite?"

"I suppose not, my lord," she acknowledged regretfully. "But would you care to tell me why?" This time the eyebrow shot up and she continued hastily, "Oh, I know it must seem a little indelicate in me to wish to know, but you see I am not much good at dissembling, and although Uncle Richard will tell me all later, I would so much rather hear it from you. After all, if we are not to meet again, it cannot matter what you think of me, and if we are, then it is better that you should know of my penchant for plain speaking."

"But I do know," he said softly. "I'm sure you will not mind my pointing out that I was made painfully aware of it last evening."

Minerva caught her lower lip between rather handsome pearly teeth. "Yes, I was afraid that might rankle with you. It was one of my less admirable impulses and one for which I can only beg your pardon. But I was curious to know what you were like, you see . . ."

"Indeed I do see, ma'am." The marquess answered brusquely. "I daresay in time I shall even become used to being the object of such curiosity, though I confess that until now no one has actually invaded my home in order to satisfy their prurient curiosity."

"Prurient?" Minerva frowned. "I'm not sure I understand."

He rose and swung around on her, his face dark with anger. "Oh, come—is this your idea of plain speaking? Well, I will be plain with you. I refer to my newfound notoriety, which seems destined to precede me everywhere—even here. You know, I really had no idea that having one's name linked with an unnatural death could evoke so much morbid interest among complete strangers. And you need not play the innocent, for your uncle is certainly well versed in all the details, and I will not believe that he has not passed them on to you."

"Oh, that!" Minerva's face cleared. "Yes, Uncle Richard did tell me about the murder over dinner last evening, but that wasn't why I so rudely imposed myself upon you!"

The marquess felt almost light-headed for a moment; he thought he knew all the reactions to his present situation—everything from jocular encouragement, to embarrassment, to the final humiliation of being cut by those he had once thought to call friend. What he had never until now encountered was Miss Braithwaite's quite genuine dismissal of it as a subject worthy of interest. For the first time he found himself warming to her.

"So—if it was not in the hope of surprising a murder suspect in his hideaway, Miss Braithwaite, why did you come?"

Minerva had the grace to blush. "I doubt you will find the answer to your liking, my lord."

"I doubt I will, ma'am, but pray do not seek to spare my feelings."

"As you please, sir. First of all, you should know that my visit last evening was in no way premeditated. But we found ourselves passing your door, and I thought . . ." Her mouth felt very dry, all of a sudden. She met his eyes and quickly looked away. "You see, until now Uncle Richard's idea of who would be acceptable to me as a husband has differed so vastly from my own that I thought this time I would like to see you for myself before making any commitment."

For a moment the marquess appeared stunned. Then his laugh rang out.

The sound penetrated to the drawing room. Sir Richard and Mrs. Peach exchanged glances.

"Dear sir, whatever can it mean?"

"I have no idea, ma'am. Extraordinary!" He glanced at the clock. "Should I go in, do you think?"

She clutched her shawl of Norwich silk closer about her. "I hardly know what to advise! It was quite an optimistic sound, and it would be a pity to destroy what might be the delicate beginnings of an understanding. Perhaps," she suggested diffidently, "you might leave them for a few more minutes?"

In the yellow saloon the marquess had resumed his seat, but now he leaned forward, his eyes keenly assessing Minerva. "I wish I knew what to make of you.

You are, without doubt, a most unusual young woman."

"But not one with whom you would care to share your life?" He made no immediate reply, and emboldened by what she construed as uncertainty, she hurried on, "May I know your reasons, my lord? Believe me, I do not ask lightly, for your answer is of great importance to me. You see, if you have taken me in aversion, then there is little I can do to mend matters, for I am what I am and cannot vouchsafe to change my ways. But if it is merely a question of the money and how oddly it is arranged, then I see no insurmountable barrier other than foolish pride."

His brows drew together. "You think pride foolish, then?"

"I do when one deliberately allows it to stand in the way of one's own best interests," she answered without hesitation.

The marquess rose and stood glowering down at her. "That, if I may say so, is a typically feminine observation."

Minerva met his look unflinchingly. "Oh, we have our pride, too, my lord. It is simply that girl children are discouraged from the cradle upward from ever displaying it openly. I thank God my father was more enlightened than most men."

"He certainly seems to have held a very high opinion of your ability to assume responsibility."

"In leaving the control of the mills in my hands, do you mean? Well, you see, Pa had hoped for a son, but when he was left with me, he decided that I would have to do. And so he trained me well." She regarded the marquess, head on one side. "Is that what rankles with you? The thought of being beholden to me? Because there is no reason why you should be. After all, as I am sure Uncle Richard has explained, it was Pa who stipulated the amount to be set aside for my dowry, and I would hazard that a hundred thousand pounds should prove more than adequate to put your affairs in order.

Once that is accomplished and your estate is again flourishing, you may look the world in the face with confidence."

"You are too kind, madam!"

The heavy sarcasm in his voice made her look at him more closely. There was a flagrant arrogance in his stance that irked her—as though he were doing her the favor. It made her speak more sharply than she had intended. "Well, it is certainly handsome under the circumstances. What is more, I doubt you would be so stiff-rumped if Lord Winterton had made you such a generous proposition instead of some jumped-up mill owner's daughter who is so vulgarly ill-bred as to speak to you of money!"

Minerva regretted the words almost before they were out. She saw the pain flare momentarily in his eyes, turning their slate gray depths to flame and then to chill night-black. "I'm sorry!" she exclaimed. "My wretched tongue. I had not meant . . . would not dream . . ." Her words had no effect, if indeed he even heard them, for although his gaze remained fixed upon her, she had the feeling that his thoughts were somewhere else entirely.

The marquess had at first been obliged to bite very hard on the retort that fought to find utterance, all of the more charitable feelings he had begun to experience with regard to Miss Braithwaite forgotten. And then, irresistibly, his thoughts were drawn to Lavinia Winterton as he had last seen her, her beauty drowned in tears as he had put her pliant body resolutely from him. Her incoherent pleas that he not permit her father to part them still had the power to tear at his senses whenever he sought uselessly for some new and magical solution that would enable them to be together. Every sensation in him screamed that it was Lavinia he wanted for his wife, not this self-possessed female who talked too much and probably hadn't a pliant bone in her body.

"My lord," Minerva surprised herself by asking

impulsively, "is your case with Miss Winterton quite hopeless?"

This brought him to with a jolt. "Oh, quite hopeless, Miss Braithwaite!" He ground the words out harshly. "Financial ruin is bad enough, but fortunes *can* be reversed. A tainted name, however, must render one forever ineligible."

The words hung in the air. Then: "Not to me, my lord," she said quietly. His glance sharpened as she continued. "I would be the first to admit that upon first acquaintance I found you arrogant and overbearing, but despite the violence of your reactions—quite justifiable in the circumstances, even if you had not been three parts disguised," she conceded handsomely as he opened his mouth to protest. "But even were it otherwise, nothing in your behavior then or now would persuade me that you are a murderer, though I would not for one moment blame you if you had killed that dreadful man. And if you could bring yourself to overlook my own imperfections of character, and accept the rather odd way my father has left matters, I would esteem it an honor to be your wife."

This time the silence lasted rather longer, and was charged with so many conflicting emotions that the very air seemed to vibrate. Then the marquess spoke.

"The devil you would!" he said softly. "You are, I repeat, a most unusual young woman. I came here today fully determined to return a polite but firm refusal to your uncle's original tentative proposition."

"And now?" Minerva found her breath catching in her throat, so important had his answer suddenly become to her.

"Now?" He ran a hand through his carefully disarranged hair as she had seen him do on the previous evening, and as before it reduced him in a single gesture from arrogant rake to a bewildered young man too preoccupied to mind his language. "I'm damned if I know! Every instinct urges me to hold my resolve, but you have a disarmingly tenacious and indeed perceptive way with an argument, ma'am."

Minerva's smile was rueful. "Some would be less kind and call it stubborn self-interest. It is a trait not universally admired in a woman, especially, I imagine, a young woman aspiring to enter fashionable society, but equally I promise you would never have cause to be ashamed of me." This drew from him a vague lift of the eyebrow. Emboldened by it, she continued impetuously, "My lord, I know that I can never be what you hoped for, but my disposition is not romantical and while I am willing to be your wife in the fullest sense of the word if that is what you wish—" to her chagrin, Minerva found herself blushing beneath his gaze, and it took every ounce of resolution to continue—"I shall not expect anything more than you feel able to give. Having said that, as matters stand, what have you to lose?"

"What indeed?" he answered, and she did not miss the note of bitter irony in his voice. "More to the point, Miss Braithwaite, what have *you* to gain?"

Piqued by his attitude, she became defiant. Her chin lifted. "I should have thought that was obvious, my lord. A title—and a place in that society I spoke of."

"As to that, ma'am, I can manage the first easily enough—indeed, it is all I do have to give. But if the second is important to you, then I urge you to reconsider, for it is by no means certain that the polite world will not shun me."

He had looked away from Minerva to stare down into the fire, hunched a little—one hand on the mantelshelf, one foot propped on the hearth. The bitterness was still there, and with it a kind of dejection that brought a lump, unbidden, to her throat; brought with it, too, a fierce longing to have the right to comfort him, which was absurd under the circumstances.

"Humgudgeon!" she said bracingly, and stood up; while this did not put them on equal terms, it did at least lessen the difference sufficiently to enable her to look him in the eye as he turned. "Only one thing might tempt me to reconsider, and that is the prospect of being married to a man who is so poor-spirited that he will allow his life to be ruined by the tittle-tattle of an ill-intentioned minority."

Slowly, his shoulders straightened and she couldn't be sure whether his expression was occasioned by anger or some less fathomable emotion. For a long moment their glances locked. Then: "Tell me, do you make a habit of being provoking, Miss Braithwaite?" he asked with a curious intensity.

"More often that I ought, sir," she admitted. "But I would rather do that than stand meekly aside and watch someone sink into a decline."

"Have a care, madam. Provoke me too far, and you may regret it."

His voice was silky soft, yet her laughing, mock-demure apology aroused in him a kind of exhilaration that was something akin to the thrill of battle, something he hadn't felt since returning home. Miss Braithwaite, Minerva—ridiculous name!—could never arouse in him those feelings which the mere thought of Lavinia set racing through his blood, but, that stubborn chin notwithstanding, he might find life with her far from dull. Would he be quite mad to contemplate it? He decided to test her further.

"And suppose that in this case you are wrong, and the tattlemongers are right?"

"Then I suppose you will wring my neck, and I shall be well served for my deplorable lack of judgment," she said calmly. His spontaneous laughter encouraged her to continue: "But it would take a great deal to convince me that someone who acquitted himself with as much credit as you did in the army, would commit the glaring strategical blunder of setting himself up as a prime suspect by killing a man with whom he had quarreled so violently only two days previously."

"Even if he were desperate?"

"Even then," she averred.

The marquess stepped closer and took her hand. She allowed it to rest quite passively in his as she looked up at him inquiringly. "How old are you, Miss Braithwaite?"

"Almost twenty, my lord."

"And so wise," he murmured. "Well then." He lifted her hand to his lips, his smile a little awry. "Perhaps we might be good for one another, after all. What do you say, ma'am? Will you take one rather tarnished marquess to husband?"

"With the greatest pleasure, my lord," Minerva said, and was surprised to find that she meant it.

4

"MARRIED?" EXCLAIMED Pelham, startled out of the rather pleasant state of torpor induced by a successful couple of hours' shooting. He even went so far as to leave his comfortable chair in order to peer more closely and with deepest suspicion at the marquess. "You *are* bamming us? I mean—not like you to be in your cups this early in the day!" Pelham's glance took in the unwrinkled splendor of the buckskin breeches, the olive coat—say what you would, Dominic had a pair of shoulders a man might envy, for all that he liked his coats so he could shrug his way into 'em. "Tell you what, though, Charles—he does have a certain look about him, wouldn't you say so?"

Charles Lowdon lifted his quizzing glass with languid indifference. "Did Weston make that coat, Dominic?"

There was a gleam in Claireux's eyes. "No. It's one of Scott's."

"I thought so. Ah, well—love is blind, or so the great bard would have us believe, if indeed love comes into it." The noted Corinthian lowered his glass, allowing it to swing gently on its riband. "Do you mean to tell us the name of this short-sighted paragon?"

"Miss Braithwaite."

"Braithwaite? Now where the devil have I. . . ?" Pelham's face cleared. "Of course! Your mysterious visitor of last evening. You should have seen her, Charles—a veritible Juno!" He cuffed the marquess affectionately on the shoulder. "You sly dog! Keeping her to yourself all this time, putting us off the scent by allowing us to think you were still sighing over the fair Lavinia."

Charles Lowdon, watching Claireux's face from beneath veiled lids throughout this exchange, was very much aware of the hastily-bitten-back word, the white line around a mouth compressed by anger, or maybe it was distress. "Known her long, Dominic?" he asked quietly.

"Not really. She is niece to Sir Richard Standish." The marquess walked unhurriedly to the sideboard and poured himself a brandy which he downed immediately, then refilled his glass. "And since I am sure Pelham will have far too much delicacy to ask," he added with deep irony, "yes, she is a considerable heiress. And she is not Juno, but Minerva."

Pelham choked a little and then grinned, unabashed. "Well, it could be worse, dear old fellow—only consider, she might have been some dreadful Friday-faced creature! Your luck could even be on the change at last."

The wedding was to be soon; since neither party seemed disposed to dally, they waited only upon the calling of the banns. It would be a quiet affair, presided over by the present incumbent of the little church in the valley where the Reverend Peach and Mrs. Peach had spent so many happy years.

"Shall you mind a local wedding, my lord?" Minerva had asked anxiously, and the marquess, relieved that she was not hankering after a showy London affair, had been quick to assure her that he did not. "You see, the local people will feel cheated if they do not see Hezekiah Braithwaite's daughter properly wed," she explained.

She did not add "to a lord," but from his expression, it was clear that he understood only too well.

"But your bride clothes, my love?" Mrs. Peach exclaimed, much troubled by the unseemly haste with which Minerva was rushing upon her fate. Her young friend's blithe assumption that the merest necessities would suffice for the present as she meant to shop for the rest later in the most fashionable salons to be found in London or Paris, far from reassuring her, aroused the severest misgivings about *repenting at leisure* in her motherly bosom. Her fears, when confided to Sir Richard, found a sympathetic ear. However, having watched the young couple together, he had rather more faith in his niece's ability to cope with any situation that might arise, though he tactfully refrained from saying so.

Whatever else Minerva might be tempted to forgo, her wedding dress was to be a miracle of perfection fashioned by the excellent dressmaker in Leeds who had sewn regularly for Miss Braithwaite over the years. Time was short, but by working long days and far into the night, Mrs. Snib and her workroom girls managed to create a gown worthy of a marchioness-to-be; of dull ivory satin, it was demurely closed high at the neck with a row of tiny mother of pearl buttons, and the brief fitted bodice was liberally appliquéd with lover's knots in shimmering cream silk, which were repeated on the gown's narrow court train and again on the enchanting cap around which Matthews would arrange her rich brown hair.

The late March day behaved beautifully, with white clouds scudding gently across an azure sky, the sun slanting on tender new greenery and picking up the echoing drifts of color beneath the trees where early bluebells bowed their heads in obeisance to the breeze; and as Minerva walked down the short path to the church on her uncle's arm, well-wishers were already gathering for a glimpse of her. Many of them were weavers from the mill further down the valley bottom, half-hidden among the trees where the river ran, who had been given time off in order to pay their respects.

Sir Richard had come to stay several days earlier, while the marquess and his friends racked up overnight in Leeds. They drove out the following morning, Lord Claireux looking, as someone in the crowd declared, every inch the nob in a wine-colored coat with quite singular silver filigree buttons, a drift of white for a cravat and dove-gray pantaloons.

The ceremony was brief, the bride and groom made their responses clearly and unemotionally, and Mrs. Peach wept copiously into her handkerchief throughout. They emerged into the sunshine once more to find that the crowd had swelled considerably and as Minerva and the marquess covered the short distance between the church porch and the ancient lych gate, they were pelted with bluebell heads amid much merriment, several voices rising above the rest.

"Picture, en't she?"

"Every inch a lady, just like 'er ma, God rest her!"

"Eh, but her father'd be that proud of 'er . . ."

"They make a right bonny pair, say what you will . . ."

"Just like a fairy tale . . ."

In the carriage, Minerva turned a rueful smile on her new husband. His profile was not in the least lover-like, and she feared that the innocent enjoyment of the crowd was not to his liking. "I'm sorry about all that. They don't have many causes for celebration, you see."

He made an impatient gesture with his hand, and her heart sank. Just for a few moments she had been seduced by the warm enthusiasm of the people—her people—into believing their fairy tale. How could she have been so foolish? She stared straight ahead with sudden bleakness, and in this way they traveled some distance in silence before she felt his fingers close on hers.

"Forgive me," he said tersely. When she turned to meet his eyes, she found him frowning at her. "They were right about you," he said in a puzzled way, as if he were seeing her for the first time. "You do indeed look a picture. Quite lovely, in fact. I should have told you so much earlier."

And would have, no doubt, she thought, had I been Lavinia Winterton. Aloud she said lightly, "Thank you, my lord. It is kind of you to notice. But I hope you will not feel obliged to be forever paying me compliments. I promise you I shall not in the general way expect pretty speeches. Pa never praised my looks, that I can remember, though he occasionally complimented me upon the way I kept a set of books, so you must not fear that I shall fall into the suds if you fail to notice every time I wear a new bonnet."

Her words revealed rather more than she realized. Clearly she had loved her father, their very closeness was apparent in the way she spoke of him, yet his obsession with treating her as he would a son must surely have contributed in no small measure to the formation of her rather odd, forthright character. That it had not detracted from her femininity was remarkable, the more so when one remembered she had lost her mother so young. He found himself making the effort to return lightness with lightness.

"And do you mean to purchase a great many new bonnets, madam wife?"

"Oh, as to that, my lord, you will have to wait and see."

Minerva blushed as he showed not the slightest disposition to release her hand. "Then I reserve my right to comment upon them as and when I see fit. And do you suppose, my dear Minerva, that you could refrain from calling me *my lord* in that rather grand manner? I would much prefer that you called me Dominic."

Her murmured assent interested him: the blush deepened and her voice sounded almost diffident. So, she was not always quite so sure of herself! For no particular reason that he could fathom, the thought cheered him no end. His fingers curled around hers with a new possessive sureness.

The road had been rising along the rim of the valley and now swept around in a wide curve as it took the private road to High Fold. The carriage drew up on the wide forecourt and Minerva sensed rather than heard the marquess draw in his breath at his first sight of the handsome yet unpretentious house built of good sound Yorkshire stone. Joshua climbed down and stood waiting while the marquess continued to sit, taking in both the building and the unrivaled choice of setting.

"Pa had it built so that he could oversee the fruits of his labor—the first small kingdom he created," Minerva said with quiet pride. "It was Grandfather who began it all, of course. He used to ride all over Yorkshire and beyond with a string of pack horses, collecting the finest fleece at shearing time and delivering it to the combers and then the spinners and weavers in small cottages, sometimes miles apart. It was a hard life out in all weathers, and as soon as Pa was old enough, he went with him. Often as he grew, he had visions of simplifying the work by assembling all the various parties together under one roof, and when Grandpa died, he made a start by buying up a derelict water mill down there where the river runs in beneath those trees." She pointed to a rooftop just visible through the trees on the valley bottom. "He rebuilt and enlarged the mill and millhouse and added a row of cottages nearby. That was the beginning. Of course, he went on accepting fresh challenges all through his life, but this was his first love—his dream." Minerva turned impulsively to the marquess. "I know it will seem like an extravagance, but I should very much like to keep this house, if you would not mind?"

There was a pregnant silence. Then: "Why on earth should I mind? The house is yours to do with as you will," he said abruptly, and as the sound of an approaching carriage reached their ears, he withdrew his hand from hers and prepared to climb down.

Minerva cursed her tactlessness, while inwardly railing against this constant need to guard her tongue. It did not come easily for her, and only the knowledge of how galling the situation must be to his pride, made her continue to try.

"My lord . . . Dominic?" she began as he turned to assist her down the steps.

The unconscious pleading in her tone brought from him a muffled exclamation which she took to be self-admonitory, though his voice did not soften appreciably. "Take no notice of me. Keep your house, by all means. It is perfectly natural that you should wish to do so. Besides," a gleam came into his eyes, "you will need somewhere to stay when you come to oversee your domains!"

She wanted to say *when we come*, but it was neither the time nor the place to begin a contentious discussion, for Mrs. Peach was coming toward them on Sir Richard's arm, and Mr. Grassington and Mr. Lowdon were not far behind.

The small informal reception had its awkward moments, although everyone tried to make it appear otherwise. For once, Minerva allowed Mrs. Peach full rein, and she fluttered about happily among those few of her father's friends from the surrounding area who had been invited back to High Fold, while Sir Richard took care of Dominic's two friends. Minerva was not sorry that she and the marquess had elected to leave by midafternoon. She was on the point of going to change out of her wedding gown when Mr. Grassington came up to her and drew her a little to one side.

"Just wanted to say, ma'am," he confided with disarming candor, "believe you'll do very well for Dominic."

Minerva's eyes twinkled. "Why, thank you, sir. I hope you may be right."

Pelham grinned sheepishly. "Thing is, Dominic ain't an easy man to help. We've tried, Charles and I, so I know! It isn't like him—this skulking away up here in solitary misery. Splendid fellow, full of go in the ordinary way of things. Don't suffer fools, mind, but there's no one I'd leifer turn to in a fix. Only when it's the other way around . . ." He shook his head. "Not much *I* could have done, mind, but Charles ain't short of the blunt, yet not a penny would Dominic take! Deuced high in the instep when he chooses to be!"

"I have noticed."

"Splendid fellow, though," Pelham reiterated hastily, lest she should form the wrong impression. "Lord Wellington thought highly of him—one of the best junior staff officers he ever had, though even he found him hard to hold when he'd taken the bit. Told my august parent so in Brussels last year!"

Minerva was fascinated by this fresh insight into the marquess's character, and said so.

"Ah, well you ain't seen his best side, I daresay. It's his curst pride, d'you see. I mean, can you imagine it? Bad enough being told your father's turned up his toes and you have to come home to do your duty by the family name, without finding that the same aforesaid parent has also squandered the family fortunes and sold his soul to the Jews! Enough to sour the most amiable nature! Small wonder if Dominic did kill that Hagarth fellow—not that he did, mind . . ."

"No, of course he didn't," Minerva agreed. "But you know, I have been thinking about that, and wondering whether we ought to make a push to find out who did, if only to restore Lord Claireux's self-esteem."

Pelham stared at her with new respect. "By Jove! What a capital notion! I knew I wasn't mistaken in you! Lavinia Winterton may be all delicacy and grace, but she would never have come up with such a corker of an idea . . . been a millstone around his neck, I shouldn't wonder, whereas *you* are a positive Amazon among women!"

"Thank you, Mr. Grassington," Minerva said, trying hard not to find the comparison odious. "But I beg you will do and say absolutely nothing for the present, especially to his lordship. It is really no more than an idea, and I would not wish him to take against it before I have been able to test its merit."

In spite of his eager promise, Minerva was already regretting having confided to him what had until that moment been no more than a half-formed thought at the back of her mind. She had scant opinion of Mr. Grassington's ability to guard his tongue, but consoled herself with the fact that since she and Lord Claireux would soon be beyond his reach, he would have no opportunity to blurt anything out to Dominic in the immediate future, and for the rest she could only trust to Providence that he would not alert the true culprit. For now, she had other things to worry about.

The question of a honeymoon, raised in all innocence by Mrs. Peach, had resulted in a few embarrassing moments for the young couple. Minerva had scarcely given it a thought, since the reason for which the custom had been ordained—the desire of a newly married couple to be blissfully alone together—could hardly be said to pertain in their case. If she were honest, the thought of being closeted with the marquess in the unrelieved isolation of some cozy country retreat filled her with apprehension, and she suspected that his lordship's feelings for once coincided with hers.

"But, my love, you must have a honeymoon!" the good lady exlaimed. "It will appear so odd if you do not!"

Minerva and the marquess exchanged glances. She supposed they could go to Claireux Priory, the marquess's family seat in Berkshire. He had already been down there to discuss improvements with his estate manager, and had returned with the news that the house itself needed decorating throughout, but that he thought it best to await her views on patterns and the like before anything was decided. She would have been perfectly happy to go straight there—at least there would be plenty to keep them both busy. But Mrs. Peach had thrown up her hands in horror.

And so, because she had a deep unsatisfied craving for travel, Minerva suggested Paris.

"Good God!" the marquess had exclaimed. "Are you serious?"

"Why not?" she demanded, laughing at his look of disgust. "It is very well for you—you have been to so many places. But I have not been anywhere. And besides, it would be such fun! And if we tire of Paris, we can go on to Rome or Florence or—anywhere!"

Her sheer zest for life and adventure was infectious, reminding him irresistibly of himself not so many years ago. Its very wholeheartedness silenced the crushing retort he had been about to deliver that they couldn't afford it; an argument that was no longer relevant. For the first time in months, the terrible weight of despair seemed less all-enveloping, and if he were to be completely honest with himself, much of the credit must go to this odd, unpredictable girl. Which was as good an argument as any for going along with this, her latest crazy scheme. Perhaps a little fun was exactly what he needed. He shrugged and gave her a slow, lopsided grin.

"Very well," he said. "Paris it shall be."

So all had been arranged. They were to travel post chaise to Dover where Charles Lowdon had a nice little sloop-rigged yacht which he willingly put at their disposal. Joshua's sensibilities had been soothed by persuading him that for him to be driving them all the way to Dover would leave Mrs. Peach without any means of getting about for the best part of a week.

And now the moment had come. The post chaise, hired from Leeds, was at the door, and with it a second carriage to convey Matthews and the baggage, while Drummond, unable to face the thought of being cooped up for so long with the prim-faced maid, elected to ride his faithful roan, Billy, who had carried him safely over some of the most treacherous terrain God had ever devised.

Minerva stood ready in her soft blue-gray traveling dress and pelisse of good Yorkshire cloth. Good-byes had already been said, but she hugged Mrs. Peach once more, begging her to invite whomsoever she chose to stay, so that she might not be lonely.

"Have no fear, m'dear," Sir Richard assured her. "I'll not allow her to mope, eh ma'am?"

Mrs. Peach smiled mistily and hoped that she would not do anything so foolish.

"Good. And my uncle will hold you to that, I know. And you shall come to stay with us the moment we are home and settled, shall she not, my lord?"

The marquess gave her a highly quizzical look, but bowed over Mrs. Peach's hand and smiled into her eyes. "We will be deeply offended if you do not, ma'am."

Mrs. Peach murmured something incoherent, and as they drove away, her last sight of Minerva through the mist of her tears, was of her elegant close-fitting toque trimmed with miniver lying close with a touching intimacy against the folds of her husband's shoulder capes.

5

MINERVA LOVED Paris from the moment they emerged from the crumbling poverty of the outer suburbs where carts and lumbering *diligences* jostled for position amid the unconcerned rabble, and where it sometimes seemed that no light could ever penetrate the perilously overhanging houses that crowded the evil smelling, treachously paved *allées*. By comparison, the wide tree-lined boulevards at the heart of the city made her exclaim with delight.

It had been a long and at times tedious journey, for she very quickly discovered that the marquess preferred to travel fast and with as few breaks in his journey as could be managed. There were indeed times when she wondered whether he was testing her endurance, and resolved that he should have no cause to complain of her fitness to stand the pace. She only hoped the same might be true of poor Matthews.

Her resolve had weakened considerably long before they reached Grantham very late on that first day, and put up at the George Inn. Indeed, she was so weary that any romantical apprehension she might have been cherishing with regard to the imminent consummation of their union had long since vanished; by the time they had snatched a late supper, every bone in her body ached so abominably that she no longer cared what happened to her. In the event, nothing did. To her everlasting mortification, she fell asleep over the dregs of her coffee cup, and thereafter was only vaguely aware of his arms lifting her as though she were feather-light, and of his soft laughter in her ear as he laid her on the bed. This is it, a tiny voice said somewhere at the back of her mind.

The next thing Minerva knew, it was morning and she was beneath the blankets, wearing only her underslip. Of the marquess there was no sign. But Matthews came in as if on cue, bearing a ewer of water and looking little better for her night's rest; poor Matthews, who had suffered agonies on the journey and kept going only by frequent recourse to the hartshorn and salts, and the passionate determination that nothing short of death would part her from her mistress, so that she had been packed off to bed the moment they arrived. Which meant, Minerva realized with a jolt, that her maid could have had no hand in putting her to bed. She glanced across at her dress hanging neatly over a chair, and pulled the blanket close around her neck as she felt the blush spreading slowly up from her toes.

"Did you sleep well?" she asked, as if hoping for a miracle.

"I did, from the moment my head touched the pillow," said the maid grimly. "And much good it will do, if we're to have a repeat of yesterday."

"Oh, poor Mattie!" For a moment Minerva's embarrassment was laid aside in her very genuine concern for this woman who, despite her bluntness, had served her with unstinting devotion as she had served her mother before her. "Would you like me to ask his lordship if we could perhaps rest for a day or maybe two? We are in no particular hurry, after all."

"Thank you, madam, but I'd as lief go on. Whether it be today or in two days' time, I'll feel just as bad, so it's best to get it over and done with."

"Well, if that is really how you want it," Minerva

said. "But I'm sure Lord Claireux would understand." Actually she was far from sure that he would, though she thought it worth a try.

But it seemed that Mattie shared her skepticism, for she only gave her a dour look. "I wouldn't count on it. He's down in the coffee room at this moment shouting for his breakfast, and sending that Drummond hither and thither to make sure that all is ready for setting off prompt. Speaking of which, madam," she added dryly, "it might be as well to complete your toilette before Lord Claireux comes looking for you."

Minerva needed no further bidding. In a remarkably short space of time she was dressed and as ready as she would ever be to face the marquess.

"Ah, there you are," he said, standing up as she came into the dining room. "Now then, what will you have?"

She wrinkled her nose at his plate of cold roast beef and bespoke bread and butter and coffee.

"Is that all? My dear girl, we have another long day ahead of us. Bread and butter won't put a lining on your stomach. You'd do better to have some ham and eggs. Allow me to order some for you." He was already beckoning the waiter as she declined once again, with rather more force this time. "As you will," he said, and addressed himself once more to his own plate.

He was a different person, she realized with some surprise—as though he had suddenly come alive. The thought gave her unexpected pleasure. "Do you miss your army life?" she asked suddenly.

He looked up. "What an odd question." He shrugged. "I suppose I miss certain aspects of it, though it wasn't all thrills and the intoxication of battle, by any means. There were long periods of unutterable boredom to be got through as best we could—hare coursing provided some lively sport if we were out in the wilds, and if we were billeted in a town or village—" he grinned—"we could usually pass our time tolerably well among the local beauties."

"For shame! What a thing to confess to your wife on your honeymoon!" she exclaimed, and then blushed crimson.

The marquess watched the color come into her face and guessed its cause. Did she have the least idea, he wondered, how close she had come last night to becoming a wife in fact as well as name? He recalled how her hair had come loose and spread in shining waves across the pillow as he laid her on the bed; how she had sighed and yielded to his touch as he removed her dress. It would have been all too easy at that moment to rouse her pliant body to passion. So why had he not done so? Stupid tenets of chivalry such as "honor" and "not taking advantage" sprang to mind. Oh, she would have responded! He had no doubt of that, but how would she have felt about it in the cold light of morning? Betrayed? Used? He cursed himself for a fool and resolved to leave any further exploration of the intimacies of marriage until they were settled in Paris.

The remainder of the journey passed off without incident—the sea crossing was an exhilarating experience (though Mattie might not have agreed) and a kind of comradeship developed between Minerva and the marquess out of their shared enjoyment. And if she was puzzled by his seeming reluctance to consummate the marriage, she reminded herself of Lavinia Winterton and resolved to be patient.

And now they were in Paris, in a hired house just off the Champs Elysées, which they had taken in preference to the restrictions of a hotel. The marquess had raised a disbelieving eyebrow when they had their first sight of the imposing mansion, set against a backcloth of giant chestnut trees already fat with buds. But the agent to whom they had been recommended had explained with a persuasive, ingenuous charm that it had been saved from destruction during the Terror by an ambitious builder, who found himself *persona non grata* with the return of the royal family and all their train, and thought it politic to hire out his prestigious home at a modest rent to the many visitors who were flocking to Paris and retire for the present to the comfortable obscurity of his country retreat.

"There are many such," said the agent with a fatalistic little shrug. "It is the way of things. And for you it is most advantageous, as the servants are already installed and there is a town coach in the stables and a pair of fine carriage horses."

It was, as Minerva quite reasonably said, far too good a bargain to pass over. Dominic, though quiet, made no objection, and so it was decided.

"You know," she said when they were installed, "we really could do with a pair of good riding horses, and I don't see why you shouldn't have a phaeton or some-such for your own use. I'm sure you would enjoy driving down the Champs Elysées in your own carriage."

"Isn't that taking things to excess? We are only here for a short time." The old grating note was back in his voice, but in her general exuberance she did not notice it.

"What if we are? I have been talking to Batiste—he is our major domo, a most knowledgeable man—and he was telling me that you can pick one up for next to nothing. So many people here are hard-pressed for money, it seems . . ."

At last something in the atmosphere penetrated her total absorption with planning ahead. She looked up and saw on his face an expression she hadn't seen for weeks. She laid an impulsive hand on his arm.

"I'm sorry. Was I being dreadfully tactless?"

He removed her hand and held it for a moment, staring down at it. "My dear girl, you can hardly be expected to take every word out and look at it before you speak," he said, his voice coolly unemotional. "War deprives men of many things—their sight, their limbs, sometimes even their lives. Set against all that, money is relatively unimportant." His thumb was rhythmically smoothing the back of her hand, though she doubted he was aware of doing it. "Except," he concluded bleakly, releasing her, "when it is constantly being thrust down one's throat."

"Dominic!"

He was already halfway to the door when his name squeezed past the constriction in her throat. He made the dismissive gesture Minerva had already grown to know, but his step never faltered.

"Oh, damn!" She muttered in a most unladylike fashion.

Batiste just happened to be passing the salon as monsieur, the marquess, swept out with a face like Judgment Day. *Dieu me suave*! So much for the English phlegm! Life, it seemed, would not be dull in the weeks to come! The major domo had seen many people come and go since Monsieur Ribalt had begun to let the premises. One would suppose that the whole world wished to satisfy their curiosity about the destiny of his beloved city. Well, she had known the best and the worst in her time, and he was not yet sure how she would fare with *Louis Gros*.

The marquess meanwhile strode out, heedless of his surroundings. He had come briefly to Paris with the army of occupation and knew his way about reasonably well, but his mind was not on where he was going. He had behaved badly—he knew it, but the knowledge only made him more angry. So it was that he did not immediately hear his name being called; not in fact until a carriage rattled past and pulled up just ahead of him, and the window was let down to reveal a familiar head.

"Damme, but your attention is uncommonly difficult to engage, major," said his grace, the Duke of Wellington, his blue eyes snapping with all their customary keenness, as Dominic, his ill temper forgotten, stepped up to seize the hand extended to him. "Your thoughts were not pleasant ones, I think?"

"A trifling matter, my lord. Already forgotten. Oh,

but it is good to see you! I had thought you would be at Cambrai by now."

"So I am, dear boy, so I am. But the headquarters goes on very well without me most of the time, you know, and I have a great affection for this city," said Wellington jovially. "And what of you? Your father died, as I remember. Bad business. Still, we are all mortal, what?"

"Yes, indeed." Clearly, no hint of his subsequent troubles had reached the duke's ears, and Dominic saw no good reason to enlighten him at the present time. "As a matter of fact, my lord, I am recently married."

"Are you, by Jove!" The blue eyes gleamed. "Do I know your bride?"

The likelihood was so remote as to render supposition a mere formality. "I think not, my lord. Minerva is from Yorkshire. She was a Braithwaite."

"Braithwaite?" As expected, the duke shook his head. "Ah well, no matter. Look here, major, Sir Charles Stuart is giving a ball on Friday at the Embassy. You must come and bring your Minerva," and as Dominic began tactfully to refuse—"Yes, yes, my boy, I insist. Sir Charles won't mind. I have Fitzroy with me and young Cathcart. They will never forgive me if I allow you to escape. Besides," his familiar, neighing laugh rang out, "you always acquitted yourself well on the dance floor."

Dominic laughed too, and shrugged. "You make it difficult for me to refuse, sir. Thank you, you are most kind."

"Not at all. Don't forget now." The duke leaned forward to tap the front panel with his cane. "Until Friday."

The carriage moved smartly away and Dominic stood watching it out of sight. Then he turned and retraced his steps. Batiste appeared almost before the powdered lackey on the door had admitted him. Dominic had the feeling that nothing in the house escaped their major domo's vigilance. He was typically Parisian, superficially bland, dapper almost to the point of dandyism with his black macassared hair, but with eyes as sharp as a hawk on the wing.

"Madame has retired to the upstairs salon, monseigneur—not ten minutes since."

Dominic inclined his head. "I am obliged. I don't know if Madame has mentioned the matter to you, but she will be requiring a dressmaker with some urgency. Perhaps you can advise her?"

"I shall be most happy to do so, monseigneur."

"Also," Dominic continued sweepingly, "you were telling Madame, I believe that should I consider purchasing an equipage for my own use, you might well know of one?"

"Indeed, yes. If monseigneur will be so good as to advise me of his requirements, it will be but the work of a moment to arrange."

"My requirements are simple," said Dominic dryly. "Something sporting, reliable, and not too expensive, and, most important, a pair of good blood horses."

Batiste bowed. "Leave all with me. You wish also a groom?"

"Certainly not. Drummond has the best pair of hands of anyone I know. What I will need, however, is a valet, if Drummond is to have charge of the horses."

The major domo's eyebrows quivered at this latest oddity of English behaviour—*a groom who serves also as a valet, enfin!*—but his murmured assent betrayed nothing of his innermost thoughts.

At the foot of the curving staircase the marquess turned. "Oh, and Batiste . . ."

"Monseigneur?"

"Have the town carriage brought around in about ten minutes." Dominic found himself whistling as he took the stairs two at a time—something he had not done in a long time.

Minerva had spent a wretched hour, her mood

veering between remorse and indignation. To be sure, her remark about purse-pinched Frenchmen might be deemed a little insensitive, but it surely did not merit the kind of treatment meeted out to her—as if, she thought, gloomily contemplating a particularly hideous, ornately gilded commode, Dominic supposed her to be vulgarly preoccupied with money, which she was not.

As if her thought had conjured him up, he was suddenly there in the room, a focus for her indignation. There was a light in his eyes, a spring in his step, and an odiously cheerful air of authority and purpose about him before which any lingering desire to conciliate him fled. She was afforded little time to wonder what had caused the change in him.

"Ah, good," he said. "Batiste told me you were here. Pray don your most fetching bonnet, madam wife. We are going out."

She stared at him frostily. "Just like that?"

"Just like that," he agreed.

"Regardless of whether I wish to go?"

"Don't be idiotish," he said, still not understanding. "Whyever would you not wish to go?"

Minerva drew herself up, the picture of injured innocence. "You have a mighty convenient memory, my lord, if you cannot recall how you stormed out of here, not above an hour since, full of injured pride, and not giving me the slightest chance to make amends! Now it seems your humor is magically restored and I am expected to receive you as though nothing had happened!" She stopped to draw fresh breath, but was afforded no time to continue.

"My God, I believe you mean to sulk!" He advanced ruthlessly upon her and grasped her arms before she had time to back away. "Now, you just listen to me," he said, his eyes glinting blackly down at her. "You have many admirable qualities, notwithstanding your strong inclination to wish to manage everything and everybody —and the fault for that lies at your father's door rather than yours—"

"Don't you dare to criticize my father. He was worth ten of most of the men I know!" To her dismay, tears threatened to choke her voice. She tried to pull away and could not.

"So you keep telling me, though he had a strange way of rearing daughters—no, be still, little termagent, I haven't finished with you yet!" Dominic suppressed a strong and unexpected desire to crush her in his arms and kiss her into submission. He did, however, pull her closer, his voice silky-soft. "I don't mind a good clean fight, but if you wish us to deal together, I advise you strongly not to sulk."

"I never sulk!" she exclaimed indignantly, while a corner of her mind registered the fact that he had called her *little*—something which at five feet seven came as a distinct novelty, a not unpleasing novelty. She caught his eye and saw that he was regarding her quizzically, and suddenly the stupidity of her behavior made her ashamed. "Was I very bad?" she asked, blinking away the stinging sensation in her eyes.

He laughed aloud then. "I've seen worse," he said, and then with a magnanimity she had not supposed him capable of exhibiting, "and you had every justification. My own behavior was abominable. Pray accept my apologies." He raised each of her hands in turn and pressed a kiss within the palm. Then he smiled at her in a way that took her breath clean away. "There. Am I forgiven?"

Minerva's reply was incoherent, but it appeared to satisfy him. "Then will you please fetch your bonnet before those long-suffering carriage horses grow tired of waiting? We have some shopping to do."

As he pushed her gently in the direction of the door she turned back, her eyes alight with eagerness. "Did you say shopping?"

"I did indeed. You, my dear Minerva, are invited to a ball."

6

AT FIRST sight, Madame Gerishe's establishment in the Rue de la Paix lacked the grandeur one instinctively associated with a Parisian modiste. But her reputation, avowed Batiste, was unsurpassed.

"Trust me, milady—and trust Gerishe," he confided. 'She will not flatter you, no—but you must not mind her oddness, because she is a genius and will know here—" he tapped his head with an air of deep reverence—"exactly what you must have. She is never wrong."

Minerva could not wait to meet this paragon, and laughingly speculated as they drove to the Rue de la Paix whether the wily Batiste might perhaps receive commission from Madame for putting business her way in the form of guileless foreigners.

"I had no idea you were so cynical, my dear," drawled her husband, stretched out in his corner of the coach and enjoying himself rather more than he had thought to do.

Minerva chuckled. "Not cynical. Realistic. That shrewd corner of my brain which you choose to despise tells me what a wonderful opportunity for gain it would be."

The establishment in the Rue de la Paix certainly did not impress from the outside; a modest front, discreetly curtained windows, and although the steps were spotlessly clean, they were also well worn. The marquess was all for going somewhere else, there and then.

"There was never any shortage of mantua makers in Paris in the past, and nothing seems to have changed," he said. "We must have passed at least ten first-rate places on our way here."

Minerva was surprised. He had appeared totally disinterested in the passing scene as he told her about his meeting with the Duke of Wellington and the subsequent invitation to the Embassy ball. And she, hanging on his every word, had certainly been too engrossed to notice anything. But it made little difference, for she was determined to at least meet Batiste's prodigy; quite apart from her curiosity value, and the fact that she would not know how to look her major domo in the eye if she ignored his recommendation, Minerva was aware of the vague prickling up the back of her neck which always presaged something of unusual importance, and which seldom if ever led her astray. She had had the same sensation, she remembered, on the night she first met Dominic.

A plump elderly woman admitted them and waddled before them in a hushed silence up a short narrow staircase, and just as Minerva became aware of "I told you so" coming in thought waves from Dominic at her back, they were ushered into a salon of such startling contrast that she stopped short, stepping on his foot.

"Oh, I'm sorry," she said in a dazed way.

"Think nothing of it," he murmured.

His magnanimity quite passed Minerva by, so intrigued was she by her surroundings. The room was spacious, luxuriously carpeted, and exuded an air of quiet elegance; neutral colors bathed in a soft light from two giant chandeliers made a perfect backdrop against which all colors would appear at their best. There were long mirrors everywhere one looked and comfortable chairs placed in groups here and there. The plump woman indicated that they should be seated and vanished through a curtained alcove into a smaller salon beyond.

"Well," said the marquess, stretching out his long legs, "so far, so good. Of course, you do realize there may be problems of communication?" he added wickedly. "The Gerishe woman probably won't speak a word of English, and my French is strictly of the army variety!"

Minerva threw him a look, but was given no chance to reply for the curtains in the alcove had parted once more to frame a diminutive figure in a simple black dress. Madame Gerishe, for it could be no other, was thin almost to the point of frailty, but her pointed features and short black hair windswept in the fashion of a man, exuded the indefinable chic of the true Parisienne. She came forward with quick little steps, amid a torrent of words.

"Good God!" Dominic murmured. "She looks exactly like a clipped poodle."

Minerva kept her countenance with difficulty, for it was true—the hair, the face, the manner—all conveyed the exact combination of hauteur and excitability of a well-bred poodle! She waited for Madame to pause for breath in order to elicit whether she spoke English.

"A trifling amount, milady—and very badly. Also, to create in English is *impossible*! It is better that we converse in French, *enfin*." Without troubling herself as to Minerva's ability to understand, she launched once more into rapid speech. And Minerva, thanking Providence and the Ladies' Seminary for the two years of rigorous instruction by Mademoiselle Sophie, whom everyone had hated, endeavored to keep up with her. "So—you will oblige me, if you please, by walking across the salon? Ah, it is good! You have excellent carriage! Women of such a height so often stoop, like so." Mme. Gerishe proceeded to demonstrate. "As for that pelisse! It is of too hard a color—and the line . . ." She shuddered. "But no matter. I shall create for you a toilette that will make you weep for joy!"

Minerva dared not meet her husband's eye; she was having trouble enough suppressing a strong desire to go off into peals of laughter, and not for anything would she forgo what promised to be the most entertaining encounter of her life to date. And so it proved. Her shortcomings, it appeared, were prodigious, but nothing so drastic that Madame could not cure it with her superb artistry.

Dominic had expected to be bored long before the session had been brought to a satisfactory conclusion, but the sight of Minerva knee-deep in swatches of material, valiantly arguing with *La Gerishe* over the rival merits of blond satin against the finest *eau de nile* silk or the delicacy of a *mousseline de soie*, provided him with almost constant amusement. Only when they vanished into the mysterious area beyond the curtains did he find the time hanging heavy, although even then, Madame had thoughtfully provided him with refreshment in the form of an excellent Madeira which made him warm afresh to her.

They had never been so much in harmony as on the journey home, laughing together over Madame's absurdities, Dominic, with his hat tipped over his eyes, mimicking her fast-talking assessment of Minerva's good and bad points. "*Alas, we cannot hope to achieve miracles! Milady's stature precludes the frail look . . . but I shall create for her an original look that will turn all heads!*"

"Oh, do stop!" Minerva begged. "I declare, I am not sure whether to be outraged or flattered at being so comprehensively taken apart and put together again."

"My dear girl, the woman may be a genius of a kind, but design the outer casing as she may, I defy her to change you one iota. That *would* require a miracle!"

"And how am I to take that, pray?"

He turned his head against the squab to look at her, a smile still lingering in his eyes. "As a compliment, of course. What else?"

She shook her head, but blushed a little just the same.

And when the mood continued throughout the day, she began to hope that there had been a subtle but important change in their relationship. In the evening, a visit to the theater, supper *á deux* in a nearby café, and a stroll through the Tuileries gardens, all in the utmost harmony, seemed to add credence to her expectations.

At bedtime she was all fingers and thumbs, and several times she caught Matthews looking at her strangely.

"All this gadding about and foreign food," muttered the maid, who was barely recovered from the rigors of the journey. "Feverish, I shouldn't wonder. Next road up, you'll be sickening for something, mark my words, and no Dr. Barton to set you right!"

"Nonsense, Mattie. I'm as fit as a flea!" Minerva declared, but when the maid had finished brushing her hair until the roots screamed, and had gone off to her own bed, she studied her reflection in the mirror. Was it the candlelight that made her eyes seem so bright, her skin so pale? Would Dominic come tonight? Oh, why were all her nightgowns so eminently sensible!

She climbed at last into the great herb-scented bed—yet another of the owner's gilded monstrosities—and lay with thumping heart, eyes closed, listening for the slightest sound of movement next door. The herbs wove themselves into her senses, and gradually the strain of concentration induced a kind of trancelike drowsiness so that he was already in the room before Minerva became aware of the tall figure in a handsome dressing gown.

She shot upright with a small incoherent exclamation, her hair spilling around her shoulders in disorder, her senses in even worse disarray, and all her good intentions of being very adult about the whole thing flown out of the window.

To Dominic, standing at the foot of the bed, it seemed that he had misjudged his moment, after all. He had been encouraged by the easy progress in their relationship throughout the day—had been so sure over supper that she was actively encouraging him. But now, God help him, she looked about twelve with her lovely hair falling in drifts about her face and sheer panic staring out at him from wide unblinking eyes.

"I'm sorry," he said abruptly. "I disturbed you. You were asleep . . ."

As he turned to leave, she was suddenly galvanized into action. "No! No, truly, you didn't . . . I wasn't! Oh please, don't go!" Her voice was tremulous, pleading, and he glanced back to see that she had flung back the bedclothes in her agitation and was already swinging her legs around to come after him. She looked tumbled, wholesome—even a shade wanton! Not in the least like that practical, sure-of-herself young lady who had on more than one occasion in the past few days driven him to the brandy glass in lieu of her arms.

He covered the distance between them in a few swift strides and gathered her into his arms, the moment dissolving unromantically into laughter as sheet and nightgown became inextricably intertwined. Just as the whole thing seemed destined to descend to the realms of farce, his mouth moved seductively close to her ear. "My dear, there is really only one course left to me . . ." and she felt his fingers loosening the buttons of her nightgown, one by one.

Minerva awoke with a languorous feeling of well-being. At first she did not even wonder at its cause; not in fact until she became aware that she was not alone, that something lay heavily across her, impeding movement. And then she remembered and smiled to herself. All that agonizing speculation among the girls at the Seminary—such a fuss, she thought, about a very natural act, although she suspected that Dominic's skillful and—yes—enjoyable lovemaking owed much to experience, but even in her ignorance of such matters she was also aware that he had been more than usually gentle and considerate of her feelings.

She had no idea of the time, but one of the curtains

had been caught back against a chair, sending a shaft of pale early light across the bed. Impelled by curiosity, she cautiously raised herself on one elbow and turned to look down at the man who, for good or ill, now belonged to her and she to him. Dominic lay half-turned toward her, the sheet pushed down, and one arm flung across her in a gesture of careless possession. In sleep his face had lost the look of strain which never entirely left him during waking hours, and even with the blue shadow of stubble on his chin, he looked younger than his twenty-nine years. She leaned a little closer, drawn by the soft vulnerability of his mouth, wanting to touch it. She was still wondering if she dared when his hand came up without warning to close round the nape of her neck, pulling her mouth inexorably down to meet his.

"Hussy!" he chided, his voice muffled, buried in her hair. "A complete innocent. That's what I expected!"

"So I was, but my teacher was an expert!" His fingers began to wander, and she chuckled as she caught his hand and removed it from temptation's way. "You will have to go, soon. Mattie will be coming in."

"Let her come," he said magnanimously, releasing her and rolling over to lie on his back with his arms folded behind his head. "You have your marriage lines, signed and witnessed."

"Oh, do stop teasing," she implored him. "You know very well that she would be dreadfully embarrassed!"

"I fail to see why."

"You *know* why!" A touch of panic edged the whispered plea. "She isn't used . . . besides, my nightgown is still lying in a heap on the floor."

"Well, if you wish to reclaim it, I won't try to stop you." Dominic's eyes laughed mockingly into hers, daring her, enjoying her confusion. Then, slowly, his glance moved down. "You know, I often wondered how far a blush could spread!"

"Beast!" Minerva cried in mock indignation, trying

without much success to drag the sheet around her.

"Ah well, I can take a hint," he said, planting a swift kiss between her breasts before throwing back the bedclothes and reaching across to a nearby chair to retrieve his frogged dressing gown. As he stood to shrug his way into it, she was afforded a brief glimpse of his fine muscular body etched like alabaster in the half-light. Then he was tying the gold-tasseled cord and walking around to her side of the bed. He stooped and picked up the crumpled heap of cambric. "Your nightgown, I believe, ma'am," he said, presenting it with a flourish and noting with a curious, possessive pride, a new softened, almost luminous quality about her face. "Now you really look like a bride," he said softly.

Much later, Minerva realized that he had never actually mentioned that he loved her. Was it possible to commit yourself so totally and not love? She remembered Mrs. Peach's stumbling and quite ineffectual efforts to prepare her for what was to come. "Gentlemen, my love," she had explained, "have certain . . . needs that must be satisfied. I daresay you will think it all very strange . . . for it has very little to do with *love*, as you and I might perceive it . . . but there it is . . . Our duty is clear, to submit ourselves to our husbands, as St. Paul tells us . . . and if we are so blessed, there will be love as well . . . and perhaps, children, though in my case, it was not to be."

At the time, Minerva had felt only a kind of mingled pity and amusement, that poor dear Mrs. Peach had suffered those strange unnamed things to be done to her by the Reverend Peach without even one baby to show for it. And yet, for all that, she had clearly been devoted to the Reverend Peach, and he, so far as Minerva could remember, had held his wife in great affection. But with a sudden blinding sureness she knew that Dominic's affection was not what she craved. She had tasted of the fruit and found it good, and could not, would not now be satisfied with anything less than total commitment, total fulfillment. Something special had happened between Dominic and herself, something she was too inexperienced to analyze. But it was a beginning. In time might she even make him forget his Lavinia and see her instead as the embodiment of all his dreams?

7

DRUMMOND WAS in his element once more. Not only were his days as a valet behind him (for good, he hoped) but he now had charge of the sweetest pair of matched bays it had ever been his privilege to behold—regular good'uns, complete to a shade—and a sporting curricle worthy of his lordship's undoubted talent. Of course, a curricle and four would have been preferable, but he doubted there were many Froggies who'd be capable of handling such a turn-out.

His opinion of Lady Claireux, not high at the first, had risen steadily since the wedding—a skimble-skamble affair, as he had been unwise enough to describe it to that sour-faced maid, reckoning his lordship could have done better for himself, notwithstanding his spot of bother. But her ladyship had a frank open way with her that suited him, and he couldn't deny that the marquess had cheered up no end in the last few days.

Batiste congratulated himself that he was really doing rather well for Lord Claireux. Not only had he secured for monseigneur a very great bargain in the acquiring of a most admirable equipage, but—more importantly in his opinion—he had only that morning received word of the untimely death of an English aristocrat on a visit to Paris, a gentleman who had long been envied by his peers for the excellence of his valet, now sadly stranded in a foreign land with neither master nor credentials. He at once made arrangements for Lord Claireux to interview him.

Moss was, upon first acquaintance, intimidating. A neat individual of indeterminate years and moderate height, he was himself impeccably though unobtrusively attired, and exhibited a faint air of hauteur which he wore almost as a badge of office. His late lamented employer, Sir Greville Pinkly-Hartington, had been for some years a most dedicated arbiter of Fashion, and would no doubt have continued so for many years to come had he not been carried off by a sudden and, as it had transpired, fatal inflammation of the lungs, brought on in Moss's opinion by recklessly venturing out in the damp air of the previous Monday evening.

Sir Greville was, however, like many such gentlemen, niggardly when it came to parting with the gilt, and had most disobligingly gone to his Maker owing six months' wages to his valet and a month's rent on the rooms he had taken in the Rue de Varenne, the latter situation being rectified by the instant reclamation of the premises by the landlord.

One might be forgiven therefore for supposing that Moss would regard Lord Claireux's appearance upon the scene as little short of an Act of God. But his manner suggested otherwise. He viewed his lordship's attire with severe misgivings—his shirt points were modest, his cravat, though crisply laundered, owed little to artistic imagination, and not a single fob adorned the plain gold chain across his waistcoat, the sole redeeming feature being a quizzing glass on a plain black riband. However, desperation obliged him to acknowledge that the marquess was not quite beyond reclamation. He had a fine pair of shoulders, an excellent leg—one would never have to resort to discreet padding, as in Sir Greville's case, and if his lordship might in the fullness of time be persuaded to patronize Weston instead of Scott . . .

"He has agreed to give me a month's trial," the marquess told Minerva over dinner that evening.

"*He* has agreed to give *you* . . ." She stared. "Oh, come, Dominic, you are funning?"

"By no means, my dear. Moss is clearly a prince among valets, and as such, I must be a sad letdown to him. Indeed, I gained the distinct impression that he comes to me much against his better judgment, and only because his patriotic principles will not permit him to engage himself to a Frenchman. He did not say so in as many words, but I suspect I am his eventual ticket back to England where he will doubtless soon find himself a more discerning employer, deserving of his talents."

"Humgudgeon!" declared Minerva with a chuckle. "Monstrous behavior! I should send him to the right-about here and now!"

"Ah, but you have the redoubtable Matthews to wait upon you and pander to your every whim," he said mournfully. "Whereas, now that I have lost Drummond to those beauties in the stables, which you talked me into buying, if you remember, I am bereft of help."

"Ha!" exclaimed his unsympathetic wife. "Helpless indeed! I would like to see that, I must say!"

"And besides, who knows—a few weeks under Moss's expert tutelage and I might emerge as the second Brummell."

But this was too much for Minerva, who cried "God forbid!" and went off into peals of laughter. Dominic pretended indignation, but her laughter was infectious and he was soon joining in.

Minerva was truly nervous for almost the first time in her life on the night of the Embassy ball.

"For the lord's sake, will you stop fidgeting, m'lady," grumbled the exasperated Matthews. "How on earth I'm expected to get this pearl fillet threaded into your hair with you turning this way and that, I don't know!"

"Sorry, Mattie! But do hurry . . . I don't want to keep his lordship waiting."

"And no more you will, if you'll just be still for a moment more. There. That should hold well enough."

Minerva stared at her reflection as though at a stranger. Mattie had dressed her hair high, falling in clusters of curls from the highest point, with a few soft wisps about her face. Her eyes glittered strangely in the candlelight, half apprehension, half excitement. She stood up slowly and the folds of peach-bloom satin whispered soundlessly around her as she moved in order to allow the ruched hem to sweep back into its short train. The ruching, the gown's only ornamentation, was repeated on the low-cut neckline of the brief bodice, and around her neck she wore a string of perfectly matched pearls, her father's gift to her when she was eighteen.

"Oh, Mattie, will I do? It is *so* important that I should be accepted as a lady!"

As Matthews stared at her, her eyes dimmed for a moment and she saw Minerva's mother at much the same age—smaller, slighter, but with that same look, and with a similar distracted cry, "Oh, Mattie! I do *so* want Papa to like Hezekiah!" She cleared her throat to say with her usual gift for understatement, "I don't know about a *lady*, but I reckon as they'll see nowt better there tonight!"

Dominic was waiting at the foot of the stairs. Minerva had seen him many times in his formal black and white, but the influence of Moss was already clearly evident in those deft little touches which raise careless elegance to the realms of excellence. She paused, impressed and unaccountably shy. Then she descended the last few steps, very conscious of his quizzing glass raised to mark her progress. Reaching the last step, she halted and blurted out: "Well? Please tell me what you think—truthfully."

He was slow to answer. In truth, she had somewhat taken his breath away. Her taste had always been good, but the genius of Madame Gerishe had given it a new dimension; from the pearl fillet, his gift to her, nestling in her burnished hair, to the pearl-studded pumps which exactly matched her gown, she was entirely delightful to behold.

"You surely don't need me to tell you," he said slowly.

"Oh, but I do!" she implored him. "This is something entirely new for me, you see—moving in first circles—and I don't want to let you down. I know you occasionally think me brash and outspoken, but I will try to think before I speak, and if I can feel that I look right, it will be such a help."

Dominic stepped forward and took her hand. He raised it to his lips and looked up at her with no hint of mockery in his smile. "My dear, beautiful wife, I have never doubted your ability to hold your own in any circles, first or otherwise. And if you are not successful in doing so this evening, I shall own myself very much surprised."

"But do I look elegant?"

He laughed. "That's doing it a bit brown, my girl! Too many compliments and you'll be getting above yourself." He saw that Matthews had followed her down with a wrap over her arm of matching satin edged with swansdown. He took it from her and draped over Minerva's shoulders, "There," he said. "Ready?"

The British Embassy occupied a prestigious position on the Rue du Fauberg St. Honoré. It had belonged in its time to a variety of people, Dominic told her as they approached the high, impregnable walls which set the building aloof from the world beyond. Most notable were the Dukes of Charost for whom it had been built in the early eighteen hundreds, and latterly, Napoleon's lovely nymphomaniac sister Pauline, Princess Borghese, from whom Wellington had acquired it, lock, stock, and barrel, for the British Government in 1814. It stood high *entre cour et jardin*, and on that evening the lofty gates were flung wide to admit the steady stream of carriages.

"Oh, it is lovely," Minerva said softly as they stepped into the hall where marbled columns rose either side of an elegant curving staircase with an exquisite handrail, and the marbled walls and painted panels in *trompe-l'oeil*. But each room seemed lovelier than the last until finally they reached the ballroom where the Duke of Wellington waited with the ambassador, Sir Charles Stuart, and his wife to receive the guests.

Sir Charles greeted the marquess amiably, reminding him of their last meeting in the heady days after Waterloo when the Allies had triumphally entered Paris for the second time in fourteen months. "I'm told we have something in common, my lord—both newly wed?" His smile extended to Minerva. "My congratulations, ma'am. May I present my wife, Lady Elizabeth?" The young ambassadress greeted them shyly. Minerva felt sorry for her. She was indisputably plain, and although the daughter of an earl, was as yet unused to the duties expected of her. But she bore the ordeal with a quiet, endearing fortitude.

"Ah, Dominic—you came. Good." The duke's eyes were already turning from him to Minerva, a decided gleam in their blue depths. The marquess, amused, presented her. "Enchanted, ma'am. I knew your husband had good taste, but he has surpassed himself. We shall meet later, no doubt, when all this formal nonsense is over. Dominic, you will find Fitzroy somewhere about—he'll look after you, introduce you to people." But his eyes still lingered on Minerva as they turned to leave him.

Dominic was shaking with silent laughter as he guided Minerva through the press of people, but when she asked him why, he would only shake his head and murmur "Later!" He was clearly looking for someone and presently advanced upon a handsome, rather serious looking young man with his right sleeve unostentatiously affixed to his coat. "Fitz! At last. Allow me to present my wife. Minerva, this is Lord Fitzroy Somerset." Minerva smiled as she returned his greeting. "Fitz and I go a long way back—to those heady Pennsular days when we served together as staff officers to Lord Wellington. Not many of the old family left now, eh, Fitz?"

"No, indeed." Lord Fitzroy sighed. "D'you know, I still miss Gordon. Cathcart is here with us—did his lordship tell you?—but most of the old guard who were left are scattered. Not a lot to stay on for, I suppose."

"Yet you have remained," the marquess interposed before he could ask awkward questions. They would doubtless come later. "Intrepid fellow, this, Minerva. Secretary to the great man—lost his right arm at Waterloo, and in no time at all was learning to write with his left."

A smile lit the square, serious face. "We suit one another, his lordship and I."

"He seems in good form, does old nosey!" Dominic began to chuckle again, and this time Minerva demanded to know why. "Obviously you didn't notice the way he was looking at you. Watch out, my love, or he will have you for one of his flirts! Tell her, Fitz."

"Hush, Dominic," his friend reproved. "He is teasing you, ma'am, though it is true that the duke does have an eye for a beautiful woman, and if I may say so, one really could not blame him if his glance did stray in your direction."

She blushed, but not so much at the compliment as at the memory of Dominic's having called her "my love," without, she guessed, even realizing he had done so. She was allowed little time to dwell on the tempting vistas opened up by this revelation, for Lord Fitzroy was at that moment summoned by the duke. Hastily, he introduced them to a Monsieur and Madame Gironde, and then left them, promising to return as soon as he could do so.

The French couple conversed amiably for a few moments, exclaiming over the beauty of the Embassy in general and the ballroom in particular, it being their first visit. From that they went on to inquire how long the marquess and his so charming wife were intending to stay in Paris, to which no certain answer could be vouchsafed, and just when the conversation seemed in danger of floundering, there was a slight disturbance in a nearby group of people, a sudden swirl of skirts, and a gay, laughing voice exclaimed: "Minerva Braithwaite! But this is famous! Of all places, I never expected to find you here!"

Minerva found her hands seized by a pretty dark-haired young lady with laughing brown eyes. "Georgie! Oh, famous indeed!" she cried, and they fell upon one another, both talking at once. It was a few moments before she even remembered Dominic and the Girondes. She turned swiftly to apologize, but Dominic, with a faint quirk of the eyebrow, was already moving aside with the French couple, who dismissed her apologies, insisting that they had seen some friends signaling to them from across the room.

Minerva smiled happily and turned back to her friend. "Georgie! Georgie! How good it is to see you!"

"So you say, wicked creature! But why have I never heard a word from you since we left the Seminary? You promised faithfully that you would write."

Minerva was hard put to it to provide a plausible explanation as to why she had not kept in touch with Lady Georgiana Lees, who had been quite the best friend of her school days. She had been then, as she was now, a lively, uncomplicated girl with a friendly, open manner, and there was no reason to doubt that she would have been delighted to pursue their relationship beyond the schoolroom. She began to explain about her father's death, but Georgiana's tongue was already running on, not waiting for explanations.

"We have been here almost two weeks. Papa is on one of his diplomatic missions, and Mama decided it was high time I saw something of the world—" she grinned impishly— "and gained a little Parisian polish!"

Minerva doubted that she needed any such thing. A

London Season had already given her a thin veneer of sophistication, and her half dress of ivory silk over a white satin slip, which bespoke Paris in every line, merely added a further dimension.

"You must come along and meet Mama and Papa, and my dear friend Vinnie, who has been terribly down-pin recently and has been dispatched to Paris with us for a cure!" Georgiana chuckled. "Actually, I believe Lord Cathcart is rather smitten with her, which would be the very best thing that could happen . . . But here I am, prattling on, when what I *really* want to know is how you come to be here? Are you with friends?"

"As a matter of fact," Minerva said, feeling unaccountably shy, "I am not Minerva Braithwaite any longer. I am here on my honeymoon."

"My dear!" Georgiana's squeak of excitement made one or two heads turn, close by. "But how wonderful! Tell me at once—is it anyone I know?"

For the first time, Minerva felt the faint stirrings of unease, for if her friend had spent any time recently in London, she could hardly be ignorant of the scandal surrounding Dominic. And if she were, it was almost a certainty that her parents weren't. In the circumstances, there was nothing to be done now but to brazen it out.

"You must allow me to introduce you," she said with admirable composure, and looked around to see if her husband had managed to free himself of the Girondes.

He had. He was, in fact, no more than a few feet away, standing absolutely still, looking not at her but at someone at little beyond her—and with an expression in his eyes that shook Minerva to the very core of her being. She turned slowly, following the direction of his gaze to the group from which Georgiana had broken away, and from them to a young woman who stood a little apart from them. She was, without doubt, the loveliest, most fragile looking creature Minerva had ever seen. Silver-fair ringlets accentuated a pale, heart-shaped face, a vulnerable mouth that seemed to tremble even as she watched, and enormous long-lashed eyes of a deep gentian blue, now wide with shock.

Amid the buzz of conversation the orchestra could be heard tuning up, but the imminence of the dance, in fact time itself, ceased to have any meaning as Minerva felt her heart being squeezed until the pain of it made her feel momentarily dizzy. For this was the moment she had secretly dreaded. She did not need to be told who Georgiana's ailing friend Vinnie was. She was Lavinia Winterton.

8

"MINERVA? ARE you all right?" Georgiana's voice seemed to come from a long way off. She drew a shuddering breath, summoned up every ounce of pride she possessed, called her husband back from the abyss into which he appeared destined to plunge at any moment, and introduced him to her friend, explaining how it came about that they knew one another so well.

Georgiana's face was a study. "Oh, Lud!" she ex claimed, her dismay almost comical, and he—recovering his composure with remarkable ease—said ironically, "Just so, Lady Georgiana. I infer my fame has gone before me?"

"Yes . . . that is, no!" She glanced over her shoulder toward her family group with something like despair. "Oh, heavens! Whatever am I to do?"

"Do?" His face had taken on that shuttered look Minerva knew so well. Any minute now he would say something cutting.

She laid a hand on his arm and said calmly, "Quite simply, Dominic, poor Georgiana has a problem." It was as though someone else had taken over her mind and body, Minerva thought, amazed by the ease with which she was able to handle the situation. Later the pain would return, but not now. Now she was Hezekiah's daughter, and nothing and no one was going to find her wanting. "Miss Winterton is presently the guest of the Earl and Countess of Lanyon, Georgie's parents." Minerva's fingers tightened on his arm as if willing him to be generous. "Her dilemma is in deciding how best to proceed without causing Miss Winterton unnecessary pain."

The marquess looked sharply down at her, as if suspecting her of sarcasm, but there was only concern in her eyes, though he detected a certain steely resolve about her chin. He studiously avoided looking across at Lavinia as he bowed and said with clipped formality, "My dear Lady Georgiana, what can I say, except to assure you that I will do all in my power to avoid any embarrassment."

An elegant young man had appeared at Georgiana's side, and executed a punctilious little bow. "Lady Georgiana . . ." he rolled the name out proudly. "It is the first dance. You are promised to me, yes?"

"*Monsieur le vicomte!* Yes indeed . . . I . . ." She threw Minerva an anguished glance. "My dear, I must go! We shall meet later, I am sure, but . . ." Very conscious of the marquess standing in ominous silence, she lowered her voice. "May I call on you tomorrow?"

"Yes, of course." Minerva gave her the address and watched her depart on the arm of her French beau. There was an unconscious wistfulness in the slight droop of her mouth which penetrated the blackness of the marquess's mood. I warned you how it would be! he wanted to shout, but he could not do it. This was, after all, her debut, arranged by him. It meant a lot to her, and the least he could do was to play his part.

"Come," he said abruptly, and taking her hand, swept her off into one of the sets that were forming up on the dance floor. Neither of them looked toward the Lanyons' party as they passed, nor were they aware of the slight flurry of activity as Miss Winterton uttered a faint sigh and slipped to the floor in a swoon.

Minerva almost forgot about Miss Winterton as the evening progressed. Georgiana whispered to her as they met briefly that Vinnie had felt a trifle faint and had been taken by Lady Elizabeth Stuart to lie down. To her shame, Minerva's first sensation had been one of relief. Lord Fitzroy saw to it that she was not short of partners, and she and Dominic had received an invitation to take supper with the duke, who was, so her husband informed her, in excellent form.

Dominic, too, had been relieved to see Lavinia leaving the ballroom with Lady Elizabeth, though he was at that moment unaware of the indisposition that had necessitated her departure. The shock of seeing her so unexpectedly had affected him more deeply than he was willing to admit. To have her so near, to be so aware of her distress, and to be unable to do anything about it, was a kind of refined torture. And it was made doubly difficult by the presence of Minerva, to whom, for good or ill, he was now bound by the ties of matrimony, and who, for all her apparently prosaic approach to their union, was every day revealing qualities that intrigued and entertained him. Even her attitude concerning Lavinia was more generous than many a man might hope to find in his wife.

It was unthinkable, Dominic decided, as he watched her dancing an energetic *ecossaise* with young Cathcart and clearly enjoying every moment, that he should ever contemplate any action which would test that generosity. Though he could not offer Minerva his undying love, she had every right to expect to be treated with due honor and respect. He must put all thoughts of Lavinia out of his mind.

He had no sooner made this decision when Lady Elizabeth approached him somewhat diffidently. The favor she wished to ask of him was delicate in the extreme, and only the direst necessity obliged her to approach him . . .

Minerva found Lord Cathcart to be a most engaging young man whose eager enthusiasm reminded her irresistibly at times of Mr. Grassington. "My word!" she exclaimed as the dance came to its conclusion. "I haven't exerted myself so much in years. I am quite exhausted, and must, I am sure, look an absolute fright!"

This his lordship gallantly denied, declaring that any incapacity must be due solely to the excessive heat in the ballroom. "Pray, allow me to procure you a reviving glass of cordial, ma'am," he begged her with a solicitude that placed her firmly in the category of the matron. She kept her gravity with difficulty and declined, resisted the temptation to tell him that she was younger than he, and avowed meekly that she would instead seek out the retiring room in order to repair the ravages of her exertions.

Refusing his offer to escort her, Minerva set off in search of the retiring room, which was situated somewhere among the many anterooms. She passed the door of a smaller room which was not quite shut, though decidedly it should have been, for the conversation taking place was, to say the least, impassioned and clearly of a delicate nature. She ought not to have listened, of course but the temptation was irresistible.

"How could you do it? . . . Marriage, so soon, and to such a nonentity!" The reply was muffled and was followed by an anguished plea that trembled on the air. "Dearest, I'm sorry! Oh no, don't leave me yet!" and again a reply more distinct this time, but scarcely less urgent. "My dear, this is madness! You know very well that I should not even be here!"

It was her imagination, of course—a trick of the ear that made the man's voice seem so familiar. She moved without conscious volition to push the door wider.

They were standing very close, the fair head dropped against his breast, soft white fingers clinging to the lapels of his coat. The stifled gasp of Minerva's indrawn breath must have carried across the space between, for he looked up and their eyes met.

She had no idea how long she stood there; it seemed like hours, but it could have been no more than a moment before she closed the door, ignoring him as he called after her. Her only thought in those first moments was to remove herself as swiftly as possible from the scene. To her relief, the retiring room was deserted except for a little group of maidservants chattering in a corner. She sat down on the nearest chair, and only then realized how much her legs were trembling.

How could he? How *could* he? screamed her unmarshaled thoughts. God in heaven, she had not expected to gain his love (though foolishly she had begun to hope) but nor had she expected him to show so little resolution in the face of temptation. That was what hurt, what disappointed her so bitterly—whatever his faults, she had not thought him weak!

"Madame?" It was one of the maids, her face concerned. "Pardon, madame, but you are perhaps not well? Is there something you wish?"

Was there something she wished? Ah, yes, but unfortunately it was quite beyond her reach, and to be fair, it had never been otherwise, except in her mind. She straightened her shoulders, and smiled reassuringly at the maid. "No, nothing," she said. "Everything is fine."

Dominic was waiting for her when she emerged; not, as might have been expected, an embarrassed or even a contrite husband. He was clearly furious, taking her arm in a bruising grip as he hurried her along. "Why the devil did you rush off like that? I have been kicking my heels waiting for you—just the thing to give any gabble-grinders food for their jaded appetites!"

Her own anger at being thus gratuitiously placed in the wrong threatened to erupt with equal force, but Madame Gironde was coming toward them, a beaming smile on her comfortably plain face.

"Such a delightful evening! But, *hélas,* my poor bones will not take any more. You young people are so fortunate, are you not? *Eh bien!* When I was your age, I too could dance the night away!"

Minerva had no idea what reply she made, but it appeared to satisfy madame, who went off in high good humor.

"Perhaps we should leave also," Minerva suggested icily. "You are clearly no longer in any mood to enjoy yourself."

His hand tightened on her arm as she turned to follow Madame Gironde. "Oh, no! That really *would* be folly!"

With a sensation of shock, she realized that they were outside the very room where she had seen him with Lavinia Winterton so short a time ago. "Is she still in there . . . your paramour?" She cried, white-faced and wanting to hurt him. From his expression, she appeared to have succeeded all too well.

"Probably," he said stiffly. "Resting, I trust. And she is not— Oh, hell and the devil!" he exploded with soft force, pushing his fingers through the coiffure that Moss had arranged with such skill, and quite ruining it. "Look, Minerva, I can't explain now. It would take too long, and besides . . ."

"You needn't bother." She wrenched herself free. "I am not interested in your explanations!"

For a moment they stood glaring at one another, she with her eyes sheening with unshed tears. Dominic saw them and silently cursed. "Very well," he said stiffly. "But do, I beg you, have a care how you behave—for your own sake, if not for mine."

He was right. She knew it. With a shuddering sigh, she lifted her head high. "You needn't worry. I won't let you down."

And she kept her word. For the rest of the evening she was excellent company. Without putting herself forward unbecomingly, she found herself much in demand, responding to the duke's flirtatious overtures during supper with just the right degree of sense and good humor, so that Wellington was heard to say later to the marquess that he had a veritable treasure in Minerva and had best look to his laurels, by God, for he was like to find his drawing room constantly beseiged by her admirers.

Poor Georgiana had been obliged to leave the ball early. "The most tiresome thing to happen, just when I was enjoying myself so prodigiously," she wailed, finding Minerva in one of her few brief respites from dancing. "I shall not easily forgive Vinnie for thwarting my pursuit of the Vicomte de Beauville . . . a divine creature and such charming manners!" She kissed her fingers to him.

"I am sorry," Minerva said. "I do feel that we are very much to blame for Miss Winterton's indisposition. If we had known she was in Paris, Dominic would never have come, I know." Or would he? she thought.

"Stuff!" retorted her friend with scant concern. "Why should you forgo your pleasures on Vinnie's account? You might as easily have met in London, after all. In any case, for all that she is a friend, I don't mind telling you that she can be exceedingly peevish if she don't get her own way, and is not above creating a scene. I fear Mama's fingers have been itching to slap her more than once since she has been with us! I'd say your Dominic can count himself fortunate to have you instead of her! I do think he is rather gorgeous, incidentally—something of the rakehell about him . . . and all that delicious scandal! Only fancy, one would never have expected you to be so dashing!"

Since Georgiana was unaware of the small drama that had taken place earlier, there was little to be said other than to murmur some kind of agreement. "I'm sorry about your vicomte, though," Minerva said sympathetically.

"Don't be." Georgiana grinned. "I have discovered that there is nothing like a trifling setback to encourage an eager suitor! If the vicomte is not on the doorstep tomorrow, I shall own myself very much surprised!"

It was well past midnight when Dominic finally managed to secure Minerva for a waltz, and only then by ruthlessly cutting out Lord Cathcart. "That was very unkind," she protested breathlessly as he hurried her on to the floor. "Poor Lord Cathcart! I promised him this waltz ages ago. He was quite cast down!"

"My heart bleeds for him," drawled the marquess, and with his mouth against her ear as they dipped and swirled to the haunting rhythm, "Do try to look pleased, my dear. We are newly married, or have you been enjoying yourself so much that you had forgotten?"

"There is nothing wrong with *my* memory," she retorted, smiling brilliantly up at him.

He laughed—a brittle, reckless sound—as for answer he whirled her ever faster until all coherent thought spun away and only sensation remained. The pressure of his hand was warm against her back, the hard muscular line of his thigh merging with hers as he almost lifted her off the ground. All combined with the sensual lilt of the music to remind her of a myriad delights of exploration and recognition—of drowning in the intimate touch and taste of him. The light from the crystal chandeliers whirled into brilliant dizzying fragments above their heads, and unconsciously she pressed closer.

And then the music ended. They stood for a moment unmoving, heedless of everyone else leaving the floor.

"Minerva?" he said softly, an unfamiliar note of uncertainty in his voice.

How much had she betrayed her feelings? she wondered in blind panic as reality returned. For if this

9

IT WAS A little after dawn when the lone horse and rider left the house in the Rue St. Jacques and, after a moment's hesitation, turned swiftly in the direction of the Bois de Boulogne. There was little sign of life—the occasional carriage returning with its weary occupants from a night of revelry (Minerva winced at the thought)—and here and there a beggar, scrabbling among the drifting rubbish in the street.

Minerva rode at a brisk canter, resisting the urge to break into a gallop along the Champs-Elysées. She had hoped that the early morning air would clear her head, which ached from fruitlessly reliving the events of the previous evening.

It had been well into the early hours of the morning when they returned home, and she had been too restless to sleep. Dominic had made no attempt to come near her—indeed, she would have been astonished if he had, for he had been conspicuously silent since that last waltz. But when daylight began to show and sleep seemed as far away as ever, she had put on her riding habit and gone silently down to the stables.

Drummond was already up and going slowly about his chores, years of army discipline having trained him to sleep little and rise at the first hint of light. He was at first surprised and then disapproving when his mistress had requested him to put her saddle on the bay mare.

"Now, why would you want to go riding around foreign streets as ain't even been aired, m'lady?" he muttered. "Who's to say what nasty piece of work might not be lurking about."

"At this hour?" Minerva said dryly. "Surely not. And in any case, I am particularly fond of riding very early in the morning. Some of my most important decisions have been made while riding across the moors at the break of dawn."

Drummond could recognize a stubborn woman when he saw one, and he knew it wouldn't be aha'porth of use trying to argue, even had it been his place to do so. Even so, he was far from happy when she politely but firmly declined to accept the protection of his company. He was even less happy when his lordship appeared not ten minues after she'd left, and demanded to know in that soft silky way of his, what the *so-and-so* he'd been thinking about, letting her ladyship go off on her own—an awesome turn of phrase, had his lordship, when he was roused. Best to keep your head low and wait for the storm to pass, in a manner of speaking!

Minerva had already reached the Bois and put the mare to the gallop along the deserted Allée de la Reine Marguerite which ran straight and clear through its center when she heard the sound of hoofbeats coming fast behind her. For a moment she was apprehensive, remembering Drummond's admonitions, but a swift glance over her shoulder brought, if not reassurance exactly, relief from any fear of physical attack.

Nevertheless, she swerved from the road to take a lesser path beneath the trees leading to the Petit Lac. She had no illusions about his ability to overtake her and so made no attempt to outride him. Instead, having reached the lakeside, she reined in the mare, slipped easily from her back, and tied her to the branch of a nearby tree.

By the time Dominic had tied his own horse up alongside, Minerva was standing motionless at the lake's edge, staring out over the water, a trim, erect figure in bronze green velvet. The snap of a twig disturbed the silence as he strode angrily toward her, and a pigeon in the tree above crooned a protest and flew away.

"Well?" Dominic demanded shortly.

She drew in a deep, unhurried breath. "How very peaceful it is. Did you know that the people skate here in the winter? They have galas and light fires and hang lanterns all along the route. It must be very pretty."

The marquess, incensed, seized her by the shoulders and spun her around. "What the devil do you think you are doing?"

Minerva gazed up at him from beneath the brim of a chic black shako, her expression tranquil. "I'm not really doing anything—except taking an early morning ride. It is an occasional habit of mine."

"So Drummond informed me. But the Bois de Boulogne is not the Yorkshire moors, as you must know! I'd be willing to wager that even now there are thieves and vagabonds lying in wait for people like you who think what a splendid idea it would be to come here all alone to admire the beauties of nature!"

"And they lay violent hands upon them?" she inquired pointedly, stung by his sarcasm.

He released her at once, as though his fingers burned. "I know perfectly well why you felt the need to get out. I didn't sleep, either. Dammit, Minerva, we have to talk. You must let me explain about last night."

"No." She turned abruptly away, looking out again across the lake. "I don't want to know. Oh, not because of jealousy or pique or any such silliness." She swallowed over a painful constriction in her throat. "I was angry at the time, because it was so unexpected. But it must have been even worse for you . . . and I do understand, you see, what it must be like to know that someone you love very much is miserable, and that you are powerless to help her."

"Minerva, stop it!" Dominic took hold of her again, but gently this time. "You are making me feel like the worst kind of knave."

"Humgudgeon!" she said with a resolute smile. "I married you—in fact, you might say I almost forced myself upon you—knowing full well how you felt about Miss Winterton, and since you could hardly hope to go for long without meeting her, something like this was bound to happen sooner or later. Perhaps it's better sooner. I don't know about you, but I always like to get anything difficult or unpleasant over with as soon as possible."

He was searching her face, trying to read into the prosaic calmness of her manner some hidden distress. But, saving a certain unnatural brightness in the blue-gray candor of her eyes, there was nothing to be discerned.

"It won't happen again," he said.

"I know that."

He looked puzzled as he kissed her mouth lightly. "Have I ever told you that you are a most unusual girl?"

Minerva's smile remained steady. "I believe you have, my lord." She put her hand in his. "Shall we go home now?"

Total innocence of the world into which her marriage had catapulted her found Minerva unprepared for the number of visitors who called or left cards in the days following the Embassy ball. Invitations proliferated, gathering like an unseasonal drift of pasteboard snow along the mantelshelf, and Batiste, scenting the possibility that the marquess and his charming bride would eventually be called upon to return such hospitality, began to preen himself and make preparations.

Minerva's very first, and perhaps most surprising caller on that first morning was Lady Elizabeth Stuart. Minerva greeted the shy young ambassadress warmly, and in response to a tentative inquiry as to whether they were likely to be interrupted, carried her off to her own private sitting room and gave precise instructions to Batiste that should anyone else call, he was to show them into the yellow salon and inform monsieur. Also, she would like coffee brought up as soon as possible.

Bien sûr, madame," replied Batiste with a flourishing bow.

The sitting room on the first floor was small by the standard of the other rooms and relatively unembellished by gilt and furbelows. It looked over the rear gardens and let in the morning sun. Without appearing to notice the way her guest twisted the strings of her reticule between nervous fingers, Minerva kept up a stream of inconsequential talk as she settled Lady Elizabeth in the most comfortable chair.

"How fortuitous that you should call," she said with a smile. "I was on the point of writing to thank you for making us so very welcome last evening." And in an attempt to put her visitor at ease, added confidingly, "I have spent most of my life in Yorkshire, you know, and am not yet wholly comfortable in society, so your friendliness and warmth were very much appreciated."

"How kind! One would never have thought . . ." Lady Elizabeth's voice was unconsciously wistful. "I, too, am finding it a trifle difficult to manage everything. It is foolish, I know, but I still find public functions quite terrifying . . . . and make silly mistakes. My husband is very patient with me, of course . . ."

"I don't consider it in the least foolish," declared Minerva with more conviction than absolute truth. "The mere thought of them quite sinks me!"

"Do you really think so?" The confidences, once begun, could not be stopped. "I had to be presented, you know . . . . the Duchess d'Angoulême, the daughter of Marie Antoinette, received me at the Tuileries, but I was so stupidly tongue-tied. She is such a very daunting, sad lady, I could think of nothing to say!"

Batiste came in with the coffee, putting period for the

present to melancholy reflections. Minerva, sorry though she was for Lady Elizabeth, greeted his arrival with some relief as her lack of sleep was in danger of catching up with her. The major domo poured and served the coffee with great ceremony. When he finally left the room, she said with determined cheerfulness, "Well, in my opinion you underestimate yourself. My own failing, as I am sure you will have noticed by now, is the reverse of yours, and just as tiresome, as *my* husband would no doubt tell you. I am, by nature, outspoken, and frequently speak my mind without due thought." She sipped her coffee and studied Lady Elizabeth over the rim of her cup. "Forgive me, but at the risk of proving my point, your visit isn't concerned with some supposed omission on your part last evening? Because if so, I confess I am mystified."

"Then perhaps . . . but Sir Charles insisted that I should come."

Minerva's tone was at its most bracing. "Well, whatever it is, you had much better get it off your chest, as my father was used to say."

This brought a faint smile from her visitor. "Yes, you are quite right. It concerns poor Miss Winterton." In her anxiety to explain, Lady Elizabeth failed to notice the guarded look that came into Minerva's eyes. "Sir Charles was quite cross with me for involving Lord Claireux, but I couldn't think what else to do . . . even poor Lady Lanyon was at her wit's end. Miss Winterton was distraught, you see . . . almost hysterically so, and would not take the mild draught of laudanum we had prepared for her until she had spoken to your husband." Lady Elizabeth's voice trembled. "Sir Charles said that if you were anything but a most charming, sensible young lady, you might well have taken the strongest exception . . ." She glanced anxiously at Minerva. "I do *hope* you were not angry or distressed?"

Minerva, striving to adjust her confused thoughts, and remembering all too well how angry she had been, was slow to answer. If only she had allowed Dominic to explain! But she must not think of that now. Lady Elizabeth's mind must be set at ease.

"No," she said, "I was not upset. In fact," and it was true, "I do most sincerely feel for Miss Winterton. Unrequited love must be a terrible blow to endure." To lend conviction, she defied the gods by adding, "When one is fortunate enough to be happily married, it is doubly distressing to know that one's state may, however unwittingly, have contributed to someone else's unhappiness."

"Such unselfish sentiments are just what I would expect, Lady Claireux," came the trembling reply. "Truly noble!"

But this was altogether too much for Minerva, who gave a soft gurgle of laughter. "Oh no, dear ma'am! I am not the least noble, I assure you. Now, do pray let me give you some fresh coffee and we will speak of other things."

When Lady Elizabeth had left, feeling much cheered by her visit, it was Minerva's turn to grow pensive. Could she be blamed for having jumped to conclusions? Or was it simply the quixotic cruelty of fate that had shown her as clearly as could be that her husband, though innocent of ignoble intent, had not altered in his affections toward Lavinia Winterton? That being the case, her only problem was in deciding whether to confess to him that she now knew what had taken place in that small room at the Embassy last night, or whether to leave well enough alone. On reflection, the latter course seemed preferable. Nothing, after all, would be changed by telling him and to drag it all up again might damage the delicate balance of their relationship yet again.

Minerva was allowed little time to brood, however, for she entered the yellow salon to find Georgiana attempting to flirt with Dominic under the faintly disapproving eye of her mother. Lady Lanyon was not enjoying her visit to Paris. She had anticipated it with such pleasure. From one cause and another it was some years since she had been able to accompany her husband on a diplomatic mission, and Paris had ever been one of her favorite cities. She had looked forward to sharing its hidden treasures with her daughter, and even when Lord Winterton had begged her to include Lavinia in their party, she had foreseen no problem. Girls were ever falling in and out of love—and she would be company for Georgiana.

Oh, how heartily she had regretted that decision! Lavinia might look like an angel, and even give a passable impression of being one when all was going her way, but she had been ruined by an overindulgent father. Lady Lanyon did not know the rights and wrongs of Claireux's affairs, but if his behavior on the previous evening was anything to go by, he seemed a very proper young man with many excellent qualities—and it crossed her mind that if Georgiana's friend was even halfway as sound as she made her out to be, the marquess had done a lot better for himself than might have been the case had Winterton not eschewed him as a son-in-law.

Her initial impression of Minerva seemed to confirm her in this belief. She certainly said everything that was proper, and had a pleasant, no nonsense way of making one welcome, in which, knowing something of her background from Georgiana, the countess could discern none of those traits which so often typified the daughters of self-made men.

Dominic watched Minerva's handling of Lady Lanyon with interest, making no effort to come to her aid; not that she needed his help, he acknowledged ruefully. She was quite without artifice, and treated her ladyship much as she did Drummond, or anyone else—with her own particular brand of natural courtesy. Because he was, for the moment, an onlooker, he was amused to note how Georgiana's glance kept straying to the door, and the reason became obvious when the Vicomte de Beauville was presently announced.

Georgiana immediately lowered her head so that the wide brim of her bonnet, a most becoming creation lined with peach satin, hid her from view, but not before Dominic had observed the rosy blush which suffuced her face. The young epitome of elegance bowed with the exact degree of correctness over the hand of each lady in turn, making Dominic feel suddenly very old, and was immediately commanded by Lady Lanyon to sit beside her. He cast an anguished glance toward Georgiana—and complied.

"Rolled up, horse, foot, and guns!" Dominic murmured, chuckling beneath his breath.

Georgiana's bonnet brim tipped to one side as she glared at him and whispered back, "That sounds like some horrid army expression!" And then, reluctantly, she grinned. "Oh, well! At least I may now get a word with Minerva."

It was little more than a word, for soon more people were arriving, Lord Cathcart among them. "Goodness!" exclaimed Minerva, as the room began to fill up. "Where *have* they all come from?"

"I believe you have made a *succés fou,*" Dominic said dryly, passing her on his way to greet the Duke of Wellington, who crowned the morning with his presence.

Georgiana, now with her vicomte firmly in tow, giggled. "I believe the duke has developed a *tendre* for you, Minerva!"

"Pray, don't even think such a thing!" Minerva begged her. "I have quite enough problems without that!"

"Oh, la! That I should have such problems!" her friend chided. And then: "I have just heard Lord Cathcart asking Mama how Lavinia was! *Resting,* declared Mama in a voice that dared him to question further. Actually, she brought a doctor to her this morning who has prescribed rest and a mild sedative for the next day or two, so let us hope that she will by then have come to her senses."

Oh, what a coil, Minerva thought. But, as always when there was nothing she could do to mend a situation, she tried to put it out of her mind. And indeed, in the days that followed their social debut, she and Dominic very quickly became accepted, and not only by the English community in Paris. The French aristocracy, now firmly entrenched once more among former glories after the alarms and excursions of Napoleon's Hundred Days, very soon decided to take the English couple to their bosoms. The hint of some slight scandal surrounding the marquess, far from putting them off, lent an added picquancy to an already interesting personality.

At first, Minerva was flattered to be the center of attention, but she gradually came to realize that their interest was superficial; compliments which came trippingly off the tongue, were shallow and lacked sincerity. The discovery in no way lessened her delight at being in Paris—if anything, it added to her enjoyment, for she was able to observe with amusement the antics of a people dedicated to an unceasing round of pleasure.

There were at times disturbing undertones to all this gaiety. The old aristocracy, some no longer wealthy, looked for a new golden age, and were bitterly resentful of those who had grown in stature under Bonaparte's rule and refused to be dominated by what they saw as the remnants of a corrupt dynasty. The obese king was accepted, but not without reservations on both sides, being too indecisive to please either.

There had been some very nasty incidents in the recent past, Dominic told her—killings—and although now all was calm on the surface, there were constant hints of plots and counterplots being hatched in the dark underworld where ambition to dominate held sway. Minerva did not doubt him, but it was difficult to reconcile with the hedonistic antics of the people they met as they rode daily in the Bois, or in the evening at the inevitable soirée or ball.

Miss Winterton was soon sufficiently recovered to

resume a limited social round, the only evidence of her recent *indisposition* being an interesting pallor and an air of frailty which must have stirred all but the hardest heart to pity.

"Thank you," she would whisper in a faint voice when some eager gentleman stooped to rescue a dropped glove, leaving her sad little smile to linger in his mind for the remainder of the day.

"She even has my Etienne fooled!" Georgiana declared indignantly, as she and Minerva met at one of Madame Recamier's intimate soirées. Across the room fair ringlets shimmered in the candlelight, surrounded by a clutch of elegant young hopefuls, while Lord Cathcart kept jealous guard.

"Your Etienne?" Minerva inquired softly.

Georgiana flushed becomingly and grinned. "Well, he hasn't declared himself yet, but he will. Mama approves of him, and Papa always listens to her. Not that he would disapprove. After all, Etienne is one of the luckier ones . . . the bulk of his family's fortune was spirited away to Vienna at the start of the Revolution, so he is eligible as well as charming!"

"Well, I couldn't be happier for you," Minerva said, and meant it. It must be wonderful, she thought, to experience a love that was so wholehearted and carefree, untrammeled by complications.

Her own relationship with Dominic was not without hope; a state of amity existed between them which occasionally spilled over into a kind of loving. But Lavinia Winterton, by her very presence, inhibited them both for different reasons. Minerva had several times recently seen them talking together, his head bent close in a manner which, to her oversensitive fancy, seemed protective. She had tried to put such fancies out of her mind, but whether from this cause or a simple lack of desire on Dominic's part, they had never again attained the magical intimacy of that night when Minerva had first glimpsed the joy of total fulfillment. Perhaps, she reasoned, she was exaggerating its importance because for her it had come as a blinding revelation; men, or so Mrs. Peach had implied, viewed the act of love quite differently. But she refused to believe that it was always so. For the moment she would bide her time, but one day . . . one day she would prove that she was right.

10

THE SEASON was in full swing when the Marquess and Marchioness of Claireux arrived back in London.

Word had been sent ahead of time to Mr. Thripp, of Fingleton and Thripp, who had acted for the family for as long back as anyone could remember, to hire the best available residence with all speed, and having done so, to send down to Abbey Park where Marsham, his lordship's butler, had been living in restricted circumstances ever since the family fortunes had suffered their fatal reverse.

"Just like his father and his grandfather before him," grumbled Mr. Thripp. "Think you can work miracles. Never ask 'Can it be done?' Oh, dear me, no. His late lordship would never have found himself in the suds to such a catastrophic extent if he'd taken the advice that was there for the asking."

"Very true," agreed Mr. Fingleton with a sad shake of the head.

"I mean, where am I to find a house in London at this time of year?" The folds of Mr. Thripp's double chin wobbled with the force of his grievance. "And in the fashionable area, for it's my guess nothing less will suit, and money being no object, as you might say."

"Hm." Both men sat in a gloomy silence for some moments. Then: "What about the Bridlington place in

Grosvenor Street?" suggested Mr. Fingleton. "I heard only this morning that they have suffered a bereavement —Lord Bridlington's mother, I believe—and are preparing to close up the house and go down to Suffolk forthwith. Worth sending a note around to Appelby, who acts for them, wouldn't you think?"

So it was to Grosvenor Street that Dominic and Minerva came, rather more laden down than when they had left England almost two months previously, so that it had been necessary to lay on a much larger extra coach to accommodate Matthews and Moss plus a quantity of portmanteux and bandboxes—far more than Minerva had realized.

"Can we really have acquired so much in so short a time?" Minerva cried, staring in rueful dismay as the pile mounted.

"I reckon so," muttered Matthews, depressed by the thought of the forthcoming journey.

Batiste was almost in tears when the time came for their departure. Never, he declared, had he felt himself to be so fortunate as in the past weeks. It had been a joy, quite unparalleled, to serve them, and were it not for the impossibility of leaving his beloved Paris, he would follow them to the ends of the earth.

Minerva was touched. She had no doubt that within a week he would be sighing a little, and within a month he would remember them with a distant esteem—no more. Yet, she had grown fond of him, of his extravagances and his enthusiasms, and knew that she would miss him.

But she was not altogether sorry to be going home. A life devoted to unrelieved pleasure, even in Paris, must eventually pall, and besides, there had been frictions of late which distressed her. The Duke of Wellington eventually returned to Cambrai, for how long no one was sure, taking Lord Cathcart with him—a very miserable Cathcart, for he had proposed to Miss Winterton before leaving and had been rejected out of hand.

"Oh, I wish she might have been a little kinder!"

Minerva was moved to say when Georgiana told them as they rode in the Bois.

"Why?" Dominic said brusquely. "If a break has to be made, better a clean one that leaves no room for hope." Almost immediately he rode away, on the pretext of wishing to talk to someone.

"Lud!" exclaimed Georgiana. "Have I been indiscreet?"

"No, of course not." But Minerva wished that Dominic had not been there. His words seemed to carry a terrible significance—as though they had come straight from the heart. If only she herself had not spoken so critically in his presence.

Lavinia Winterton was not short of admirers, but it soon became clear that she was missing the single-minded attentions of Lord Cathcart. An ingenuous young man he may have been, but he was sincere—something that many of her other admirers were not. And again it seemed that she was turning more and more to Dominic. It was this, more than anything else, which precipitated Minerva's suggestion that they should return home.

As if to spite her, the journey proved much less enjoyable than the previous one. The sea crossing, though calm, made her feel queasy, and for the first time she appreciated how Matthews felt. She was never so glad as when the coach finally turned the corner into Grosvenor Street.

"Oh, but it is quite charming," she exclaimed, rousing from the doze into which she had fallen over the last few miles to catch her first glimpse of the house. "Your Mr. Thripp has been very clever, I think."

Dominic thought so too, and privately wondered how he had persuaded Bridlington to hire it out to them. It was good to see Marsham looking much more like his old self. It had been distressing, when he had gone down to Abbey Park before the wedding, to see the way the butler's thin shoulders had begun to hunch as though he were shrinking into himself. He had owned to being a trifle down-pin, but it was clear to Dominic that the old fellow suspected that he had been put out to grass. It was for this reason as much as any other that he had sent for him to take charge of the household, and that it had done the trick was evident in the jaunty step and straight back.

"May I say, my lady, how very pleased and proud I shall think myself to be serving your ladyship," he said with all the dignity that his calling demanded.

"Why, thank you, Marsham," she said with a warm smile. "Dominic has told me all about you, and about how you used to help him out of scrapes when he was a boy."

"Fancy his lordship's remembering that, my lady. Well, I never!" The butler's nose twitched several times, very fast. "Master Dominic was a good boy . . . full of fun, you know, but a good boy." He shook his head and recalled himself to his duties.

"Thank you, Minerva," Dominic said quietly when they were alone. "You could not have said anything more guaranteed to please the old fellow."

She sank into a chair and leaned her head back with a sigh of relief that they had finally stopped moving. "Well, I'm glad. He obviously thinks a great deal of you."

"I thought I might go down to Abbey Park in a day or two, to see how the work is going down there," he said. "Would you care to come?"

"Oh, Dominic, I don't believe I could face another journey for a while."

He looked at her sharply. "It isn't like you to cry enough! You are all right? I must admit you don't look in prime twig."

"How very ungallant of you to say so!" Minerva roused herself to smile at him. "Yes, of course I'm all right—just a little tired. That wretched journey! But I must write to Uncle Richard and to Mrs. Peach to tell them we are home, and invite them down whenever they wish to come. And I would like to find my way around this house."

She glanced around the comfortable drawing room and sighed. "I must say it is a great improvement on the Rue St. Jacques . . . all that gilt! Though I had grown quite attached to it by the time we left." He was still regarding her intently, and she suddenly lost patience. "Oh do, I beg of you, stop looking at me in that way. It makes me feel quite horridly peaky and plain!" And to her everlasting shame, she burst into tears.

This was so out of character that he became really worried, but he knew better than to say so. "Right, young lady," he declared in his best army bark that brooked no argument, "It's bed for you, and you stay there until I say different." And he picked her up as though she weighed no more than a feather, and carried her up the stairs, protesting and hanging on to her hat with one hand while she scrubbed away at her tears with the other.

Minerva slept the clock around and awoke feeling very much better, to find Dominic sitting in a chair near the window, reading. The sun was slanting across his bent head, teasing lights out of his dark hair, lovingly arranged by Moss in a windswept style. She lay for a few moments without moving, pondering on the thought that he might have been there all night keeping watch out of devotion to her. It was such a delightful delusion that she was loath to relinquish it, but at last, with a sigh, she sat up.

Dominic turned at once, putting down his book. "Ah, good. You are awake." He came to sit on the bed beside her, examining the flushed face, still vulnerable with sleep, lifted to him. For an instant, he longed to push his fingers into the cloud of tangled dark hair and draw her mouth to meet his, and cursed the uncertainty that held him back. "Well, you look a lot better, at any rate."

"I am. I told you I was simply tired."

"So you did. In that case, I might just allow you to

get up for dinner—just a quiet dinner for the two of us." His look grew quizzical. "Does that sound dreadfully prosaic?"

She drew a blissful breath. "It sounds like heaven. What have you been doing with yourself?"

"I strolled along to White's for an hour or so last night to see if Pelham and Charles were there."

"And were they?"

"No, but several other people were, including Cousin Gervase."

Minerva sat forward. "I didn't know you had a cousin. Oughtn't we to have invited him to the wedding?"

Dominic looked amused. "My dear, we might have invited him, but he wouldn't have come. The exertion would have quite sunk him."

"Oh, well, if he is elderly, perhaps we could ask him around to dinner one evening. Perhaps I can persuade Uncle Richard to come and stay, and I'm sure Mrs. Peach will." His shout of laughter startled her. "Now what have I said?"

"Nothing at all, my dear managing wife. It is simply that Cousin Gervase is, if I remember correctly, three and thirty—a mere four years older than me! But it takes very little to fatigue him."

"Oh, I see." But it was clear that she didn't, really.

"You will understand when you meet him."

"*Am* I managing?" she said in a small voice. "I don't mean to be."

"Only in the nicest possible way," he said, dropping a kiss on her head as he stood up. "And now that I see how much improved you are, I can go to Abbey Park with a clear conscience."

"Dominic?" She put out a hand to him. "I do *want* to see your home, you know."

"Yes, of course," he said, but she wasn't sure if he believed her.

The following day Dominic rode into Berkshire, promising not to be away for more than a day or two at the most, and Minerva set about putting her own house in order. She wrote her letters, including one to Mr. Briggs, who was in charge of her affairs in Yorkshire, familiarized herself with the house and servants, and went through her clothes with Mattie to see whether there was any urgent need for refurbishment. After which she sat down on the bed with a sigh.

"As well his lordship is away, or he would start bullying me again," she said, vexed with herself. "I don't know what's got into me."

"Happen you should consider what you've just said," said the maid cryptically. Minerva looked at her uncomprehendingly, thought about it, and then, as her blood leapt: "Oh! But it can't be . . . I'm not . . . I haven't . . . no, no, it's too soon."

"I wouldn't know about that," said Mattie dryly. "But I know you, m'lady, and I've never seen you carry on the way you've been doing the last few days. It takes different folk different ways, that much I *am* sure of." She sniffed. "Of course, I could be wrong . . ."

A baby! The thought amazed and terrified Minerva by turn. Of course she wanted children, but so soon! Would Dominic be pleased? She decided not to say anything, just for a little while. How foolish she would feel if it were a false alarm.

The marquess and Drummond made good time on the road. It was like old times, riding together. Odd how one's life could change in so short a space of time. This time last year he had been in Brussels preparing for battle with no thought in his head of leaving the army, and Waterloo had been no more than an insignificant dot on a map, though like many of those closest to Wellington at the time, he believed that his lordship already had it pinpointed as the most likely place for his final confrontation with Bonaparte.

Those had been heady days, notwithstanding the danger. He would sooner face an adversary face to face any day, then endure the kind of sniping and backbiting that had been his lot in the short time since his return home. Oddly enough, he had come close to forgetting the unpleasantness during their stay in France; not that his troubles had remained a secret, but being one step removed, as it were, no one thought to take them seriously.

It had come as something of a shock therefore on his return to find certain members at White's turning their backs on him.

"Shouldn't regard it, if I were you, dear boy," murmured his cousin, Gervase Wilmington, coming up behind him in the wake of one particularly marked cut. "Old Cornfield always was a high stickler!"

Dominic had never supposed he would be glad to see his dandified cousin; not that he disliked him, it was simply that they had absolutely nothing in common. Gervase wore showy coats very tightly waisted, and affected shirt points that made any movement of the head a virtual impossibility, and if that were not enough, his conversation seldom rose above the trivial.

"I was hoping to find Pelham here, or Lowdon," he said without comment.

"Not been in, to my knowledge. Lady Jersey is giving a soirée, as I remember. That's where they'll be, I'd lay odds on't. Sent my apologies—didn't fancy a whole evening of her la'ship's unremitting chatter!" Gervase put up his glass. "You have a new way of tying your cravat, I see. I like it—yes, decidedly I like it. You must show me the way of it."

"Lord, it's no good asking me. You had best see my valet."

"Valet?" mused his cousin. "H'm. Heard you had done rather well for yourself, dear boy. Golden leg shackles and all that," he continued with a consummate want of fact. "Just the thing to quash any lingering rumor. No news about that missing document box, I suppose?"

Dominic said shortly that there was not.

"Only wondered. I mean, whoever does have it might

well be tempted to make use of the contents. Could be quite a profitable little operation."

"And dangerous, since that person almost certainly murdered Hagarth."

"How very true," agreed Gervase softly. "I had not considered that! But then, I have often envied you your perspicacity. However," he added, eyeing his cousin's grim face with a degree of trepidation, "I daresay you would as lief not talk of such unpleasant things. Tell me instead about your bride."

Dominic had never felt less like doing so, and was in consequence less than enthusiastic on the subject, which would, he supposed later, have given Gervase quite the wrong impression, but since what Gervase might think had never unduly concerned him, he found little difficulty in putting the matter from his mind.

The visit to Abbey Park cheered him no end, for the whole place, as Marshal had ventured to remark, was slowly coming back to life—the gardens cleared and the gardeners hard at work, the home farm too showing a decided improvement with the increase in the workforce; even the windows of the house shone, giving clear evidence that it was being cared for once more, though most of the interior decorations were being left for Minerva to choose. This was the place Dominic had always thought of as home—not an elegant house by any means, having been much altered, and not always wisely, from its pre-Reformation days when it had belonged to the monks of Claireux, but it was the place where much of his childhood had been spent, and he could only be thankful that the entail had prevented his father from disposing of it along with so much else.

He must be pleased, too, he told himself, that Minerva's money had made its present refurbishment possible; in fact, until his cousin's gibe about "golden leg shackles," he had almost ceased to mind. Now he consoled himself with the thought that once the place was paying its way again, he might recoup his fortunes to the point where he could hold his head up once more, something which had seemed impossible but a short time ago. All this and more he owed to Minerva; and to be fair, she had never once sought to make him feel beholden to her, as many might.

If he had a regret, it was that the apparently total disappearance of Hagarth's document box still left a cloud hanging over his future. Financially speaking, his affairs were now on course for improvement, but he disliked unfinished business. He must have a talk with Thripp when he returned to London, he decided, to see what, if anything, could be done to clear the matter up.

Sitting alone in the library with the evening sun burnishing the shabby leather chairs, he found himself wondering about Minerva—even worrying about her. It was so uncharacteristic of her to display an anything less than robust temperament. Quite suddenly he wished to get back, to assure himself that she was recovered—even to tell her how the improvements were progressing at Abbey Park.

It was late when he and Drummond reached the outskirts of London, but after a fine day, light still lingered pale and clear in the night sky. They had not long passed Chiswick on a quiet tree-lined stretch of road when four men on foot burst from the covers and ran suicidally into their path, one of them letting off a pistol almost at the feet of Dominic's black gelding. Had the horses been ordinary mounts, they must surely have reared in panic, unseating their riders. But both Ebony and Drummond's faithful old roan, Billy, had come through many a campaign, braving fire and shell without flinching, and treated the efforts of such singularly incompetent footpads with contempt, answering the pull of the reins by swerving around and coming up behind them.

"Ware your right, m'lord!" shouted Drummond, dragging his own pistol from its holster.

Dominic half-turned and the movement probably saved his life. He felt the scorch of the bullet as it scraped his temple beneath his hat. "Hell and the

Devil!" he muttered. His own pistol cocked, he swung around and fired straight at his adversary. The man screamed and fell back. Drummond had already accounted for one of the others and the remaining two turned tail and fled, with the groom in pursuit.

Drummond was soon back, disgruntled, with the news that the miserable varmints had escaped into the trees and he could see nothing to be gained by crashing around in the dark looking for them.

"Well, we won't get anything out of these two," said Dominic, who had dismounted and was hanging onto the rein, staring down at what remained of them. Sheer unmitigated insanity, he thought, feeling sick and a little giddy.

"Hold up, major." Drummond's voice came from a long way away. Then a shoulder was under his oxter and he was being lowered gently to the ground with a tree trunk at his back. "That's a nasty-looking wound—gouged quite a deep gash, that bullet did. Just you sit still, now, while I do what I can with it."

For a moment Dominic thought he was back in the Peninsula, and then his head began to clear. "Damned careless!" he muttered in disgust. "Seven years and ne'er a scratch, and I get winged by a pesky footpad!"

"Yes, well, we might have done a lot worse," said the groom. "You wouldn't happen to have a clean handkerchief about your person, would you, m'lord?"

"I very much doubt it. You will have to use my neckcloth." He laughed weakly. "Moss won't like it, but needs must . . ."

In a very short time he was on Ebony's back once more, protesting that he was feeling fine, but Drummond kept a careful eye on him for the remainder of the journey, and was not sorry when they reached Grosvenor Steet.

Minerva had not long retired when she heard the knocker and the sounds of unusual activity below. Quickly, she pulled on her dressing gown and hurried to the stairs, guessing that Dominic must have returned.

The scene below was confusing at first; Marsham was there, and at least two of the footmen—and Drummond, who seemed to be issuing a number of instructions. Beyond them, and masked by them, she could hear Dominic's voice raised in protest. She hurried down and pushed her way through.

"Whatever . . ." she began, and then stopped as she saw him. The left side of his face was caked in dried blood which had obviously come from a roughly bound wound. Her heart stopped for a moment, and then began to thud, but she forced herself to appear calm.

Dominic did not seem to be in the least pleased to see her. He glared at her and obliged her to retire. "This is no place for you, ma'am," he stated firmly. "And the rest of you can go about your business, also. I have no desire to be mauled about, and I want no doctors. Drummond will do all that is necessary."

Marsham, clearly distressed, looked to Minerva for guidance. "Do as his lordship says," she told him quietly. "And I would be obliged if you would arrange to have a bowl of hot water and some cloths, and some basilicum powder, if we have such a thing, brought to the library." He went away, taking the footmen with him, and Minerva led the way to the library, leaving Drummond to bring up the rear with Dominic.

"More light, I think," she said, when the marquess was safely settled in a chair with a small sofa table close by, and as Drummond brought a branched candlestick and set it on top of a Chinese cabinet, "That's better."

Dominic opened his eyes, which had been closed upon first sitting down, and squinted up at her. "Stubborn as ever, I collect?"

She smiled placidly at him. "Just performing my wifely duty, my lord."

"Oh, good God!" he groaned. "Drummond, be a good fellow and pour me a large brandy."

The groom looked unhappily at Minerva, who shrugged and indicated with her fingers, unnoticed as she supposed, that it should be a small one.

"Drummond—" the marquess's voice was at its silkiest—"may I remind you that you take your orders from me, not my wife."

The groom looked unimpressed. "Yes, m'lord," he said, pouring a short measure and handing it to him. Dominic glared at him, but drank it without comment.

At this point the footman came in bearing a loaded tray. "Thank you, Robert. Put it down here, will you? If I need anything else, I will pull the bell." A little pale, but with determined cheerfulness, Minerva began to unravel the cravat and saw that it had stuck in places. "I will try not to hurt you," she said, wringing out the cloth in order to damp down the worst affected areas in order to ease them free.

"I wish you would not put yourself to the trouble," he said. "You can scarcely be fully recovered from your own indisposition."

"Oh, that! A second night's sleep cured that." That this wasn't wholly true, and took no account of her succumbing to sickness first thing in the morning, troubled Minerva not at all. "Yesterday, I may tell you, I was taken out driving by your friend, Mr. Grassington. Your cousin informed him that you had returned to town, so he came in search of you—and, not finding you, entertained me in your place. A very pleasant young man."

As she talked, Minerva peeled away the last and most stubborn piece of the neckcloth, and her eyes instinctively sought Drummond's as she laid bare the wound.

"Well?" Dominic demanded abruptly.

"We've seen worse in our time, m'lord," said the groom with a matter of factness that earned him a smile of gratitude from Minerva. "It's not as deep as I feared it might be, but you'll have a tidy scar to show for it, I reckon."

Minerva was privately much shocked by the deeply gouged laceration, three or four inches long and penetrating beyond his hairline, but her hand was steady as she bathed it gently and patted it dry. It must have hurt dreadfully, but Dominic bore it without a murmur, though there was a tell-tale white line about his mouth.

"I suppose sooner or later one of you will tell me how it happened."

"Footpads," said Dominic through shut teeth.

"Goodness!" She bound the wound with lint and bandages to give it as much protection as possible, while Drummond supplied the details.

"Four of them, there were, with pistols, my lady. We did for 'em, or most of them, anyway, but not before a bullet caught his lordship a glancing blow."

"What Drummond has omitted to mention, my dear, is that but for his presence of mind, your husband would now be lying ingloriously dead upon the road instead of merely a trifle damaged." Dominic's voice was ironical, but there was weariness too as he leaned back in the chair.

Minerva's pallor almost matched his own, but she only said quietly, "Then I shall be forever in your debt, Drummond." She glanced at Dominic and added, "I think another small tot of brandy for his lordship. And have one yourself. You have earned it."

The groom came as near to blushing as he was ever likely to do.

"And then," she continued, sitting down rather suddenly, overcome by the realization of what had so nearly happened, "I think we should get my husband up to his bed. Perhaps you would be so kind as to ring for Marsham so that it can be arranged."

She found Drummond at her side, pushing a glass into her own hand, with a brusque nod to her to drink it. She sipped the fiery liquid and managed not to choke on it.

Dominic uttered something remarkably like a weary chuckle. "You are enjoying all this, are you not?" he muttered, his voice a little slurred, his eyes closed. "Getting some of your own back . . . Think you've got the upper hand. But I shall come about soon enough, you'll see."

Minerva, feeling better already, took a deep breath and said in what she hoped was her normal voice, "I haven't the least doubt of it, my dear sir. But for the moment, pray indulge me. If you will drink the brandy Drummond has brought you, we may set about making you more comfortable."

He opened one eye, squinting at her. "Yes, ma'am," he said, sketching a salute.

"Don't you take no notice of him, m'lady," Drummond advised her with a lugubrious sniff. "He could have a touch of concussion, besides losing a fair deal of blood, which has likely made him a bit light-headed. I've seen it afor often enough."

The same bleary eye was turned on Drummond, more in sorrow than in anger. *"Et tu, Brute?"*

"If you say so, m'lord," Drummond agreed. And as the door opened to admit Marsham, "But for now, if you please, we'll just get you upstairs."

11

BY MORNING the marquess was showing some evidence of fever. Minerva had reluctantly agreed to take some rest herself, having seen Dominic made comfortable by his valet, assisted by Drummond and a footman. But she was up early, ignoring Mattie's silent disapproval, her own queasiness resolutely suppressed in her anxiety to see how he did.

She entered his room to find Moss and Drummond locked in verbal combat over their master's restively recumbent form—the former insisting that a doctor should be called without further delay. His rather protuberant eyes dared Drummond to say otherwise. He had been much put out by the presence of the groom, who had not left the marquess's side all night, and carried about his person the distinct odor of the stables. And if this were not enough, the knowledge of the bond that existed between master and groom further fueled his jealous defense of his territory.

He took advantage of her ladyship's arrival to air his superior assessment of the situation. "In my opinion, his lordship should be bled as soon as possible, ma'am. I can, if you wish, recommend a most excellent man."

"Begging your pardon, m'lady," interposed Drummond, seeing the indecision in her eyes, "but I don't hold with cupping, and neither does his lordship, except in desperate circumstances. I mean, where's the sense in bleedin' a man who's already lost more than enough?"

This further evidence of the close affinity between groom and master inflamed Moss. "I should have thought it was obvious, man. How else is one to purge the blood of its ill humors? My late employer, Sir Greville Pinkly-Hartington, found it highly efficacious on more than one occasion."

"Aye, well, with a name like that, I'm not surprised," muttered Drummond.

The battle was raging hot and strong and Minerva judged it to to be time to step in. She had already felt Dominic's forehead, which was disturbingly warm and moist to the touch, and noted his unnaturally flushed face. Now, she said firmly, the prime consideration must be to examine the wound. Her stomach threatened to rebel at the prospect, but she ruthlessly quelled the sensation of sickness and removed the dressing. The edges of the skin were rather angry looking, but the flesh showed no sign of putrefaction or unpleasant odor, so she applied fresh lint and bound it up again. This accomplished, she looked up and found that both men were still looking to her for a judgment.

Feeling a little like Solomon, she glanced from one to the other. "I must admit that I do not in principle favor blood-letting. My father, too, was very much against it. However, I think we must not totally dismiss the idea, if all else fails." She prayed that she was doing the right thing. "For the present, and before I have recourse to a doctor, I would like his lordship to be sponged down with lukewarm water every half hour or so, and we will try to get him to drink as much cordial as possible."

Minerva saw that Moss in particular looked skeptical. "I know what you must be thinking, but I have seen such methods used with great success in cases of fever." She smiled reassuringly as she turned to leave, reserving a special warmth for Drummond. "His lordship's case is far from desperate at present, you know, and with any luck we may prevent its becoming so. I am going now to dress, but I'll return very soon, and then you must both get some rest. Yes, I insist. You must be worn to a thread. Matthews is an excellent nurse and will manage very well with the help of a footman."

Back in her own room, Minerva's iron resolve deserted her and she was violently sick. Mattie grumbled as she fussed around her, muttering that some people had no more sense than they were born with.

"I shall be all right directly," Minerva said, head in hands and feeling like death. "You know it never lasts beyond the first hour or so, and anyway, I had to see how Dominic did."

"Aye," said Mattie. "So how is his lordship?"

Minerva told her, and told her also what she planned to do. "You won't mind helping, will you? I don't care to leave him in the sole charge of footmen."

"I should hope not," came the caustic reply. "Much they know!"

By afternoon, Dominic was certainly no worse, so that when Mr. Grassington called for the third afternoon in succession, his nice face puckered with concern, having learned in the extraordinary way that people do something of what had happened, she was able to reassure him. It was a source of amusement to Minerva that, out of all she told him concerning her hopes for Dominic's eventual recovery, what he leapt upon with the eagerness of a dog sighting a particularly juicy bone was the name of Dominic's valet.

"Not Pinkly Hartington's Moss?" he exclaimed in disbelief. "Dominic and the great Moss! However did that happen?" She told him. "Well, if that don't beat all! His cousin, Gervase, will be furious! He has been trying to lure the man away from Pinkly-Hartington for years! Just wait until I tell Charles. Charles ain't returned from Newmarket yet," he explained hastily, "or he'd be here like a flash!" And then, reverting to the matter in hand, "Footpads, so I heard . . . half a dozen or more . . ."

"Four actually," Minerva said. She told him as much as she knew, and he listened in awe.

"Could have been killed! Poor old Dominic. Devilish luck he's had recently. Thought all that was at an end when he married you!"

Minerva managed a smile. "So did I. But this is no more than a temporary setback, I am sure."

"Don't know if this is a good time to broach the subject, but have you given any more thought to what you said about clearing up the mystery surrounding Hagarth's death?"

Minerva had to admit that she hadn't given it another thought, and viewed alongside her present problems, the discovery of some mythical killer seemed totally irrelevant. "Surely by now all interest in the matter will be at an end?"

"Don't you believe it, ma'am. Still affords much food for gossip in the clubs—the mystery of the missing documents, they term it. There was a rumor going around White's last night that Tuffy Donnington, who was also being bled dry by Hagarth over some kind of incriminating letters he'd once written—no idea what, but he was deuced edgy—had received an anonymous note threatening him with exposure if he didn't cough up the blunt, and *his* letters were also in the document box that went missing at the time of Hagarth's death!" Mr. Grassington leaned forward eagerly. "Now, what do you make of that? Deuced odd, what? Looks as though whoever stole that box was decided to use it for gain. I suppose Dominic hasn't had any similar demands?"

But Minerva, who liked Pelham Grassington and would in the ordinary way have found the information fascinating, could only look at him in his blue superfine coat and his yellow calf-clingers and think of Dominic tossing feverishly in his bed with a scar several inches long where some thieving rogue had tried to put period to his life.

Something of her thoughts must have penetrated Mr.

Grassington's preoccupation with deeds adventurous, for he suddenly sprang up, calling himself all kinds of a crass idiot for speaking of such matters when she must be wishing him elsewhere.

"Not at all," she said a little too quickly. "It is certainly very strange, but as far as I know, Dominic has had no word of any kind."

"And at the moment you couldn't care less, and are no doubt wishing me at the devil!" He was all contrition. "No, no, you are quite right! I'll go now, and we'll speak of it again when you are less troubled." At the door he half-turned and smiled with a beguiling wistful charm. "I may come again? To ask after Dominic? Deuced fond of the fellow, y'know."

"Oh, yes! You must call as often as you wish. It is only that today I am a little distrait . . ."

"Very understandable, ma'am!" And a little jerkily, "Be sure to give Dominic my best!"

That day and night were crucial. There were times when Dominic seemed more lucid, and by morning he was certainly less feverish, but Minerva did in the end seek the reassurance of a doctor—not the one Moss would have favored, but a very good man recommended to her by Mr. Grassington, who told her that his Aunt Wilberforce, who didn't suffer fools and quacks, reckoned him to be "as sound a man as any of her acquaintance, which wasn't saying a great deal." Minerva said she would very much like to meet his aunt sometime, and promptly sent for Dr. Hitchen.

He was a man of few words, rather ascetic in appearance, but with remarkably keen eyes that missed nothing. He took his time in examining the marquess, quizzed Minerva with an economical thoroughness which aroused her admiration, and at the end of it, when they had retired to the small sitting room she had caused to be adapted for her needs close by, he expressed surprise that she had thought it necessary to call him in at all.

"You seem to be doing all the right things, Lady

Claireux. Your husband is young, strong, and fit—I doubt you have any reason to worry."

She gave him an embarrassed smile. "I suppose I wanted reassurance. There have been moments when I began to wonder if everyone else was right and I was wrong. You really don't think he ought to be bled?"

"Certainly not. Patience, madam—and the excellent care that he is getting. That is all his lordship needs." Dr. Hitchen bent his acute stare upon her. "If you must know, I am more concerned about you and your needs."

"My needs?" Minerva frowned and then turned a rosy pink. "Oh, but . . . that is, how can you possibly tell when I have only just begun to suspect it myself?"

Her embarrassment brought a faintly sardonic light to his eyes. "It is my business to know such things, though to be honest"—his eyebrow quirked amusedly—"I was not entirely sure until you so obligingly confirmed it to me."

Minerva laughed. "For shame, sir. In other words, it was pure conjecture!"

Dr. Hitchen found himself liking this young woman very well. She was quite unlike many of the spoiled rich upon whom he waited. His tone mellowed accordingly. "Not entirely, Lady Claireux. More what you might call an educated guess. It has been my experience that a woman almost always takes on a particular aura when she first becomes pregnant."

"How fascinating. Not obvious to all, I trust?"

"Hardly." The hint of arrogance was, she was sure, unintentional, and merely indicated to Minerva a dedication to his calling which she thoroughly approved. "But since in your case I have clearly been proved right, may I beg you to have consideration for yourself, ma'am, as well as for your husband. It would be a great pity to risk miscarrying for want of a little care in these early weeks—something that happens all too often, I may say."

"I will try to remember," she said meekly. "But I am by nature as fit as a flea, you know."

"That is not necessarily a recommendation, ma'am." Dr. Hitchen's reply came dryly. "Fit people frequently drive themselves too hard. Just bear that in mind."

As he picked up his bag and turned to go, Minerva decided that he was exactly the kind of doctor in whom she could repose her trust. "You will call again to see my husband?" she said quickly.

He inclined his head. "If you wish me to do so."

"I do. And . . . and it seems that I too shall have need of you?"

"My lady, I should account it an honor to serve you."

"Thank you," she said simply.

He was right about Dominic. By the following day he was sitting up and demanding good honest beef and a bottle of claret instead of the pap Moss had shown the crass stupidity of allowing a quaking young footman to put before him, and on the following morning he demanded his clothes, and nobody was allowed any peace until he got them.

Pelham Grassington and Charles Lowdon became frequent visitors and Minerva was very glad of their company and their invaluable assistance in keeping Dominic's ambitions within bounds.

"You are quite the worst patient it has ever been my misfortune to know," she told him roundly, after he had threatened to throw a soothing potion specially prepared for him by Moss at the poor man's head. "It will be no more than you deserve if Moss finds himself a more congenial position and leaves you. *I* would do so tomorrow, let me tell you, if I wasn't your wife!"

"Humgudgeon!" He mocked her with her own favorite expletive. He reached out with surprising swiftness, in view of his condition, and seized her hand, pulling her close until she collapsed on the bed beside him. "You are enjoying every minute of your dominion over me, madam wife, but it won't last! A good soldier knows well enough when to lie low and plan his counter-attack, so look to your defenses . . ." And before she knew what he was about, his hand was under her chin, insistent, and his mouth was on hers. It ought to have been a gentle salute, best suited to an invalid, but all the pent-up emotions of the past two days were released and found expression in a passionate urgency that would not be denied.

Dominic, taken by surprise, drew her closer as the tears, too-long suppressed, welled up and mingled with their kisses. Marsham, coming in to announce that Mr. Grassington and Mr. Lowdon were below, backed out unnoticed and silently closed the door.

"Oh, I shouldn't have . . . how dreadful!" Minerva tried to sit up, tried to wipe away her tears and tidy her hair, which was in danger of falling down, but he still kept a firm hold of her.

"I didn't think it dreadful at all. In fact, I quite enjoyed it. *In fact,"* he murmured, warming to his theme, "it has probably done me far more good than any physic that fancy doctor could prescribe!"

"He isn't fancy," she protested. "I was very much impressed with him, I may tell you."

"Were you, indeed?" His eyes were upon her and, embarrassed, she could not meet their searching scutiny. She made a determined effort to free herself.

"I was. And furthermore, he is coming to see you again, so you may as well get used to the idea." She seized her moment and moved swiftly out of reach. "Heavens, I must look a mess!"

Dominic studied her fine, strong-boned face, its sometimes luminous quality never more marked than now, flushed as it was and streaked with tears, and he thought that she had never looked more beautiful. He wanted to tell her so, but his head ached and the only words he could call to mind seemed inadequate. I'll tell her tomorrow, was his last coherent thought as his eyes closed.

* * *

His determination to get back on his feet in the days that followed surprised everyone, proving much greater than anyone's power to stop him, so that even Dr. Hitchen when appealed to gave it as his opinion that to frustrate him would probably do him more harm than good. "His own strength will dictate how much or, more likely, how little his lordship does," he prophesied, and so it proved.

Dominic's temper, however, was uncertain, and Minerva lived in hourly expectation of Moss's giving notice, but to everyone's surprise, the valet seemed to show remarkable patience with his lordship's ill humor. In fact, the many years spent pandering to the uncertain whims of a petulant Sir Greville had long since innured him to displays of temperament.

Minerva thanked heaven for the times when his friends were around to lift his spirits with their ridiculous cameraderie, and as he improved, to take him out for drives. The scar had healed better than she had ever thought possible.

"Very dashing thing to have—a scar," Pelham observed, eyeing it judiciously when it was given its first airing. "Intrigues the ladies no end! Wouldn't mind acquiring one myself."

Charles Lowdon put up his glass. "My dear Pel," he drawled with deepest irony, "I had no idea you cherished any such ambition! Had you, Dominic?"

"None at all. But I'm sure it can be arranged. In fact, if you will but be patient a while, I will personally attend to the matter."

Alarm flickered and was replaced by a sleepy smile. "Have done, both of you. No call to take a fellow so literally!"

They were all sitting together in the library one afternoon when Marsham announced Mr. Gervase Wilmington. Minerva heard Dominic swear beneath his breath, and she saw Pelham and Charles exchange a highly quizzical glance. For her part, she could not wait to see Dominic's much discussed cousin.

It was as well that comments let slip from time to time had prepared her for the sight of Gervase Wilmington in all the glory of a pink coat, dove-gray pantaloons, and a purple striped waistcoat. He was not ill-looking, she thought, striving to be fair, though he resembled Dominic not at all, being somewhat florid of countenance and of a much neater build. And it was a little unfortunate that the excessive height of his collar gave him such a misplaced air of consequence. He started and then exclaimed with joy upon seeing Dominic, not at death's door as he had expected; and his bow to Mineva upon being introduced was a miracle of correctness so that it was all she could do to respond without laughing in his face, and she dared not look at her companions.

"Please sit down, Mr. Wilmington." She indicated a chair and watched him lower himself with extreme caution, his neckwear rendering him unable to look down to see where he was going. "Would you care for a glass of Madeira?"

"Too kind, cousin. I may call you cousin, may I not? And you will call me Gervase. I beg that there will be no standing upon ceremony, for we are family, after all!"

Minerva assured him that it would give her the greatest pleasure, and expressed her regret that she had not made his acquaintance sooner.

"My sentiments, entirely. But you have been abroad, I collect, since the happy occasion of your marriage, news of which, alas, reached me much too late to felicitate you." He turned a reproachful glance upon Dominic. "However, it would be too unkind in me to scold your poor husband in view of his recent misfortune. My dear coz, I was never so shocked as when I learned that you were laid low . . . and to think that we were talking together not above a week ago! You may conceive of my feelings . . . such horrid rumors! Rascally footpads, bullet wounds, escaping death by a whisker! I simply had to come to see for myself, though I declare, I dreaded to think what I would find!"

"Your concern is touching, coz." Dominic was at his most sardonic. "But you may be easy. I am not in any danger of closing my account, so you will be spared the burden of assuming the title for a little longer."

Minerva scarcely knew where to look as Gervase turned as red as a turkeycock and protested that nothing had been further from his mind, and that only the greatest concern for Dominic's health had prompted him to come at all. "You must *know* how the sickroom affects me! Even as a child, I could not bear to witness the afflictions of others. Just to look now at that dreadful scar . . . !" He pressed a lace-edged kerchief to his lips.

"Oh, cut line, Gervase, for the love of God!" Dominic snapped. "Methinks you do protest too much!"

"Well! If this is all the thanks I am to receive . . ."

Minerva judged it to be time to intervene. She apologized for her husband's bad temper, her frown daring him to contradict her, and explained to Gervase that her husband's indisposition had made him exceedingly crabby, as she could testify, and begged that he would overlook any unintentional slight. Throughout, Dominic wore a look of angry disdain which she mistrusted, Charles regarded the toe of one shining hessian boot through his quizzing glass, and Pelham seemed in severe danger of exploding at any second.

Gervase, only slightly mollified, tossed back what remained of his Madeira and rose majestically to his feet. "I offer no reproaches, Cousin Minerva, largely, I may say, out of consideration for your feelings. And now, if you will oblige me by ringing for Marsham, I will take my leave of you all." He eyed Dominic balefully. "I trust that your health and your temper will improve in due course, cousin." He inclined his head to each in turn, and then paused before saying casually, and with an innocence which contained a hint of malice, "Oh, by the way, Dominic—you have still not had any news of those documents, I suppose? No? The word is that several other interested parties have recently received threatening letters, demanding substantial amounts of money. Deuced odd, you must admit, remembering our recent conversation on the subject!" With a final flourish of his handkerchief, he left them.

There was an uncomfortable silence. Then: "Perhaps someone can tell me what all that was about?" Dominic said with ominous calm.

Pelham looked at Charles, who shrugged and related to him as much as they themselves knew.

"Only Tuffy Donnington?" he pressed them.

Pelham looked uncomfortable. "Rumors of others," he admitted.

"I see," Dominic said. That was all. But he looked grim.

12

ON THE morning following Gervase's visit, the marquess was up at his usual time, scoffing at Moss's gloomy forebodings and sending the whole house into a ferment of activity as the breakfast room was hastily prepared to receive him. Her ladyship, he was told, had formed the habit of taking breakfast in her room during the time he had been indisposed.

He ate little, but denied that he had anything more than a thick head, and by the time Minerva appeared, he had his day planned; Drummond had been summoned, and a message had already been sent to Mr. Thripp announcing that he would be calling upon him later that morning.

Minerva, not yet at her best, found all this sudden activity tiresome and not a little worrying. "Surely," she pleaded, "Mr. Thripp would come to see you here if you were to ask him?"

"I'm sure he would," Dominic said. "But I prefer to go to him. Besides, when my business in the Strand is at an end, I mean to take Drummond with me to Longacre to look at carriages—something sporting in particular to replace my curricle. We did discuss it, if you remember, on our journey home."

There was a look in his eyes that dared her to argue, but she knew the look of old and was persuaded that it would be useless to try. It was true that they had talked about carriages. He had sold the curricle before leaving Paris, and she knew that he would miss it, but surely it could have waited for another day.

"Best to let him have his head when he's in this sort of a mood, m'lady," Drummond advised her like a wise old uncle. "But don't you fret none. I'll be watchin' over him like a nursemaid watching a baby, though I doubt he'll be any the worse for an outing. Indestructible, his lordship is."

With this Minerva had to be content. However, by the time Pelham called later in the morning, she was fully herself again, and feeling a sense of injury at being deprived of an outing which she had been looking forward to sharing. But perhaps it was not too late. Pelham was as putty in her hands, and within a very short space of time he was handing her into his phaeton.

So it was that when Dominic entered the warehouse in Longacre, his head throbbing from a long session with the lawyer, the first sound he heard was his wife's voice enthusiastically extolling the merits of a high-perch phaeton.

Thunderstruck, he made his way among a bewildering array of vehicles until he found her at last in the company of his best friend, arguing with Pelham as to the vehicle's suitability for a lady's use. "Never, fairest Minerva!" Pelham was declaiming. "Out of the question . . . all one's finer feelings would be outraged!" Her peal of laughter rang out, echoing around the vast area of the warehouse.

Dominic's fury was totally irrational, and was further inflamed as he strode, set-faced, toward the sounds of hilarity, only to come upon his wife, who was looking particularly attractive in a morning dress of the smoky blue color that became her so well, clearly enjoying herself with his best friend.

"Perhaps," he suggested with silky calm, "you would care to share the jest?"

Minerva turned at the sound of his voice, relief that

he was none the worse for his outing blinding her momentarily to his mood. "Ah, Dominic—so we haven't missed you. I'm glad."

"Are you?" he said sarcastically. "You're sure I am not spoiling your fun? Pray do not hesitate to be frank with me. I can always go away and come back later."

"Don't talk gammon, old fellow," Pelham put in hastily, misliking the look in his friend's eye. "Minerva had a fancy to meet you here, and I offered to drive her. Simple as that."

"Is it? Well, now you can drive her home again." Dominic drew his wife aside. "You are too busy, ma'am," he said, low-voiced. "I will not be watched and nursemaided by you or anyone else. Drummond already knows that, and the sooner you realize it, the better we shall deal."

Any sympathy Minerva might have felt vanished under the injustice of this tongue-lashing. Her own pride, every bit as ingrained as his, reared its head. "Heavens, Dominic! As if I didn't know by now that you will go to hell your own way! I came here to buy a carriage—we were to have come together, if you remember." She raised her voice, "However, Pelham will be very happy to advise me, won't you, Pel?" Mr. Grassington looked anything but happy. "And you, my dear husband, may go about your own business with a clear conscience!"

Dominic's head throbbed dully, and Minerva's lively temper did nothing to improve it. He saw her glance provocatively at the high-perch phaeton with its huge wheels and the body hung perilously above the front axle. "Very well, I will," he said grimly. "But if Pel lets you get away with buying that monstrous turn-out, he's a bigger fool than I take him for!"

He strode away with Drummond following in his wake, shaking his head at the follies of those who ought to know better.

"You all right, m'dear?" Pelham's anxious voice penetrated Minerva's tempestuous thoughts.

She turned overbright eyes on him and for a moment he was taken aback. Then her anger evaporated and she smiled wryly. "I am not the world's most tactful person, as you may have realized by now."

"Not your fault. Dominic's temper ain't always what it might be. Besides which," he added by way of comfort. "I doubt he'll be feeling quite the thing, you know."

"And I haven't made him feel a whole lot better." Minerva stopped him as he would have protested this. "No, please! I have no wish to quarrel with you as well. Let us aportion the blame equally and have done with it. I have come here to buy a carriage, and that I still mean to do."

Her glance lingered for a moment, admiring the lines of the sporting phaeton, and Mr. Grassington's heart plummeted. "You ain't seriously considering that turn-out?"

Minerva thought of the coming baby and regretfully turned her attention to something equally elegant, but altogether more circumspect. And then her thoughts turned to horses—a pair, she thought.

"If I were you," Pelham said hastily, not wishful to be on the receiving end of his friend's uncertain temper yet again, "I should leave your cattle to Dominic. Not quite the thing for a lady to visit Tattersail's, y'see—and anyway, it might go some way toward pacifying him."

"What a craven creature you are!" she teased him good-naturedly.

He grinned, but warily. "All very well for you, but Dominic has the most punishing left I ever saw, and you ain't the one he'd likely send to grass!"

"Poor Pelham! Well, come along. We shall just have to choose something to which Dominic cannot possibly take exception."

In the event, the marquess arrived home first. He retired to the library, gave strict orders that he was not to be disturbed, and slumped into a chair, relieved to be able to rest his head against its back without being obliged to answer questions concerning the state of his health. He was more tired than he would admit to, but that would pass and he needed time to think. Gervase had prompted his initial moodiness with those spiteful insinuations, catching him at a weak moment so that he had been unable to get them out of his mind. His ill humor had not been improved by an abortive session with Mr. Thripp, who had hemmed and hawed over every point put to him in a particularly irritating fashion. With white fingertips delicately steepled beneath his chin, Thripp had again gone through all the tedious details concerning his father's affairs until his senses began to spin.

"All the creditors who had claims upon the estate have now been accommodated, my lord—and as for this other unfortunate business, well, I should simply put it out of your mind. The . . . er, person who was engaged in harassing the late marquess being now deceased, and all papers concerning their somewhat irregular transactions—"

"Irregular transactions!" Dominic's laugh was bitter. "That is a deuced nice way of defining blackmail, Thripp!"

"As you say, my lord. Nonetheless, it would appear that the papers, if they still exist, are in the hands of such people as can have no possible claim upon you. The scandal, such as it was, was brought into the open at the time of his late lordship's demise, and has therefore lost any value that might have appertained to it earlier, which, I would hazard, is why you have not been approached."

The explanation was perfectly valid, if convoluted by Thripp's passion for words—Dominic had told himself much the same thing a hundred times. Yet, at the back of his mind there lurked a nagging suspicion that whoever had killed Hagarth was deliberately setting him forward yet again as the prime suspect, and since he had no real enemies that he could think of, it could only be a ploy to divert attention from the killer himself.

His head was easing and his eyelids began to droop, but before he lost consciousness, the thought came to him that if his name was ever to be cleared, he would have to tackle it himself. It was something he should have done a long time ago. After all, he had engaged in a certain amount of intelligence work for Lord Wellington, so why should he not now turn his skills to good account.

Minerva had been silent for much of the drive home, so that Pelham was surprised when she suddenly asked him if he would have any objection to making a detour through the Park.

"Delighted, m'dear. Lovely day . . . what could be more enjoyable?" Perhaps, he thought with a certain sympathy, she wanted to put off a reckoning with Dominic for as long as possible. Couldn't say he altogether blamed her. Wouldn't fancy facing him himself!

Later in the day, Hyde Park would be alive with the rattle of carriage wheels and the hum of conversation as fashionables strolled beneath the trees, eager to see and be seen, and to savor the latest scandals. But for now all was quiet. Minerva waited until they reached a place where there was no one to be seen before asking him to pull in.

"Pelham, I want to know everything you can remember about the time Baron Hagarth was killed."

He turned to her, his face lighting up. "So you do mean to pursue your idea?"

"It may come to that, but at present I'm not sure if there is anything to pursue. I had hoped the whole affair might be forgotten, but it seems someone is determined that it won't be—in which case I refuse to stand by and watch Dominic's life being dogged by insinuation, for I'm sure it is that prospect rather than the effects of his accident that is making him so out-of-reason cross."

Pelham regarded her with admiration. "Damme, if you haven't got to the nub of it! What is it that you want to know?"

"I'm not sure. Uncle Richard told me about the duel—and how it was called off. Who informed on them, do you know?"

"The usual anonymous busybody. Just as well, mind . . . the law takes a pretty hard view of such things these days." Pelham shrugged. "Some folk at the time reckoned it was Hagarth himself . . . knew Dominic was a crack shot . . . only way to save his skin without losing face. I don't see it, myself. Not that sort of man—not easily scared."

"I see. And I suppose Dominic took it badly?"

"He was furious! Brooded all day, and steadily drank himself insensible that night. It was the talk of White's for days after, or so I heard."

"You weren't there, then?" Minerva put in quickly.

" 'Fraid not." Pelham pleated the reins between his fingers. "Often blamed myself—might not have got himself in Queer Street if I'd been there."

"You mustn't think that!"

"Perhaps not. Matter of fact, though, it was good old Cousin Gervase who came to his rescue that night—incongruous thought, ain't it? Gervase Wilmington risking the despoiling of his beautiful person in order to support his drunken cousin home! Dominic had rooms in Arlington Street at the time. Said later he was willing to swear that Dominic was incapable of murdering anyone that night. Only halfway unselfish thing I've ever known him to do!"

For a moment Minerva had toyed with the notion of the absurdly effete Gervase as the villain of the piece, but on the evidence it was highly improbable. She sighed and resumed her inquisition.

"I remember Uncle Richard's saying something about a button . . ."

"Now that was a rum thing!" exclaimed Pelham. "It was found clutched in Hagarth's fist . . . and ought to have hung Dominic, by rights!" Minerva suppressed a shiver of apprehension as he rushed on. "That button, y'see, was unique, as near as dammit! It was identical to the ones on that wine-colored coat of Dominic's—you know, the silver filigree ones? And he was wearing the coat that night!"

"Then why was he not apprehended?"

"Because," said Pelham with a strong sense of the dramatic, "I was there when the Runners came to demand that the coat be produced, and every button was intact! And yet, Dominic had had it specially made in some obscure little town in Spain, buttons and all! What do you make of that?"

"It is certainly most odd," she said slowly. "Could Dominic explain it?"

Pelham grinned. "Didn't attempt to. Just looked down his nose at 'em—you know the way he can!—and showed 'em the door! But I could tell he was puzzled, just the same."

"Oh Pel! I don't know what to make of it all! It certainly seems as though someone was trying to ensure that Dominic took the blame. And is still trying. But who? And why?" Minerva suddenly felt tired and a little dispirited as the enormity of the task she had contemplated with such high hopes came home to her. "I believe I need time to think about it. But thank you for telling me, and I know I may count on you for support."

In the house, all was silence. Marsham told Minerva that his lordship was in the library and had expressed a wish not to be disturbed. "Though naturally any such restriction would not apply to your ladyship." The elderly butler's voice sank to a hushed murmur. "It is my belief, my lady, that his lordship was a trifle done up, it being his first outing, as you might say."

She smiled. "I have no doubt what you say is true. I will just put my head in, and if he *is* asleep I will not seek to wake him."

The library curtains had been half-drawn against the intrusive rays of the sun, so that the remaining light came dappling softly across plush and honeyed oak.

Dominic sat in shadow, his large frame stretched out, long legs crossed at the ankles. Moving closer she saw that sleep had relaxed the strong taut lines of his face, giving it an oddly youthful vulnerability—an illusion enhanced by the long dark eyelashes brushing his pale cheeks and an errant lock of hair which had strayed unbidden across his forehead.

The love that had been growing in Minerva suddenly welled up, catching her unawares. She stood quite still, entranced, examining every feature as though seeing them for the first time, longing to touch the long sensual fingers curled around the arm of the chair, to feel their strength clasping hers.

"Will you know me again, do you suppose?"

She let out a skirl of surprise, her glance flying to Dominic's face. He hadn't appeared to move a muscle, yet his eyes were now wide open, watching her watching him. How long he had been doing so, she had no way of knowing.

"I . . ." She stopped, steadied the uneven fluttering of her heart, the tremor in her voice, and began again. "I'm sorry. Did I disturb you? I didn't mean to."

He rolled his head lazily from side to side. "In the army you learn to sleep with your senses tuned to react to the slightest sound." He showed no inclination to move, and she remained likewise rooted to the spot. "Did you buy your carriage?"

Minerva bit her lip. "Yes. And you?"

"A rather handsome racing curricle." He paused. "You didn't succumb to that absurd vehicle, I trust?"

"No." A guarded, faintly embarrassed look crossed her face, and she saw his interest quicken. "As a matter of fact, I bought two."

"The devil you did!" One eyebrow quirked wickedly. "Such extravagance from my practical wife. Well, why not? One for weekdays and one for Sunday, I suppose?"

His gentle irony put her on the defensive. "Certainly not. A phaeton and an elegant little landaulet." Her eyes challenged him. "There is ample room in the stables and we do need some kind of town carriage . . ." For when I am no longer able to drive myself, she added silently. "But Pel thought I should leave the horses to you," she concluded with her usual disarming honesty.

"I had no idea Pel was possessed of so much tact," Dominic drawled, but the smile that accompanied the words quite melted her resistance.

"Oh, Dominic! I am sorry!" She stretched out impulsively and touched his hand. Quick as light, he moved his fingers to clasp her wrist, lightly but inescapably.

"For what? For treating a churlish husband as he deserved?"

"No! You were not churlish, or if you were," she amended, seeing the look of disbelief in his eyes, "some of the blame must be mine for appearing overprotective. Indeed, I do *try* not to rule the roost, but there is no way that I can become the submissive little woman, either."

"God forbid! I wouldn't want you any different."

"Really?" She searched his face, looking for irony, but finding none.

For answer, he turned her hand over and dropped a kiss lightly in her cupped palm. "Word of an officer and a gentleman," he averred, softly mocking, though his eyes were serious. Then he let her go and eased himself upright. "You realize," he said, reverting to practicality, "that we will need a coachman for your landaulet?"

"Yes, of course. I have already given it some thought," she said, meeting his change of mood. "The obvious answer, of course, is to send for Joshua." He began to laugh, and after a moment she saw why and joined in. "I'm doing it again, aren't I? But it would serve—if you agree?"

"Why not? I confess it would be worth it just to see Joshua's reaction to London traffic!" She smiled, but in a rather abstracted way that warned him there was more to come. "Out with it, woman—what else are you plotting?"

13

MRS. PEACH and Sir Richard arrived on a bright June day, driven by Joshua, who had much to say about London traffic in general and the ill manners of other coach drivers in particular, which Minerva took in good part. Until that moment she had not realized how much she had missed the cantankerous old fraud, though how he and Drummond would deal together she couldn't imagine.

"Oh, I am so happy to see you both!" she exclaimed, when her uncle and her old friend were comfortably ensconsed in the drawing room. "Are you both worn to a thread by the journey?"

Nothing of the kind, said Sir Richard. They had accomplished it in easy stages, resting for as long as was necessary. "We spent last night at Richmond, so that we might arrive here fresh and bright. Ain't that so, ma'am?"

"Yes, indeed. Sir Richard arranged all most admirably." Mrs. Peach's plump features dimpled. "I believe I have never enjoyed a journey more! But what of you, my dearest child? I must say you look blooming! Marriage obviously agrees with you. And his lordship—he is also well, I trust?"

This was a little awkward, but Minerva murmured something appropriate, and was temporarily saved from the catalog of questions that must inevitably follow any mention of Dominic's recent misfortune by the entrance of a footman bearing a tea tray which he set down beside her. Thus, in the course of pouring the tea, and tempting her guests with a plate of cook's best shortbread, she was able to steer the conversation toward trivialities, some anecdotes about the Paris visit and a brief account of how they had come by Lord Bridlington's house. From there, she moved on to ask how everything was going on in Yorkshire, and by the time that topic was exhausted, Sir Richard was talking of moving on to his club. He had taken the liberty of dropping his baggage off there on the way, and insisted that there was nothing he would enjoy so much as a walk, having been so long in a coach over the past few days.

Sir Richard had been adamant about staying at Brooks's from the moment the visit was first mooted, and Minerva had not sought to dissuade him when it became clear that he was genuinely looking forward to renewing acquaintance with some of his old cronies.

Mrs. Peach, on the other hand, was overjoyed at being reunited with her dear Minerva, whom she had missed sadly since her departure. Her life had become singularly lackluster without her young friend's enlivening presence and conversation. She had not realized how much she would miss it. But now there was all the time in the world.

She sighed in blissful anticipation. "Do you know, I haven't visited London since my come-out—more than thirty years ago! When Mortimer was alive, we seldom went further than Scarborough, and afterward, well . . . Only fancy! I daresay much will have changed, but what fun I shall have finding out!"

She was, thought Minerva, like a child with a newly opened box of sweetmeats. It would have been nice to talk more about Yorkshire, but it hardly seemed fair to prompt her to look back when all her mind was concentrated on expectations of things to come. Minerva hoped she would not be disappointed. She certainly was not disappointed with Dominic, who treated her with charm and courtesy, bearing all her exclamations and alarms over his scar and how he had come by it with admirable patience, thus winning her heart all over again.

"I distinctly remember, my love, how even on that very first occasion, which even now makes me blush to think of it, his lordship's courtesy was very apparent! Such kindness he showed me when it might so easily have been otherwise!"

Minerva hid a smile, for she had very different memories of that night.

"Who would have thought then, how well it would all come out? Lady Claireux! My word! And now that you are back from Paris, and with the Season well underway, I daresay you will be leading a very giddy social life. Which brings me to something I wanted to say." Mrs. Peach gazed earnestly at her young friend. "You must not be thinking that I shall expect to go hither and thither with you. In fact, even if I wished to, I doubt that I would be able to keep up with you young things!"

"Nonsense!" Minerva protested, laughing. "I'm sure I don't know what kind of life you think we lead! I am determined that you are going to enjoy every minute of your stay!"

But Minerva was vaguely troubled by Mrs. Peach's words. In Paris they had enjoyed a full social life, but here, and never having moved in London circles, she had only the vaguest idea of what to expect. True, Dominic's illness so soon after their arrival had prohibited any outing of a social nature until recently, but although a few people, old friends of Dominic's, had called and they now had a sprinkling of invitations, she suspected that there would be many among the *ton* who would not wish to know them—either because of her own unacceptable background, or because of malicious gossip concerning Dominic and the Hagarth murder. However, that was pure speculation, and for the present there was sufficient entertainment in prospect to satisfy Mrs. Peach that they were in popular demand.

A drive in the Park on the following afternoon at the fashionable hour brought an unexpected boost to their popularity. The continuous traffic made progress slow, allowing ample time for a lady in an approaching barouche to observe them. A formidable figure, she stared intently, lorgnette raised, then exclaimed and commanded her driver to halt.

Minerva hastily bade Joshua to do likewise, and as he mutteringly complied, the lady cried out in ringing tones: "Bless my soul! Esmeralda Rodway! Can it really be you?"

Mrs. Peach peered at the awesome figure, resplendent in purple silk and wearing a deep-brimmed hat bedecked with feathers upon a head that was rather more auburn than she had remembered. "Maude Freemantle! How extraordinary! Why, it must be th—" Just in time she caught the glint in the other's eyes. " . . . years since we last met," she amended hastily.

Lady Maude Bredon gave a little nod of approval. "Quite so. Before I accepted Bredon, in fact. And you married a clergyman with a ridiculous name. What was it now? Some kind of fruit, as I remember."

"Peach," came the rather subdued reply.

"That was it!" agreed her ladyship. "Went off to bury yourself in Yorkshire or somewhere. A dreadful waste everyone said at the time, such a pretty thing as you were!"

Minerva thought her quite the most dreadful woman she had ever met, but was nonetheless captivated by her.

"I was exceedingly happy with Mortimer," Mrs. Peach said in a small voice. "When he died almost four years ago, I scarcely knew what I should do without him."

"I'm sorry to hear it. But happily, you have survived. Bereavement afflicts all of us at one time or another. I lost Bredon some ten years back." The lorgnette came into play again. "So, what brings you to London?"

A note of pride came into Mrs. Peach's voice. "I am staying for a while with my dear young friend, Lady Claireux. I expect you will already know one another. No? Oh, how remiss of me!" Haltingly she made the introductions.

"Claireux?" repeated Lady Maude, staring very hard. "So you are the heiress. Hm. Not what I expected." Minerva was on the point of saying something unwise when her ladyship continued brusquely. "Pray ask that husband of yours why he has not been near me since his troubles. Hiding himself away in Yorkshire—as if that ever solved anything!"

"Dominic was not hiding away!" Minerva protested. "Whatever else he may be, he is not a coward!"

"No. A stiff-rumped young fool, more like!"

"Because he prefers to fight his own battles? I admire him for it," said Minerva with something of a martial light in her own eyes.

Being talked back to was a novel experience for Lady Maude. The daughter of a duke, she had long since become a considerable personality in her own right, and was used to being obeyed without question. Now she endeavored to stare Minerva out of countenance, while Mrs. Peach stirred uncomfortably. But Minerva, far from being discomposed, seemed to relish the encounter and, because Dominic and her ladyship seemed such an unlikely combination, found herself asking, "Do I then take it, ma'am, that you know my husband?"

"Know him? Well, of course I know him. He is my godson." Lady Maude sniffed. "Not, of course, that he would stoop to come to me for help, though my influence is considerable," she said without conceit. "Too proud by half!"

Looking her straight in the eye, Minerva said, "Then could you not have gone to him—offered him your help and support?"

"And have my head snapped off for my pains?" came the swift retort.

Minerva tried to visualize such an encounter, and laughed. "Yes. I can see your ladyship's difficulty!"

Lady Maude was much taken with Dominic's bride, though she would not go so far as to admit it. "I am having a reception on Friday evening. Try to persuade that husband of yours to come." She nodded. "I shall expect you also, Esmeralda." She rapped smartly on the box with her cane, and the barouche began to move. "Good day to you."

"Well, really!" exclaimed Mrs. Peach. "My dear, I do apologize. I hope you did not find Maude too dreadfully rude. She was ever outspoken—her upbringing, I suppose—but age has not, I fear, improved her!"

"Oh, I don't know. In an odd sort of way I rather liked her."

Dominic, however, was less sanguine when told as they sat over tea in the drawing room. "Good God! Not the grand Maude! However did you manage to get yourself noticed by her?"

"I fear the blame must be mine," put in Mrs. Peach apologetically. "I knew her as a girl, you see."

"Was Maude ever a girl?" he drawled. "I find any such creature impossible to imagine."

"That is no way to speak of your godmother," Minerva said severely.

"Ha! Told you that, did she? You *have* been exchanging confidences."

"Yes, and it may surprise you to know that she is concerned about you in her own rather brusque, high-handed way."

Dominic shrugged. "Oh, she's not such a bad old bird under all that bombast. We always dealt tolerably well together."

"Yet you did not go to her when she might have helped you?" Minerva was curious.

"Have her meddling in my affairs? God forbid!" His eyes glinted at her. "My dear girl, you are more than five, so don't tell me that you spent even a short time in her presence without observing that Maude's help would almost certainly come with strings attached. In short, one would be required to dance to her tune."

Mrs. Peach set down her cup with a nervous clatter. "I fear his lordship may be right, my dear," she ventured. "Maude always did like to rule the roost."

"So do we all, dear ma'am, Dominic included," Minerva said, giving him a challenging look. "But that in no way alters the fact that he could manage Lady Bredon with one hand tied behind his back, should he wish so to do, and as he will no doubt demonstrate when we go to her reception."

"*If* we go," he said in an uncompromising way which disconcerted her not at all.

"Dominic, we must," she urged. "I distinctly remember Georgie telling me that she is one of London's most prestigious hostesses. It is exactly the *entrée* we need. If she accepts you, so will many others who are not at present so disposed. We cannot afford not to go!"

He was looking at her in the strangest way. "It means that much to you?"

Minerva thought of all that they were up against: the doubt and suspicion; her own background and want of connections. She thought of the child she was carrying and those who would hopefully follow: for their sake and to further the restoration of Dominic's own good name, every hand offered in friendship must be grasped.

"Yes," she said quietly. "It means that much."

He stared at her a moment longer. Then: "Very well," he said, nodded abruptly to Mrs. Peach, and left the room.

"Oh dear! I do hope that my encounter with Maude will not be a cause of friction between you two young things." Mrs. Peach pleated her gown in an agitated way. "His lordship does seem a trifle displeased."

Minerva had been staring at the shut door, but now

she recollected herself and smiled brightly. "Think no more of it, ma'am. Dominic will come about. In time he may even have cause to thank you."

Benevolence was not uppermost in Dominic's breast, however, as he presently made his way to White's. It had come as something of a facer to him to find that Minerva had apparently acquired social ambitions. True, she had enjoyed her time in Paris, but he could have sworn it had never gone to her head. It was one of the things he most liked about her, that she had so little time for pretension.

He found Charles Lowdon ensconsed in a deep comfortable armchair, sleepily surveying the members who came and went. Lowdon greeted Dominic amiably, noting without comment his air of frowning preoccupation as he sat down.

"You have just missed your cousin," he commiserated. "He was carrying a fan. I swear I do not jest," he went on, pleased to see that he had engaged Dominic's interest. "It is a quite wondeful creation of chicken feathers on ivory sticks. Says he finds the present heat insupportable!"

"Poseur!" Dominic grunted.

"True. But so entertaining. I sometimes wonder what we should do without him." This produced a further grunt, unintelligible this time, though Charles was able to make a fair guess at its general drift. He sighed and waited patiently for his friend to unburden his mind of whatever was troubling him. He did not have long to wait.

"Charles? Do you have the remotest idea where Hagarth's manservant might have gone after the fuss died down?"

The question almost surprised him out of his customary lethargic pose. "Deuce take it, Dominic. What kind of a question is that?"

"A paradoxical one, I fear. But recent events have forced me to the conclusion that I must make a push to do what I should have done months ago—" Dominic leaned forward with sudden urgency—"namely, to prove my innocence to the world. And in order to do that I must discover who in fact *did* kill the bad baron, which is more than the Runners seem capable of doing."

Charles, fresh from Pelham's eager confidentialities which he had put down with, he hoped, cutting finality, was less sure how to answer Dominic. If anyone could track down the killer, it would be Dominic, but in his opinion it couldn't be done. The trail was cold.

"Do you think it's a good idea?" he began cautiously.

"Well, of course it isn't a good idea. In fact, it's damned nigh impossible—and if you can come up with something better, I shall be eternally in your debt. But I am fast coming to the conclusion that someone out there is playing a deuced deep game, with me as the quarry—and it's gone far enough."

"But how would finding Hagarth's man help you?" asked Charles, intrigued in spite of himself.

"I'm not sure," Dominic confessed ruefully. "But it occurred to me that Hagarth might have recorded his dealings in a book, somewhere apart from the documents—in his desk, perhaps."

"If he did, the Runners would surely have found it, unless . . ." Charles stopped and looked across at him.

"Precisely. Unless the manservant had already taken it."

"Which would suggest that he is the villain you're after."

Dominic sat back, deflated. "I think not. If that were the case, I would surely be among those now being pressed for payment. Unless the fellow is cleverer than I take him for, and is willing to forgo my payment in order that suspicion might continue to fall on me."

"Or," suggested Charles quietly, "he could be in league with someone else, another of Hagarth's victims, perhaps, someone smart enough to tempt the servant into becoming his accomplice, maybe even to do the actual killing, with the promise of rich pickings to come.''

Dominic found himself experiencing the sensation that often came to him just prior to battle when the enemy is almost within reach. ''Charles, you're a genius!'' He dismissed his friend's faint demur. ''No, no, that's it! I am sure we are on the right track. But, dammit, how do we set about finding the fellow and proving it?''

''Not by drawing attention to ourselves, that's for sure,'' said the other hastily. ''Your Drummond might perhaps make a few judicious inquiries in the taverns around the area. He seems to have a good head on him.''

''True. It wouldn't be the first time he's undertaken such a mission. I doubt Moss would know anything—a trifle below his touch!''

''I'll ask my man. Amazing what these fellows know sometimes.''

''Hm. And there's something else.'' Dominic, now well into the spirit of the thing, found his mind working furiously. ''Minerva's uncle is in town. He's a Justice of the Peace and may well have friends at Bow Street. After all, the more we can learn, the better place we will be to act.''

Charles sighed. ''When you say 'we,' dear boy, I do trust I will not be expected to become involved in anything of an energetic nature. Not that I wouldn't lay down my life for you should necessity demand, but I'd as lief not be called upon to go rushing about the countryside hunting down villains.''

''Gammon!'' Dominic grinned. ''That's a hum if ever I heard one, coming as it does from someone Jackson reckons has one of the most punishing rights in the game.''

''Pugilism, dear boy, as you know as well as anyone, is concerned with science and skill and timing,'' Charles said, resuming his indolent pose. "Quite different from the kind of mayhem I can envision once you begin stirring up trouble. However, we can but hope."

14

MR. ABEL Nugent arrived on the doorstep of the house in Grosvenor Street on the following morning as the marquess was finishing breakfast.

Marshal cast a disparaging eye over the portly figure in the tight-fitting blue coat and low-crowned beaver hat, and knew him at once for a Bow Street Runner. Outraged, the butler's first instinct was to cause the door to be shut in his face, but a moment's reflection brought wiser counsels to bear and instead he had Mr. Nugent shown into the small, sparsely furnished saloon immediately to the left of the door where callers of little significance inevitably found themselves. Before going to inform his lordship, however, Marsham did not scruple to favor the Runner with his opinion of persons who were so inconsiderate as to disturb a gentleman at his breakfast.

The arrival of the marquess further demoralized Mr. Nugent, who had heard daunting tales of his predecessor's encounter with his lordship, and soon discovered that his top-lofty manner had not been overstated.

"Beggin' your lordship's pardon for the inconvenience of the hour," he began hesitantly, "but dooty is dooty, and it struck me as it would be less of an embarrassment to your lordship if I was to execute mine at a time when very few folks is abroad—if you take my meaning."

"Mighty civil of you."

The sarcasm was not encouraging. Mr. Nugent took out his occurrence book and thumbed through it with more haste than accuracy. "Ah, here we are," he said at last, unnerved by the brooding silence. "My business is concerned with the foul murder of a gentleman by the name of Baron Hagarth on the night of January 3rd, and the disappearance at the said time of a box containing certain documents . . ."

"You have found it?" Dominic said tersely.

"No, m'lord. I regret that we have not as yet laid hands on the said item, but we 'ave reason to believe that someone else has, and is, as you might say, using the contents for unlawful gain."

"That much I know. Come to the point, man."

His impatience drew a reproachful glance from the Runner. "The point *is,* m'lord, that whosoever this cove might be, he waited—hopin' as we'd be lulled—afore starting up his dubious enterprise. Only he reckoned without the fury of certain parties, whose names I am not at liberty to divulge, who had complained to my superiors as they're being hounded for money—and why I'm here is to ask if your lordship would be so obliging as to tell me if you have received any such demands?"

Dominc's initial reaction was to damn him for his insolence and throw him out on his ear as he had done with his predecessor; but a moment's reflection suggested that before doing so, he might as well make what use of him, if any, that he could.

"Why me?" he asked with deceptive mildness. "Am I still under suspicion, or are you asking the same question of others?"

"I am not at liberty to divulge information of a confidential nature, m'lord," said the man, ill at ease.

"Perhaps," Dominic continued to press him, "you have a list of Hagarth's debtors?"

Mr. Nugent was by now almost squirming with embarrassment. "My lord, I'm sorry! But I am not at liberty . . ."

"To divulge information of a confidential nature. Yes, I see," said Dominic with chilling formality. "Well, you may tell your superiors that I, in return, choose not to divulge to them information which I consider to be none of their damn business. Good day to you, Nugent."

When the discomforted Runner had departed, Dominic had time to reflect on the wisdom of dismissing him so summarily, but the satisfaction it had afforded him to do so more than made up for any doubt. With Drummond already briefed as to what was required of him, the immediate priority must be to contact Sir Richard Standish. He had called in at Brooks's on his way home the previous evening, but the baronet had gone to dine with friends. He would try again this morning.

On his way upstairs, he met Minerva hurrying down. She looked a little pale, he thought, but before he could voice the thought she demanded to know if it was true that a Bow Street Runner had called. Annoyance that she had been troubled made him curt.

"Yes. But he has gone."

"But Dominic, why did he come?" she continued impetuously. "I thought they had done with all that!"

"My dear girl, you cannot expect me to discuss my private affairs on the stair." And, forestalling her next question, "In any case, there is nothing to discuss. It was no more than a query—a mere formality. Now, if you will forgive me, I have to go out." Her troubled look reproached him. He touched her cheek briefly. "Don't worry. I promise you there is no need."

With that she had to be content, though it hurt her that he did not feel able to confide in her. She resolved to see if there was not something she could do to help. An opportunity presented itself later that morning when Sir Richard came to call on them. He was full of good humor and had come to see whether Mrs. Peach might care to go to the theater. "You, too, my dear—and his lordship, if he should care to go. My friends tell me that Kean is playing in *Macbeth* at Drury Lane, and is well worth a visit. I thought I might try for a box."

Mrs. Peach was incoherent with delight. Her only worry was that her wardrobe might prove somewhat inadequate for the giddy round of gaiety that was clearly to be her lot over the next weeks, and no amount of reassurances from Minerva or Sir Richard would convince her otherwise.

"Then we shall go shopping, dear ma'am—and see what may be done to supplement any shortcomings, real or imagined," Minerva said, laughing. Mrs. Peach demurred, but was soon persuaded to go and put on her bonnet while Minerva had a private word with her uncle.

"Well now, m'dear, why all the secrecy, eh?" Sir Richard asked jovially when they were alone. "Something your old uncle can do for you, is there?"

"I'm not sure," Minerva said, so serious of a sudden that he looked at her more closely. "Uncle Richard, do you know anyone important at Bow Street?"

Mrs. Peach was quite overwhelmed by her visit to the theater. "Oh, how it takes me back!" she exclaimed, gazing about her, entranced by the elegant foyers, the circular auditorium filled with a glittering audience, and the constant buzz of conversation. "The year I came out, we visited the Theatre Royal quite frequently, and Covent Garden, of course . . . Kemble and dear Sarah Siddon! You will remember, Sir Richard?" She smiled mistily at him, and he found himself thinking how remarkably well she was looking . . . in one of the new dresses Minerva had tempted her into having, a becoming shade of lavender gray. Always had good taste, his niece. He was glad she hadn't forgotten her old friend. He came to with a start to find that Mrs. Peach was still awaiting his answer.

"The divine Sarah? Lord, yes. We young bloods were all mad for her!" he agreed hastily.

By the first interlude, opinions were divided about Edmund Kean. Minerva found his voice a little harsh, but allowed that there was something undeniably compelling about the ugly little man with the fierce, tragic eyes. Mrs. Peach was quite overcome by his passionate performance, Sir Richard admitted that he had a definite presence, while Dominic was less impressed, though he had perceived flashes of brilliance.

In fact, he would as soon not have been there at all, and only agreed to go at Minerva's most earnest entreaty—"Mrs. Peach will be so disappointed if you are not with us. It is her first *real* outing!"

It was during the second interlude that Minerva became aware of someone endeavoring to attract her attention from a box almost opposite their own. It was Georgiana. In a very short space of time, she was tapping on the door of their box.

"My dear Minerva! I could scarce believe my eyes! We only came home yesterday and I have been asking for your direction so that I might call on you. You will remember Etienne?" As she put out a hand to draw forward her escort, the special glow about her was reflected in the young vicomte's eyes so that Minerva was not in the least surprised when she added proudly, "We are betrothed!"

Minerva embraced her and offered her hand to the vicomte. "My dears, I am so happy for you both!" There were introductions all around and then she asked, "Have you arranged any date yet for your wedding?"

"Mama and I thought October." Georgiana threw her betrothed a playful glance. "Although Etienne would prefer that it was sooner, I believe!"

The vicomte gave a droll little shrug. "*Quant á ça,* with ladies the talk is all of bride clothes, I find. For the gentlemen, we do not regard such things! Is this not so, *Monsieur le marquis*?"

But Dominic threw up his hands. "Acquit me, dear boy. I long since gave up trying to fathom the workings of the female mind."

Amid general laughter, Minerva said, "Don't listen to him, Georgie. He simply enjoys being superior!"

"My love!" exclaimed Mrs. Peach, just a little shocked, though her pleasure at seeing two young people so much in love soon preoccupied her once more, to the exclusion of all else.

It was under the cover of all the general excitement that Dominic managed to draw Sir Richard to one side. "I wonder, sir, if you would be able to help me in a rather delicate matter?"

"You have but to ask, my dear Claireux, and if it is within my power, I will do all I can to oblige you." Sir Richard, affected by the general mood, was inclined to be expansive. "Haven't had the chance until now to say how indebted I am to you, how delighted at the way things have turned out. Why, I declare, I never saw my niece looking finer or happier."

Dominic was anxious not to let the moment escape him, yet even so, he found himself glancing across to where Minerva stood in animated conversation with her friends, her tall slim figure shown to advantage in her amber crepe gown. Sir Richard was right—she did look very fine. And reluctantly he had to admit that if this was the kind of life to which she aspired, she should have no difficulty in achieving her goal. He murmured something appropriate and hastened to explain his problem to Sir Richard. "So you see I was wondering if you might perhaps have some influence at Bow Street—enough perhaps to discover for me the present whereabouts of the manservant, if it is known, or at any rate whether the Runners ever found any records of the baron's dealings among his effects?"

Sir Richard seemed surprised. "But—has Minerva not yet spoken to you?"

"Minerva? What has Minerva to do with it? Did you give her some message for me?"

"Ah! No . . . that is, nothing of importance, my boy! Now, what was that about the manservant?" Sir Richard was struggling to extricate himself from an embarrassing *faux pas,* but Dominic was not prepared to leave it there.

"Sir, am I to understand that Minerva has made a similar request of you?"

Mercifully for Sir Richard, the interlude was coming to an end. Lady Georgiana and her fiancé were about to leave the box and were waiting to say their farewells. "See here, Claireux, I'll try what I can do—we'll talk about it tomorrow, what? Be able to decide then how best to proceed. Oh, by the way, what I said about Minerva—pray disregard it. Stupid of me to have confused two different things . . ."

And you are a terrible liar, Dominic thought, brooding in his corner of the box and paying no heed whatever to Mr. Kean's fine histronics throughout the remainder of the play as he pondered what the devil Minerva could be up to. He said little on the way home, either, but since Mrs. Peach scarcely drew breath, his silence went largely unremarked although he caught Minerva looking at him oddly now and then. Once she even asked him if he was all right. "Perfectly all right, thank you," he replied with scrupulous politeness.

He exercised patience while an animated discussion took place as to whether Sir Richard should come back with them or be dropped at his club, and when the latter was decided upon, he continued to remain patient throughout all the good nights and later, with the aid of the brandy bottle, while the two ladies talked on interminably until finally Mrs. Peach declared herself exhausted and she and Minerva made their way upstairs.

When he was absolutely certain that the older woman was safely tucked up in her bedchamber for the night, he made his way purposefully along to his wife's room, knocked briefly, and entered. Minerva was seated at her dressing table in the act of removing her earrings while

Mattie unpinned her hair. She watched him through the mirror as he came in; she had not imagined that odd shuttered look of his when they were in the carriage earlier—it was there still. And his voice was terse as he informed Matthews that he wished to speak to his wife —alone. Instinctively the maid looked to her mistress.

"It's all right, Mattie," Minerva said quietly. "You may go to bed now—I shall manage very well without you."

Matthews went, but reluctantly, giving his lordship a disapproving look and muttering darkly about keeping her ladyship from her rest.

"Is there something wrong, Dominic?" Minerva asked, turning to face him as the door closed behind Mattie. "I do hope that Mrs. Peach isn't annoying you with her chatter." She smiled suddenly. "Do you know, I believe Uncle Richard may be becoming a trifle smitten with her. Now that *would* be extraordinary indeed—such a confirmed old bachelor as he is!"

"Minerva," Dominic cut in without ceremony, "what in heavens name are you playing at?"

"I don't understand."

She stood up, and as her amber gown rippled over her shapely limbs, he was for a second in severe danger of forgetting why he had come. But only for a second. "Such innocence! Well, it won't wash, my girl. What I want to know is, why you were asking your uncle for information about Hagarth?"

Minerva bit her lip. "Oh, drat him! Honestly, you would think a Justice of the Peace could be relied upon to be discreet."

"I'm sure he can be the soul of discretion if he has been properly primed. And before you ask, no—he didn't give you away," Dominic said with soft force. "In fact, it was his desperate attempt *not* to do so which betrayed him, though I magnanimously allowed him to think he had succeeded."

"Oh, thank you. Poor lamb, how embarrassing for him!"

"It was devilishly embarrassing for me, I might tell you!" he declared savagely. "And you haven't answered my question."

Minerva turned her back on him on the pretense of searching in her reticule for a handkerchief, but in truth to give her a moment in which to think. But in the end, the simple truth seemed the only way. "If you must know," she said without facing him, "it was just an idea that Pelham and I had . . ."

"Pel! My God, you'd as well broadcast it to the world!" Dominic took her by the shoulders and spun her around. "Now you listen to me, Minerva. Once and for all, I will not have any interference in my affairs, not by you, or Pelham—especially Pel, for all that he's my friend."

Minerva struggled to free herself, and when she failed, her eyes blazed up at him. "Yes, he *is* your friend! And a better one than you deserve! Pel really cares what happens to you—as I care, though heaven knows why either of us should in the face of such rank ingratitude."

"Minerva . . ." he tried to stem the flow, but she would not be silenced and tears of anger rolled unheeded down her cheeks.

"So, how dare you lay down the law about what we should or shouldn't do to help you! I should have thought that you would be glad of all the f-friends you can g-et."

"Minerva!" Appalled that he had brought her to the point of tears, this strong, assured wife of his, he stopped her in the only way he could, by pulling her close and kissing her hard and long. As the salt of her tears mingled with the sweetness of her mouth, and as her resistance, which was but a token one, melted away, so the nature of their embrace changed and quickened into something altogether different. His every touch became a caress which lit fires in her she had not known existed until now.

"I'm sorry." The words fluttered softly against her skin while his lips did the most unsettling things to her ear lobes. "You are quite right. I am an ungrateful brute!"

"No, no!" she insisted. "I should not have flown up into the boughs as I did! I fear my emotions are not very stable at present . . ."

His laugh was soft. "Well, let us not come to cuffs again. I can think of a much better way to pass the time." He lifted her and carried her across to the bed.

"Dominic—my gown! Mattie will be furious if you ruin it!"

For answer, he set her on her feet and a moment later the dress was slithering to the floor. Blushing, she stepped out of it and watched him lay it ceremoniously across the chairback without taking his eyes off her.

"Now, where was I?" he said, returning to lift her up again.

She giggled into his shoulder. "Aren't you in the least curious about my emotional state?"

"Only in so far as affects me."

"And would it affect you to know that you are to become a father?" The words spilled out impetuously. Minerva had not meant to tell him for some time yet, but suddenly the moment seemed right. Now she awaited his reaction in a fever of uncertainty. Suppose he did not relish the prospect of fatherhood so soon?

Dominic sat down abruptly on the side of the bed, still holding her firmly in his arms. He was silent for so long that she grew impatient. "Dominic? Say something! You did understand—that I am pregnant?"

"Yes, of course." He sounded dazed.

"You don't care for the idea," she said flatly, attempting to withdraw herself from his arms. But he only held her more tightly and to her astonishment began to laugh. "Dominic!"

"I'm sorry, my dear, but you really do have the damndest way of going about things!" He kissed her soundly. "Idiot! Of course I am pleased. You are sure?"

"Well, of course I am sure. I have been confoundedly sickly every morning for the past few weeks . . ."

"All the time I was ill, in fact?" he put in, regarding her curiously.

"Yes. In fact, it was Dr. Hitchen who finally confirmed it to me, though Mattie had already assured me that it was so."

"Yet you devoted yourself to my needs and said nothing?"

"But of course," she said matter-of-factly. "I am your wife. And in any case, I had not intended that you should know for some time yet. I'm not altogether sure why I have told you now."

Dominic looked amost boyishly piqued. "You didn't consider that I had a right to know?"

She chuckled at this display of husbandly outrage. "In the fullness of time. But I am quite determined not to be fussed over and treated as an invalid, and I give you fair warning that if you make the least attempt to curtail my pleasures, I shall become exceedingly crabby!" She smiled into his eyes. "So you won't, will you?"

He set her on her feet and stood up. "I am making no promises, young lady, so it's no good trying to wheedle any out of me." He dropped a light kiss on her mouth, his voice softening. "For now, it is high time you were asleep."

"Oh, good God, I knew it was a mistake to tell you!" she exclaimed, holding his arm as he moved away. "A few minutes ago you were not wishing me asleep,"she coaxed him quite shamelessly. "I haven't suddenly become untouchable, you know."

He stood looking into her upturned face, his expression quizzical. "Hussy!" he said, and as her laughter gurgled deliciously, "You really want me to stay?"

"I really want you to stay," she affirmed.

and until then it is simply a cross we must bear."

"Well, I do think he is jolly lucky to have you instead of Vinnie for his wife," Georgiana declared with her usual lack of tact. "She would do nothing but cry all over him and very likely go into a decline!"

Until that moment Minerva had managed to block Lavinia Winterton from her mind, apart from a brief sinking of the heart on the previous evening when her pleasure at seeing Georgie had been tempered by the thought that Lavinia must also be back in London.

"Mama was profoundly relieved to deliver Vinnie back into her father's charge," Georgiana was saying. "She does seem to have a talent for making everyone else appear in the wrong, while looking lovely and innocent as a newborn lamb, which quite set Mama's back up on more than one occasion. And it took every ounce of my determination, I can tell you, to keep Etienne out of her beguiling clutches."

Minerva did not really want to talk about Lavinia Winterton, and was glad to seize this chance to turn the conversation into safer channels. "I am so pleased that she did not succeed. It is so delightful to see two people so obviously in love. You are fortunate indeed."

The vaguest hint of something in her voice made Georgiana saying swiftly, "Oh, but you and Dominic are happy, surely? I mean, I know it was not a love match, but you seem to deal extremely well together?"

"Yes, of course we do." Minerva could have cursed that moment of weakness. It must have been the mention of Lavinia Winterton. After all, no one could have been more loving than Dominic last night. She said brightly, "But I am sensible enough to know that it is not always so. You and I are the lucky ones."

"Well, I mean to make sure that Etienne never has cause to stray," said her friend with such conviction that Minerva laughed. "And I'm sure he will never do so!" she said. "Oh, by the way, we have been invited to Lady Bredon's reception on Friday evening. Shall you be there, do you know?"

"I can't say for sure, because we have been quite swamped with invitations, but I should think it more than likely."

"Well, I hope you are, because I shall know hardly anyone, and it would make so much difference to see a friendly face!"

"Oh, I have no doubt that you will manage beautifully." But Georgiana looked genuinely pleased, nonetheless. "And if Lady Bredon likes you, you can have little to fear, though personally, I find her quite terrifying!"

"I'm not at all sure whether she likes me, but she is Dominic's godmother and certainly seems to be fond of him. Also, she is acquainted with Mrs. Peach, who is presently staying with me."

"What a delightful name!" Georgiana exclaimed.

Minerva smiled. "Indeed. And Mrs. Peach is a delightful lady. She does not rise very early, but no doubt you will meet her in due course."

Pleased as Minerva was to see Georgie, she was not entirely sorry when she departed. One corner of her mind was obsessively occupied with thoughts of how Dominic was faring with her uncle. She had made him promise to tell her everything on his return.

"And I do think you should take Pelham into your confidence," she had said coaxingly. "Especially as Charles is already aware of what is happening. He would be so hurt if he thought he was being excluded, and besides, it would surely be better to have him under your eye where you can control him."

"Did anyone ever tell you what a devious young woman you are?" he answered with a sigh of resignation.

"On the contrary, I thought it was my frank and open ways that you most often deplored," she said meekly.

When Dominic returned from his meeting with Sir Richard, however, she saw at a glance that he had met with little success. "My uncle was not able to help?"

"Oh, I believe he did his best, but it seems the

Runners found very little that would be of help to us. Certainly, there was no journal or notebook of any kind." He sounded dispirited.

"And the manservant?"

"Vanished the day after the murder, and hasn't been seen since." He shrugged. "Drummond has visited almost every tavern which he might have been expected to frequent to little purpose except to give himself a thick head."

"Well, it sounds to me as though your theory of an accomplice may yet prove to be the right one. Though I fear a truly ruthless accomplice might well have disposed of the man the moment his usefulness was at an end."

"It does seem the most likely explanation," Dominic agreed, "but it doesn't really get us anywhere."

Even during her time in Paris, Minerva had seen nothing to equal Lady Bredon's reception in terms of sheer grandeur. Previously, her only experience of receptions had been confined to tedious business affairs in company with her father. So there was nothing to prepare her for the sight of Berkeley Square on a hot June night, jammed with vehicles of all shapes and sizes, all seeking to converge upon a house that blazed light from every open window.

"It en't reasonable—nor safe, if you arsks me—quarts into pint pots en't in it!" she heard Joshua grumble as he steered the landaulet nimbly past a more lumbering coach, whose rear wheel had somehow become inextricably caught up in one belonging to a more elegant equipage on its other side. The warm air grew warmer still with the force of the coachmen's language, which would have shocked Mrs. Peach to the core had she not, by great good fortune, become totally dazed by the whole spectacle. At one point Minerva was sure she heard Joshua chuckle to himself and say: "There—that'll learn yer!" and she smiled to herself. For all that Joshua might complain, she was convinced that he was thoroughly enjoying his stay in London, and welcomed the chance to pit his wits against his peers.

And then they were outside the house, and in a moment more were joining the seemingly endless procession of guests wending their way up the curving staircase amid the scent and profusion of flowers and the light of hundreds of candles. At the top stood Lady Maude, an imposing figure in black twilled silk and wearing a turban of the same, adorned with ostrich plumes.

"Ah, so you came," she boomed as Dominic, a sardonic glint in his eyes, raised her hand to his lips.

"But, of course, dear Lady Maude. How could I possibly ignore such a summons?"

"Pshaw!" she retorted, prodding him with her fan. "Don't give me that flim-flam! I know well enough that I owe your presence to this charming wife of yours. I hope you are taking good care of her. She's worth it. Just the kind of good honest stock your family needs." She had a carrying voice, and Minerva's face grew scarlet, much to Dominic's amusement. "This was your idea, remember," he murmured in her ear as Lady Maude turned her attention briefly to Mrs. Peach. "Go along through into the saloon," she concluded. "I daresay you haven't forgotten your way, boy."

The room was already crowded, and spilling over into a room beyond by means of two pairs of doors thrown wide. Several chandeliers, each holding anything up to a hundred candles and as many glittering lusters, showered soft light down upon the scene, and in spite of many long windows standing open to the night, adding to the general warmth.

Mrs. Peach, following behind Minerva, had to restrain her urge to hang on to her for fear of getting lost in the crush while Dominic endeavored to clear a path for them. She was never so pleased as to see a familiar figure pushing his way through toward her, a very elegant figure.

"Ah, there you are, ma'am," said Sir Richard. "Pray

take my arm and permit me to find you somewhere a little less crowded."

"Oh yes, please do!" she exclaimed a trifle faintly. "Of course it is all magnificent, but I fear I am not quite used to such gatherings."

"No more am I, ma'am. No more am I. But never mind—I have discovered a small anteroom just beyond the second room. Minerva . . ." Sir Richard managed to attract his niece's attention for long enough to explain where they were going. "So you'll know where to find us."

Minerva noted his protective manner toward Mrs. Peach as they departed and turned to share with Dominic her conviction that she had been right about the couple, whether or not they yet realized it for themselves. But the few moments' delay had been sufficient to separate her from Dominic. She glimpsed his head above the rest, some way ahead, and followed as best she could. If she were honest, she also found the crush and the heat more than a little trying. She looked up into the light of the chandelier and the prismatic brilliance of the crystal drops seemed to shiver and merge.

"A sad crush, ma'am," said a quiet voice at her side. She turned a little too quickly, grateful for a voice she knew, and felt the room swimming. Charles Lowdon's hand was under her arm in an instant, its grip surprisingly strong and comforting. "Lady Claireux, are you quite well?"

"Yes . . . yes, of course," Minerva said, her laugh a little uncertain. "It is the heat, I expect . . . and the press of people." She took a couple of deep breaths. "Ah, that is better."

"Nevertheless, I think we will get out of the center of things. There is a little more room over by the windows." He cleared a path as if by magic and soon they were standing beside an open window. The air was not much cooler, but a slight breeze moved the muslin curtains now and again. "If you wish, I will try to procure you a chair," Charles said. "And I daresay there may be some cordial available in the supper room."

Cordial would have been nice, but the dryness of her mouth was already easing. "Oh, no! Please do not go to so much trouble," she exclaimed. "Truly, I feel very much better already. You have been so kind, but I must not keep you from your friends."

"You are not," he said with a faint smile. "One does not come to such functions to see one's friends, but to be seen in the right company!"

Minerva's smile was uncertain. "That sounds very calculating."

"Oh, it is. But only if one takes it seriously," he said gently. "And besides, Dominic would never forgive me if I abandoned you here."

Minerva had never felt so much at ease with this young Corinthian as with Pelham. He was quite unlike anyone she had ever known, and she sometimes found his world-weary pose difficult to understand. There was no doubting his kindness at this moment, however, and it emboldened her to appeal to his gallantry.

"Mr. Lowdon—please promise me that you won't tell Dominic about my stupid faintness? You know what he's like," she said, striving for lightness. "He would probably insist on taking me home, and we should fall to arguing, and the whole evening would be ruined!"

He saw that the color was coming back to her cheeks, which a few moments before had matched the ivory silk of her gown. "Very well, if that is your wish, but I will stay with you for a while, I think, if you feel able to endure my company."

"I should be very glad of it," she said, and smiled at him. "We have never quite got to know one another as we should. Perhaps we can go a little way to remedy that now. For a start, do you think we might be Charles and Minerva? The other is so formal."

And so it was that they walked in amiable accord in the direction she had last seen Dominic taking. The guests had by now dispersed somewhat into groups, which made the general atmosphere much less oppressive.

It was Charles who spotted Dominic first. His immediate instinct was to lead Minerva in the opposite direction, for his friend was not alone. He was talking to Lord Winterton, and with the viscount was his daughter, looking frail and willowy and incredibly beautiful. But he was too late. Minerva had already seen the small group. Just for an instant her step faltered, and Charles found himself saying in his calm, droll fashion, "We could go and view Lady Maude's collection of jade. It is, I believe, very fine."

She threw him a grateful look. "Thank you, but I think not. Running away is never a good idea. Papa was used to say 'Always face your enemy. That way he can't stab you in the back.' It is something I have always tried to do."

Charles glanced at Minerva with renewed interest. He had dismissed her at their first meeting, and thereafter, as a pleasant, intelligent young woman but one with whom he had little in common. Only now was he beginning to realize how greatly he had underestimated her. Was Dominic aware, he wondered, of his wife's admirable qualities? "An excellent philosophy," he remarked. "Suppose we test it out."

As they approached, Minerva heard Lavinia saying with charming diffidence, "I do hope that my foolishness did not cause any difficulty between you and your w-wife." The stumble over the last was so expertly achieved that one could almost believe it to have been spontaneous. And delivered with just the right degree of humility. "I would never forgive myself."

She could tell little from Dominic's face, or from his quiet: "Lavinia, pray forget what happened. No damage has been done, I promise you."

"So kind!" she murmured, with just a hint of tragedy bravely concealed. If it had not concerned her so deeply, Minerva would have found the performance vastly entertaining. But gentlemen were so much more susceptible to that kind of thing, and she had no intention of permitting Lavinia to exercise her wiles on Dominic.

As she and Charles approached, the limpid gaze was turned on her. "Dear Lady Claireux, how delightfully you are looking! May I introduce my father to you? Papa, this is Dominic's wife—" no break in the voice this time. "And Mr. Lowdon, how do you do?"

Lord Winterton was a bluff, jovial man, clearly besotted with his daughter—and why not, for she was beautiful enough, and Minerva suspected, clever enough to enslave any man, even her father. The only surprise was that she had not managed to persuade him to overlook all obstacles and accept Dominic as a son-in-law. But every man, she supposed, had his sticking point.

"I do hope we can be friends," Lavinia was saying with a charming, diffident smile. "I fear I was not at my best in Paris. In fact, I was not at all well when I first went there with Lady Lanyon, was I, Papa?"

"Indeed you were not, my love," Lord Winterton agreed indulgently, while carefully averting his gaze from the marquess, whose expression was inscrutable. "So low in spirits she was, Lady Claireux, that at one point our physician almost feared for her life!"

With eyes demurely lowered, Lavinia continued, "Lady Lanyon was most forbearing, for indeed there were moments when I scare knew what I was doing!"

But Minerva could take no more from this slight angelic creature who always succeeded in making her feel large and awkward. "I understand perfectly how it was," she said, with a look that left her in little doubt of her meaning. "However," she continued briskly, "what is past is done with, as my Papa often used to say. I am sure you will presently have any number of beaux flocking around you, so pretty as you are, and nothing is so guaranteed to lift the spirits as to find oneself the center of attention." She put her hand possessively on

Dominic's arm. "And now, if you will forgive me, I mean to steal my husband away from you, for there is someone I very much wish him to meet." Dominic looked at her rather hard. Was it his imagination that she looked pale and a trifle strained? But she only smiled at him.

"Bravo!" murmured Charles in her ear. "Your father would be proud of you."

"And what was that all about?" Dominic said tersely as they moved away.

"We were proving a philosophical point," drawled Charles.

Dominic glanced from one to the other. "You two are mighty close, all of a sudden. I mislike people who talk in riddles. So, who is this person you so urgently wished me to meet?"

The two looked at one another blankly for a moment, then Charles, at his most charmingly quizzical, murmured, "Why, your wife, of course, my dear fellow. You were separated by the crowd and I was sure you would wish to have her restored to you with all speed!"

"Vastly obliged, Charles." He regarded his friend through narrowed eyes. "Strange. It ain't like you to meddle."

"Meddle? Such an ugly word." Charles considered it. "But you are quite right. Not my style at all. I shall seek a quiet corner somewhere and ponder my illogical behavior." He made an elegant leg. "Your servant ma'am," and added with a faint smile, "any time."

"Well," said Dominic, feeling slightly aggrieved without quite knowing why, "I am delighted that you and Charles seem to be getting along so well together."

"Yes, so am I," she answered, her expression tranquil.

He was silent for a moment, then he said, "You have no need to worry about Lavinia, you know. What is past is done with, as you so pointedly remarked."

"I know," she said. "I just wanted to make sure that she knew it, too."

He raised her hand to his lips. "I have the feeling that you could be quite ruthless if anyone attempted to cross you."

"Let us hope," she said with a curious intentness, "that I never have cause to prove it."

Close by, a quizzing glass was raised, regarding them intently. A moment later, the unmistakable drawl of Gervase Wilmington broke in upon them. "My word, a husband and wife demonstrating their affection in public! It won't do, my dears—deuced unfashionable, don't y'know!"

"Gervase. I did not expect to see you here." Dominic's greeting could hardly be said to be encouraging, but his cousin seemed immune to the lack of warmth.

"One might have said the same of you, dear boy! But then, Lady Maude is your godmother, I collect—and when one is sorely in need of support socially, who better to turn to than the most influential hostess in town? I would have done exactly the same in your shoes!"

Minerva sensed that Dominic was on the point of exploding, and dug her fingers very hard into his sleeve. "I'm sure you would, cousin," she said sweetly. "One senses in you immediately the conviction that you would, if necessary, climb over your dying mother in order to be seen in the right place!"

His face flushed a dull red above the intricacy of his cravat. He bowed jerkily—"Servant"—and departed with less grace than was his wont.

"Minerva!" There was a touch of awe in Dominic's soft exclamation.

"I'm sorry," she said, only half contrite. "I seem to have proved your point, don't I? But he is such a posturing creature, and I was so angry about what he said, especially as it was I who persuaded you to come!"

To her surprise, Dominic laughed suddenly. "Well, all I can say, my dear termagent of a wife, is that I am glad you are for me and not against!"

The rest of the evening passed off without incident. During supper, they came upon Sir Richard and Mrs. Peach, who seemed to be well content with each other's company. Sir Richard had met several people he knew, but showed no inclination to abandon his partner in their favor.

Lord and Lady Lanyon arrived a little late, and were most encouragingly cordial to Minerva and Dominic, while under Lady Maude's intimidating eyes, several people who might in different circumstances have looked the other way, were constrained to be pleasant.

"I trust," she said as they left, her words addressed pointedly to Dominic, "that I shall be seeing much more of you in the future than I have done heretofore."

"I promise," said Minerva.

16

MINERVA MIGHT never have known about the accident to the curricle if the sky had not cleared suddenly after a spate of showers that had continued for several days. The air was fresh, the sun shone with a new brilliance, and she was alone. Dominic had gone with Drummond to try out the paces of a new pair of horses, and would undoubtedly finish up at White's in hopes of showing them off to Pelham and Charles if they should be there, and Mrs. Peach was, most unusually, lying down with a headache.

After prowling restlessly for a while, unable to settle to anything, Minerva decided to take a drive through Hyde Park. It was not long past noon and with any luck, there would be little traffic to spoil her pleasure. She would have liked to ride, but Dr. Hitchen had advised her not to, for a week or two at least. "A little care now, my lady, is worth twice as much later on," he had said, and since she had no wish to jeopardize her baby's progress, she must heed his words.

"You shouldn't ought to be a'driving that perilous thing without someone along of you," Joshua said with a sniff of disapproval as the stable boy led out the gelding to put it between the shafts.

Minerva looked at her genteel lady's phaeton and laughed. "Humgudgeon!"

"So you say, but you don't have to answer to his lordship. Tongue as sharp as a razor, he's got, when things baint be to his liking! And that Drummond en't here—never is when he's wanted—so it's down to me or the boy."

"I appreciate your concern, Joshua," she said, stifling her exasperation, "but I believe I shall survive without you. The carriage is not exactly a sporting vehicle and the gelding is as meek as a lamb. Even if I were ham-handed, which I am not, I could hardly come to any harm with either of them!"

Joshua finally let her go, muttering dire prophecies.

As she had expected, the Park was quiet. Even the nursemaids had taken their charges home to luncheon. Everything looked very green after the rain—beautiful, ordered, civilized. She found her throat catching with an overwhelming yearning for the moors—those great sweeping miles of open land which knew no order, which in places were wild and bleak, but had a beauty all of their own, and where you could spend whole days of glorious liberty, untrammeled by conventions, with the sun and the wind on your face. Shaken by the unexpectedness of this longing for Yorkshire and home, she drew in to the side and sat for a while allowing her emotions free rein.

The moment passed, of course, and she was soon admonishing herself for what she termed mawkish sentimentality. "This is what you wanted, my girl, and this is what you've got. And the moors will still be there when you've a mind to go back—as you must anyway, sooner or later."

When she felt quite calm once more, she set the horse in motion and trotted on, past the Stanhope Gate and along by the Serpentine, intending to come full circle. In the far distance a small carriage, a tilbury or something similar, was being driven at a spanking pace. She smiled. Some young blood trying out its paces, rather like Dominic.

And then, some few yards ahead, she noticed that a

curricle had been involved in an accident. It had veered off the path and ended up half on its side against a tree. The horses had been released and two people were bent down, apparently with their shoulders against the curricle, endeavoring to right it. Minerva slowed down and was about to call out to ask if there was any way in which she could be of assistance when, to her horror, she saw Drummond's head appear as he stood up.

In that moment, when time seemed to have no meaning, she heard him say: "Cut through, m'lord—clean as you please! Lucky as we wasn't both killed!"

Minerva stopped, secured the reins, and jumped down, running across the grass with only one thought in her mind. Please God, not again!

"Dominic? Are you all right?" She stumbled around the end of the curricle and they met face to face as he hurriedly straightened up.

"Minerva! What in the name of God are you doing here?"

"Oh, never mind all that!" Breathless from running, she gasped the words out. "Are you hurt? What happened? Oh, please tell me!"

He held her, steadied her. "Minerva, this isn't like you! It's nothing. One of the traces broke, that's all."

"All? You might have been killed—I heard Drummond say so!"

Dominic cast the groom a look of exasperation.

"Well, I wasn't to know her ladyship would hear, was I?" Drummond muttered in an aggrieved voice.

But Minerva had by now recovered her breath—and her wits. "You also said 'cut through,' as I remember," she said more calmly. "And don't try to gammon me, either of you. I may not have your benefit of years, but I cut my eye teeth a long time ago."

Dominic shrugged, his eyes crinkled up, but whether from exasperation or the brightness of the sun she did not know. And she did not care. Without further comment, he led her around to the side of the curricle which leaned against the tree and showed her the two pieces of the leather strap. Two thirds of the break on each side were sliced clean, and the small amount remaining was ragged where the pressures exerted upon them had pulled the two pieces apart.

Minerva stared in shocked silence, feeling a little sick. "Who would do such a thing? And why?"

"Would that I could answer you," he said. "But I fear I am as much in the dark as you. However, since you have arrived so opportunely—" he made no reference to her being out alone, though she sensed the unspoken criticism— "You shall have the pleasure of driving me home. Drummond can ride one of the horses and lead the other, and the curricle will have to remain where it is until he can get someone out to replace the trace."

The silence was heavy between them as they drove home, broken only occasionally, as when Dominic observed quietly, "You have good hands." She could have sworn his mind had been quite elsewhere, and was therefore doubly pleased by the compliment.

"Dominic," she said presently, "I have had a thought which I am sure must have crossed your mind also. If this mischief was deliberate, as it must have been, then it could conceivably put a different complexion on the attack made on you at Chiswick. Or am I being over-fanciful?"

"I wish I could say that you were, my dear, but you wouldn't believe me." He ran a thoughtful finger along the scar. "I just wish that the thing made sense. I must be missing some vital clue, somewhere."

"Perhaps," she suggested, "the time has come for a council of war?"

The curricle was recovered without any undue attention being drawn to it; by the time Minerva returned to the Park later that afternoon with Mrs. Peach, it had gone.

It was much pleasanter these days, driving out at the fashionable hour, mostly due, Minerva had to admit, to the good offices of Lady Maude. Such was her influence that people who would previously have considered her beneath their touch now smiled a greeting, and in some cases actually condescended to speak. Among their number were several of the doyens of Almack's, notably Lady Cowper, who was both pretty and charming, and Lady Jersey, who overcame her scruples concerning Minerva's plebeian background to the extent of according her a civil greeting.

The likelihood of her receiving vouchers for the famous Almack's was slim, though this deprivation caused her no loss of sleep. "If it takes your fancy to go, I'll arrange it, never fear," said Lady Maude. "But I can't stand the place myself—a lot of pretentious people playing off their airs, and condescending to partake of bread and butter and lukewarm tea such as they'd throw at their chef if he dared serve it to 'em at home! But well enough, I suppose, if you've a daughter to bring out and wish to get her noticed!" Minerva thought it all sounded a little dull, and unless something happened to change her mind, decided that she could manage very well without it. She doubted there was much that the patronesses of Almack's could do for her that Lady Maude couldn't do just as well.

The Lanyons, too, went out of their way to include them in their many soirées and receptions, and invitations had already arrived for the ball they were to give to celebrate the engagement between Georgiana and the vicomte. So, in fact, the social life of Lord and Lady Claireux had taken a decided upward turn in spite of the rumors which still fluctuated concerning Dominic's affairs.

Yet, Minerva could not be easy. Rumor was one thing, but actually making not one, but two attempts on Dominic's life was quite another matter, one almost too frightening to contemplate. People, madmen excepted, almost always killed for a reason. But what possible reason could anyone have for wanting to kill Dominic?

It was a question that vexed the minds of the four

people who sat around the library late that night when Mrs. Peach had gone to bed. The gentlemen had their brandy and Minerva, a tray of tea.

"We could, of course, be jumping to quite the wrong conclusions," Dominic said, though his very voice denied the words. "It could have been a demonstration of spite, or a particularly stupid prank that went badly wrong."

"Well, I don't know of anyone who'd play a damnfool trick like that," Pelham exclaimed. "Do you? And what of the other business?"

"Coincidence?" Dominic suggested.

"Devil a bit! Oh, my pardon, Minerva."

She brushed aside his apology. "I agree with Pel. I'm sure the two are connected. What I can't understand is why. I can quite see that it could be convenient for whoever has the document box to make it look as though Dominic has it, in order to divert suspicion from himself. But if that is so, then it would be stupid to kill him."

Charles was the only one who hadn't spoken. He lay back in his chair, his eyeglass trained on his gleaming hessians—a sure sign that he was deep in thought.

"Perhaps," he said at last, "there are two needles in the haystack, and we are concentrating on the wrong one."

Pelham raised eyes to heaven. "Pray don't start talking in riddles, dear fellow. We are having enough trouble understanding what's going on without searching for deuced needles!"

"No, Pel!" Mienrva sat forward eagerly. "I see exactly what Charles is getting at . . . that the person trying to kill Dominic is doing so from motives not entirely connected with the documents."

"You mean we are looking for two people?" Pelham leaned his head in his hand. "This is all getting too much for me!"

"Not two people, Pelham," Charles said. "At least, I

think not. But I do think the motive all along has been more complex than we have supposed."

Dominic stood up and began to pace the room, his fingers as usual ruining Moss's handiwork as his mind began to race through possibilities.

"All right, let's go through it all, step by step, and see where it gets us. Let us suppose that someone, with the help of the manservant, kills Hagarth and steals the box —presumably because he like many others owes more money than he can repay—and with it all the relevant information about each debtor. I am the obvious suspect, but just to make sure, he disposes of the manservant, thus covering all tracks that might lead back to himself. Then he gets greedy and decides to recoup his own losses by, as it were, taking up where Hagarth left off—"

"With you as the only exception," Minerva put in.

"So it would seem." He had come to lean on the back of her chair, and one finger absently caressed her neck. "Thus resurrecting the flagging interest in me as the original suspect."

"In which case," said Pelham, "he would have to be a bit loose in the attic to kill off his alibi."

"Or much cleverer than we have given him credit for," Charles concluded softly.

Pelham threw up his hands. "Now you've lost me again."

"Suppose the original crime had a dual purpose— one, to rid the perpetrator of his most pressing debts at a stroke, and two, to implicate Dominic to the extent that he confidently expected him to be arrested and charged with Hagarth's murder. Hence the timing—Dominic's violent attack on Hagarth in the presence of witnesses, the aborted duel. It should have needed only the discovery of that rather singular button clasped tight in the baron's fist, and the missing documents to clinch the evidence against Dominic—enough, one would think, to hang any man."

"It was deuced odd about that button," Pelham mused. "Thought so at the time."

"What I find even odder," said Minerva, "is why anyone would wish to kill Dominic? I know he can be tiresomely overbearing at times . . ." She glanced up at him with a sudden humor that lightened the mood, skillfully avoiding his attempt to cuff her ear. "In any case, you had been abroad for years . . ."

"And, being the kind of person you are," Charles suggested, "the chances were that you might not survive the war?"

"But I don't see . . ." Minerva said.

Dominic's eyes narrowed. "Oh, but I do!" he murmured, his eyes suddenly keen as they met Charles's.

"Well, I wish I did," complained Pelham, pausing in the act of refilling his glass. "Can't stand people who talk in riddles, and there's been a deuced lot of't this evening."

But his words fell on the empty air. The candle flames shivered as in a sudden draught, and Minerva, sitting very still, felt as though they were all on the edge of some momentous discovery.

"But he hasn't the stomach for it," Dominic said.

"Stomach enough, dear boy—and guile enough, make no mistake. He would simply engage others to do the unpleasant part."

Dominic began to prowl again. "I'm not convinced . . . too many imponderables. Besides, although we don't exactly love one another, I had not thought he hated me enough to kill me!"

"Not just hate, dear boy," Charles said. "Envy, too. It is no secret that he has coveted the marquessate for years, or that for some considerable time he had grown to expect that, with just a little bit of luck on his side, it might be his sooner rather than later."

"Excuse me," Pelham said with an exaggerated politeness induced by the amount of brandy he had consumed, "but are we to infer that you are speaking of the unspeakable Gervase?"

"Your cousin?" Minerva exclaimed. "Oh, surely not. He is much too . . ." she struggled to find the words to describe Gervase Wilmington, ". . . too effete to kill anyone!"

"Don't judge by appearances, my dear," Dominic said. "He was the kind of little boy who pulls the wings off flies."

She shuddered.

"Think about it, Dominic," Charles urged him. "Who just happened to be around the night Hagarth was killed—when you got so badly disguised?"

"Gervase, by damn! He even helped me drown my evil temper."

"And also obligingly helped you home and delivered you into Drummond's hands, which gave him ample opportunity to remove a button from your coat—"

"Ah, but he didn't, you see. When Drummond produced that coat on the following morning at the Runner's behest, the buttons were all intact. And as you are aware, they are quite unique."

There was something nagging away at the back of Mineva's mind, but she was too tired to pin it down.

"Which rather leaves us at stalemate, don't you think?" Dominic concluded. "I mean, leaving the button aside, I can accept that Gervase could well have seized his opportunity and contrived the Hagarth business, but the other incidents. . . ?" He shook his head. "Why would he suddenly develop such a burning compulsion to kill me, for God's sake?"

Charles sat up, setting his wineglass down on the table with careful precision. "My dear fellow, the reason is obvious, and if we do not make considerable haste to prove his guilt, he may yet succeed."

"Well, it ain't obvious to me," Pelham complained. "So I'd be glad if someone would explain it to me."

It was Minerva, feeling suddenly a little sick, who said

quietly, "It really is very simple, Pel. Dominic married me."

Charles glanced at her in quick approval. "That's it exactly. Quite simply, my friends, the moment Dominic married, the prospect of a direct heir became a distinct possibility and the likelihood of Gervase's inheriting the marquessate was by comparison diminished. Hence his increasing panic."

Minerva and Dominic looked at each other in silence for a moment, and then she nodded briefly.

"Then, strictly between the four of us," Dominic said, "we have even less time to stop him than we thought."

17

SIR RICHARD was to call the next day to take Mrs. Peach to a musical afternoon at the home of a friend of Lady Maude's. Minerva found the thought of her uncle attending such a gathering highly entertaining.

"Strange," she said, as they awaited his arrival, "I have never known him to be in the least musical."

Mrs. Peach blushed and avoided Minerva's eyes. "He is not," she confessed. "I was never more surprised . . . that is, Maude suggested he should accompany me, and I do think it was noble of him in the extreme to agree so readily, when he cannot have wished . . . I told him that I should not mind in the least if he did not like the idea . . . and I am sure it cannot have been fear of Maude that made him agree, for he was quite short with her only the other day when she criticized my new straw bonnet."

"Oh, I think Uncle Richard is afraid of very little," Minerva said gravely.

When presently he came, she noticed that he wore a new coat of dark blue superfine, and that everything about him had an extra polish; even his side whiskers had been burnished to a gleaming white. There was something wholly endearing in the sight of her uncle handing Mrs. Peach into the carriage with all the courtesy of former years. She sighed and wished that life could always be like that.

She and Dominic had talked little after Charles and Pelham had left last night. She had been willing enough, but he declined, saying that there had been enough talk for one evening and he needed to think. "Besides," he added, not ungently, "you look worn to a thread."

Matthew said much the same thing in her blunt, uncompromising way. "Carrying on as though nothing had changed," she muttered. "Not that you'll heed anything I say."

"That rather depends on what you say," Minerva teased her. "After all, women have been having babies since the beginning of time, a good many of them in far less privileged conditions than mine, so I doubt I will come to any real harm."

"Hmp!" had been the ambiguous retort.

Minerva could hardly tell her that the look of strain was not due to any physical cause, but to the almost unbearable worry of letting Dominic out of her sight for fear of some further attempt on his life; that his friends had pledged themselves to shadow his every move was of some small comfort to her, but she knew how it would irk Dominic beyond endurance to be constantly watched, and if the situation continued for any length of time, she dreaded that sooner or later his impatience would drive him to behave rashly.

How much Drummond knew, she wasn't sure, but she resolved to speak to him at the first opportunity. That opportunity came when Dominic set off for the day with a party of friends including Gentleman Jackson, the famous pugilist, to watch some particularly promising mill. In such company, he could surely come to no harm.

Drummond, it transpired had been told very little beyond being cautioned to be more than usually vigilant. This seemed less than practical to Minerva; if the groom was to adequately protect Dominic, he should at least know what he was likely to be up against, though she did not go so far as to name Gervase Wilmington.

"Well, I can't say it comes as a surprise, m'lady, not taking all in all. Got a nose for trouble, I have, and what with all that's been going on lately, I suspicioned there was skulduggery at the bottom of it somewheres!" Drummond scratched his head consideringly. "That lot as set on us—I never reckoned them as your regular footpads."

"No." She shuddered as she remembered how close they had come. "You will realize, of course, that I have told you this in confidence—and why?"

"Surely, my lady. And don't you fret—I'll watch out for the major, same as I alus have. He'll not come to any harm while Jack Drummond's there to prevent it."

"Thank you. I knew I could rely on you." Something just below her consciousness that had been eluding Minerva suddenly clicked into place. "Drummond, do you remember the night Baron Hagarth was killed? My husband's cousin brought him home, did he not?"

"Aye, m'lady, he did." There was a note of reserve in his voice, the reason for which became apparent when he added, "A bit under the weather, his lordship was."

She smiled. "More than a bit, I think."

Drummond's face cleared. "I disremember seeing him in such a bad way, except perhaps after Bajados. That was a regular bloodbath, beggin' your pardon. But this other business, now—it took Mr. Wilmington and meself all our time to get him upstairs."

"His clothes would have been in a bit of a state, too, I daresay?"

He was surprised by the question, but ladies set more store by such things, no doubt. "Took me a deal of a time sponging his coat clean, I can tell you. Meant a lot to him, that coat did—specially made for him in Spain."

"So I heard. And the missing button?" she said casually.

"Button, my lady? There was no button missing, as

the Runners found when they asked to see that coat the next morning. Unique, them buttons were!" He was sharp, but not quite sharp enough to deceive her.

"Which is why you acquired several spare ones when the coat was made," she said calmly.

"Now, however did you know that?"

"Oh, it was just a guess. It seemed to be the only possible answer."

There was admiration in his sheepish grin. "No pullin' the wool with you, is there? Not even his lordship knew about them spares. It was just as I thought it'd be as well to have one or two."

"And there *was* one missing from the coat on that evening?"

"Yes, my lady. I didn't know how important it was when the Runners came, of course—and his lordship was in no state to know what was what. It was only later I heard all about it, so I just kept mum, knowin' as how his lordship wouldn't go around killing people in that hole and corner fashion, even in his cups!"

Minerva felt herself closer to tears than she had been in a long time. "Thank you, Drummond," she said huskily. "What a treasure you are, to be sure. Just one more small point, if you can remember—had the button been torn off, or cut?"

"Oh, cut, m'lady—not a doubt of it, because I remember thinkin' at the time that it was a bit odd."

"That is exactly what I hoped you would say. Would you mind if I told his lordship? Or you may do so yourself if you prefer." She saw his reluctance and added persuasively, "It is rather important—the last piece of a puzzle, you might say. I'm sure he won't be angry with you for not telling him before now."

"Lord bless you, ma'am, I've been cussed up and down by the major often enough in the past! You tell him whatever seems right to you."

It was the following morning at breakfast before she

had a chance to tell Dominic. Her morning sickness had abated sufficiently now for her to resume her normal habits, and although he was not usually very talkative at that time of day, she preferred that he should know.

He took it almost without surprise, if anything with a kind of casual good humor. "The old rogue! I might have guessed—it's him all over, saving me from myself. Like a deuced mother hen! Wait till I see him."

"You won't be angry with him, will you? He was doing it from the best of motives, and it did save your skin."

Dominic looked at her over the top of his *Morning Post*, a faint glint in his eyes. "My dear, you are almost as bad as Drummond. Rest assured, he doesn't need protecting from me—we understand one another much too well."

"Yes, of course." She sipped her tea. "And it does solve the mystery of the button." But he was immersed in his paper once more, and she fell to turning over in her mind something that had been occupying it on and off for some time.

"Dominic," she said at last, "I don't believe I ever asked you where your old family home in London was?"

"Portland Place," he said without looking up. "A dreadful mausoleum of a house. Father sold it to some ambitious cit for an astronimical sum, I believe—and promptly lost most of the money to the horses and bad investments, hoping as always to make a killing."

"So you wouldn't want it back, always supposing we could persuade the man to sell?"

"Good God, no! Whatever put an idea like that into your head?"

"Well, we are all right for now, but I thought how much nicer it would be if we had a place of our own in London."

Resignedly, he put down his paper. He had been thinking how pleasant it was to have her sitting opposite him at breakfast again; surprisingly, he had missed her these past weeks. But she was not usually so confoundedly talkative.

"Is that really necessary? We already have Abbey Park and Claireux Lodge, not to mention your own High Fold. We can always rent a house in London for the Season as so many others do."

"Yes, but if we had our own place, we could come to London whenever we wished."

"You do know how much such a place would cost?"

"Yes, of course, but we could regard it as an investment, and it wouldn't have to be terribly grand. I'm sure your Mr. Thripp could keep his eyes and ears open for us."

Dominic frowned, suddenly flicked on the raw. "For us? For you, rather. You have clearly made up your mind and will doubtless do as you please. After all, it's . . ." He had been about to say "your money", but a fleeting glimpse of the hurt in her eyes stopped him just in time. "I'm sorry," he said tersely. "I thought I had got over my touchiness on that score. It's this other business."

"Yes, I know," she said quickly. "I do understand." And then, with the thought of getting him away, hopefully out of reach of Gervase, she said: "Dominic, speaking of Abbey Park—do you think we might go there next week, after Lady Lanyon's ball?"

But he was strangely reluctant, finding all manner of excuses for remaining in town, which she for the most part countered, including the problem of what to do with Mrs. Peach.

"She can come too," Minerva said. "And Uncle Richard, since they seem loath to be parted."

"My dear girl, the place is hardly in a fit state to house visitors. The interior is still badly in need of refurbishment, which awaits your approval."

"Well then?" she said. "What better reason for going? They won't mind if things are not exactly as they should be."

"I . . . I don't know. I'll think about it."

And with that, she judged it wiser to be content.

Sir Richard had made up his mind.

It had not been an easy decision; he was well into his fifty-fifth year and a bachelor. It was a way of life that had always suited him—no one else to please, an agreeable circle of friends who were there when he felt like being sociable, his magisterial duties which he took seriously and enjoyed.

To even contemplate embracing the married state at his age smacked of having windmills in one's head—something not so different, he suspected, from the strange giddiness which seemed to afflict him whenever Mrs. Peach leaned on his arm for support and smiled up at him. It was, he had suddenly realized, the first time anyone had ever looked to him for anything.

There was no guarantee that she would accept him, of course, although he had surely not imagined her partiality for his company. Emboldened by this thought, he decided to take the plunge and propose. This much decided, he determined to do the thing in style. A picnic in Richmond Park. Tomorrow. Esmeralda would like that. (Only in his imagination had he ever made so bold as to address her with such familiarity!) He would call in at Gunters this very day to arrange for one of their best hampers. Then he had but to hire a barouche for the day.

Mrs. Peach thought the picnic in Richmond Park a delightful idea and when the following morning proved to exhibit just that trifling degree of mist which so often heralds a beautiful day, she knew that everything was going to be perfect. But nothing quite prepared her for what happened when the lobster patties and chicken had been consumed and the champagne bottle all but emptied. For that was when Sir Richard, having surreptitiously assured himself that they were quite alone except for the driver of the barouche, who was dozing under the shade of a distant tree, went down on one knee in the prescribed fashion and asked her to be his wife.

"Oh!" Her breath expired on the tiniest of sighs. "Oh, was there ever anything quite so romantic! I had not thought . . . had not expected . . ." She grew rosy pink with confusion.

"Well, to be honest, I feel slightly ridiculous kneeling here, ma'am, but the thing had to be done properly, y'know." His snowy whiskers twitched. "Still, I'd be grateful if you would put me out of my misery. Quite understand if you don't care for the idea . . ."

"Oh, no! Dear Sir Richard! I care for it very much! Dear me, yes!" Her hand went out to him. "But pray, do get up at once . . . you must be horridly uncomfortable, and if there should be any lingering dampness in the ground . . ."

They both began to laugh as she helped him to his feet, and dusted him down. "Just like a wife!" he chortled, and then bent to gently kiss her cheek. "You have made me a very happy man, m'dear!"

Minerva knew the moment she saw them. Like children, guilt and joy shone out of them in equal measure. "I cannot say that I am surprised . . ."

"What?" Sir Richard exclaimed. "You're never saying that you guessed?"

She laughed. "It has been written all over both of you for ages, but I am truly delighted for you, my two most favorite people! Have you decided where or when?"

"We thought here, because we want you to be present," said Mrs. Peach. "But very quiet, you know . . . perhaps fairly early in the morning."

"I'm arranging a special license," Sir Richard added gruffly. "No sense in wasting time . . . we're not children, after all."

Minerva could not wait to tell Dominic. "They looked so sweet," she said with a sigh.

He threw her a sanguine look. "I must say, I had not

expected you to go into raptures over prospective bridals."

"Oh, but this is different. I only wish you had been there to see them—holding hands, and with Uncle Richard looking decidedly sheepish!"

"Well he might, a man of his age."

"Oh, what a cynic you are," Minerva scoffed. "They are to go to Brighton for two or three weeks after they are married, so there will be no problem about our going to Abbey Park."

"If we go," Dominic said.

"Oh, but I thought . . ."

His eyes narrowed. "I'm not at all sure this isn't some devious ploy to get me out of my cousin's reach." He ignored her protest. "Because if it is, you are wasting your time, my dear. Gervase knows Abbey Park and its environs almost as intimately as I do myself."

"Dominic, I wouldn't dream of attempting to arrange your life to such an extent!"

"Ha! Would you not?" he exclaimed. "You, my sweet, innocent-looking wife, are about as devious as they come." He pointed an accusing finger. "Who was it, pray, who charged Drummond with the task of standing guard over me like some damned sheepdog?"

"Is that what he told you?" she said, playing for time.

"Oh, he didn't tell me anything. He didn't *have* to tell me. It is simply that I find I can scarce turn around nowadays without falling over him!"

Minerva bit her lip. "Well, that is hardly surprising, after all that has happened recently," she said reasonably. "I fail to see why you should lay the blame at my door."

"Because," he said in his silkiest voice, "it's 'my lady' this, and 'her ladyship wouldn't like that'! I tell you, it was bad enough having Pel and Charles dogging my steps, but between the lot of you, I'm beginning to feel like a deuced monkey on a string!"

"It's only because we all care!"

"Well, I wish to goodness you'd do it less obviously, because I give you fair warning that the present situation is fast becoming intolerable!"

Minerva bit back the retort his ungraciousness provoked, for she knew that it sprang solely from frustration. In fact, it was what she had been fearing would happen; an enemy that he could see and do something about was one thing, but not knowing how or when or in what form an attack might come was a constant gnawing menace. Without proof, there was little that could be done, but she was not sure how long he would stomach the situation before attempting to force some kind of confrontation.

She said as lightly as she could manage, "Then I suppose if I ventured to suggest that I would like to visit Yorkshire before too long, you would suspect me of having an ulterior motive for that, too! Well, I have. I must go sometime, to see that all is well at the mills, and if I don't go before winter, I shall find the journey excessively uncomfortable—and in any case, I love the moors in early autumn."

"Well, that shouldn't be any problem," he returned with an angry flippancy. "By the autumn Gervase will have been brought to book or I shall be dead."

"Don't!" she cried. "Not even in jest!"

As he scraped back his chair, a look of anguish crossed his face. "Oh ye of little faith!" he said in soft accusation. And he left the room.

"Oh dear!" Minerva sighed, infinitely distressed.

In the days that followed, Dominic was out a good deal, and she was glad to have the preparations for Mrs. Peach's wedding to take her mind off what he might or might not be doing. He did, however, make a special effort for the wedding itself, which was celebrated at a small local church on a perfect summer morning with only Dominic and herself and an old friend of her Uncle Richard's as witnesses. Mrs. Peach, soon to be Lady

Standish, wore blue and approached the ceremony with all the shy shining certainty of a young bride.

Minerva did not usually cry at weddings, but she came very close to it that day. And Dominic, as if sensing how she felt, was more gentle and attentive than he had been for some time. But later in the day, when the happy couple had been seen off after a simple family luncheon, he asked Marsham to have his curricle brought around and departed, saying that he would be out for most of the evening.

18

DRUMMOND WAS not at all happy with the way things were going. His loyalties were divided—Lady Claireux, he knew, was relying upon him to keep his lordship out of trouble, and indeed, he had given his word that he would do his utmost to see he came to no harm. But when his lordship was plainly bent on mischief and as good as told you that either you was with him or against him, there was really no alternative, choose how!

"I know well enough what it is you're about, major," he said, reverting as he so often did in times of stress to the old ways, "but I can't see what's to be gained from drawing the enemy's fire when all you're going to end up catching is some poor little perisher who's acting under orders and don't know the why or wherefore!"

"Perhaps. But anything is better than sitting back and waiting to be picked off," said his lordship with that set to his chin that told you his mind was made up. "Besides, I know the why and wherefore—what I need is proof. And if we can flush out a few *little perishers*, as you call them, they might well lead us right into the enemy camp."

It irked Dominic to have to be polite to his cousin when they met at the club, or at some function or other. He longed to smash his fist into that smiling painted face and expose the rottenness beneath. But such behavior would not help his case in the slightest, and he was becoming totally single-minded in his determination to bring Gervase to his knees.

He had tried all the straightforward legal avenues—Sir Richard had failed to uncover anything that might be of help. And Hagarth's manservant, he suspicioned, was probably at the bottom of the Thames, well weighted down to ensure that he stayed there.

So, if he was ever to resume a normal life, he must go on the offensive and see if he could not rattle his cousin to the point where he would grow careless. And in doing this, he had no intention of risking the lives of his friends; in any case, he would do better alone, with Drummond to back him up.

Minerva must likewise remain in ignorance of his decision; already the atmosphere between them was strained, and it would inevitably become more so as a result of behavior which he could not explain. He was surprised to find how much he minded forfeiting her good opinion of him. The bond between them had grown almost imperceptibly from those early tentative beginnings into a deepening friendship warmed by her uninhibited physical acceptance of him, which just occasionally had shown glimpses of a passion which might yet take them into the realms of something quite special. If he was right, then it would survive a temporary estrangement, but either way, he could not afford to risk her involvement. If Gervase learned about the baby, her own life would be in the gravest danger. Yet, knowing her as he now did, if she got the least hint of what he was about, involve herself she would!

Lady Lanyon's ball was clearly destined to be the shining success of the Season. The earl had spared no expense to ensure that everything would go well.

"Over five hundred acceptances," Georgiana told Minerva gleefully, seemingly oblivious of her friend's preoccupation. "That is more than Cleonie Gordon had for her coming-out, and everyone agreed that hers was an outstanding event! We are to have the band of the Scot's Greys to play during supper, and the Duke of Wellington has engaged to come if at all possible. You know him, of course, from your time in Paris!" Georgiana giggled. "And as a final accolade, the Duke of York is to look in during the evening—he and Papa are friends, you know."

Minerva realized that a show of enthusiasm was expected of her, and endeavored to oblige. "It all sounds tremendously exciting. How impressed Etienne will be!"

"Oh, I do hope so! He is due back from France at any moment. He has been making all the final arrangements for our tour through Italy. Only think of it! And then to be living in Paris! It will be the greatest fun!"

Minerva suspected that life would always be the greatest fun to Georgie. She was not the kind that tragedy ever touched.

"And you must come and stay, you and Dominic, just as soon as we are settled."

"Thank you, we should like that," Minerva said absently. "That is, if it is possible."

"Possible? Whyever should it not be possible? Unless . . ." Georgiana's eyes widened. "Minerva—you aren't, are you?"

Minerva affected not to understand her, but it was to no avail; a betraying tide of color had already let her down. Georgiana clapped her hands in delight.

"Georgie," she pleaded, "promise me that you won't tell a soul? Not anyone, *please*—it is most important!"

Her friend looked a little put out. "Well, of course I won't, if that is what you really want, though I'm sure I can't for the life of me see why you should wish to keep it such a dark secret! Does Dominic know?"

"Oh yes."

"Well then?"

Minerva hedged desperately. "Well, for one thing,

it's early days and I should feel such a fool if it should prove a false alarm. And anyway," she concluded, "we did rather want to keep it to ourselves for a little longer."

This idea appealed much more to Georgiana's romantic notions, and she swore that not a word would pass her lips. Minerva, knowing her of old, placed little reliance on her ability to live up to such promises, but there was nothing more she could do. As long as word didn't reach Gervase, the rest mattered little.

On the morning of Lady Lanyon's ball, Dominic seemed in much better humor than of late. There was a kind of indefinable buoyancy about him that she couldn't remember having noticed in all the time she had known him, and which, considering the time he had come in, well into the early hours—hours in which she had lain awake worrying about him—seemed grossly unfair. However, she was so thankful for the improvement that, when he went so far as to tell her how very much in looks she was, she thanked him kindly and reminded him of the evening's festivities ahead.

He groaned, but more in mockery than dismay, for he did not dislike the Lanyons. As he turned the page of his newspaper, Minerva noticed scratch marks on his knuckles.

"You've grazed your hand," she said.

"Oh, that." Dominic glanced at it with, she thought, a certain satisfaction. "It's nothing. The outcome of a slight contretemps, that's all—a flush hit, actually."

Minerva shook her head at him. "You and your mills!"

He grinned, remembering the bruiser—one of two he and Drummond had jumped in the early hours of the morning, lying in wait for him on the approach to the stables. One had run off with a badly blooded nose, but his confederate had been less fortunate; hampered by a twisted ankle, he had been obliged to endure a decidedly uncomfortable interrogation which only produced results after heavy hints about the protracted and hideous fate of a French spy they had caught just prior to Waterloo—"Poor perisher!" Drummond had muttered with a shake of the head. Once the man's tongue was loosened, he couldn't talk fast enough, and although he didn't know Gervase by name, his description was sufficiently detailed to satisfy Dominic.

Once they were sure they had all the information the man could give them, he was allowed to escape and, with Drummond as his invisible shadow, he limped away, hopefully to give Gervase his dismal account of what had happened. Dominic amused himself with the thought of his cousin's fury. It was a beginning, but more than anything, the fact that he was fighting back had given him back his pride.

The ballroom occupied an enormous area at the rear of Lord Lanyon's house in Grosvenor Square, which by the time Minerva arrived with Dominic was already so crowded with elegant persons that someone was heard to remark that the whole of fashionable London must be present. And indeed, to Minerva it scarcely seemed an exaggeration.

The whole scene was one of brilliance and color and beauty which was given an added glitter by the almost casual proliferation of precious jewels adorning the more fortunate, of whom there were many. But it was Lady Georgiana's evening, and none was more beautiful than she, who wore no diamonds but radiated a happiness unmatched by the most priceless of jewels as she opened the ball partnered by her handsome vicomte. And among the dancers, the spangles of her silvery spider gauze caught the light with every swaying movement.

Minerva had taken especial pains with her own appearance, choosing one of her favorite Paris dresses of palest apricot silk appliquéd with tiny ivory gauze butterflies. The dress, softly gathered, fell straight from a high brief bodice, and both flattered and concealed—not, as Mattie had dryly observed when buttoning her into it, that there was yet anything worth concealing.

She and Dominic took no part in that first country dance, but it was followed by a waltz which was their particular favorite. If Georgiana and Etienne had shone in the previous dance, it was Minerva and Dominic who drew all eyes now—he with his imposing height, and she tall enough to compliment him—they were the epitomy of grace as they dipped and swirled effortlessly around the floor. Minerva wished the moment would never end; every nerve end tingled with her awareness of him. Once their eyes met, and against the giddy spinning lights, they held and locked together with an intensity that took away her breath.

"Are you all right?" he said abruptly as the music ended and she stood clinging to him. Unable to speak, breathless and still under the spell of him, she nodded. "I'm a thoughtless fool," he muttered, and with a hand firmly under her arm, led her over to the nearest vacant chair.

"Don't be silly," she chided him as breath and reality returned. "I haven't enjoyed anything so much in a long time!" Over his shoulder she saw Gervase Wilmington watching them, and removed her arm from Dominic's clasp on the instant. "I certainly don't want to sit down," she declared with a laugh. "I am already promised to several excellent partners and intend to have a marvelous evening! See, here comes Charles—Charles, isn't this a splendid ballroom? I declare, I have never seen a finer one!"

She was gabbling, she knew; knew too that they were both looking at her as if she had taken leave of her senses, Dominic more puzzled than annoyed. But a further glance assured her that Gervase had moved away, and she was able to relax.

"And what, pray, was all that about?" Charles asked

when Dominic's attention had been claimed by an old friend from his army days.

She told him about Gervase. "It was something about the way he was looking at me—as though he thought it odd that a mere waltz appeared to have exhausted me. But I didn't want to spoil Dominic's evening with my silly suspicions, especially as he has been in such good spirits all day." She smiled at Charles. "I have no idea what you were up to last night, but whatever it was, the effect on him was highly beneficial."

"You don't say so," drawled Charles, his face giving nothing away. "He didn't tell you about it?"

Minerva gave a cheerful shrug. "I didn't ask, though I gathered it had something to do with your occasional preoccupation with pugilism, if his grazed knuckles were anything to go by! I had no idea these sporting activities went on so late into the night."

"Ah, well, you know how it is."

"I do, indeed." She laughed. "It becomes clearer to me by the minute that you are all boys at heart!"

"Quite so." But Charles was thoughtful as he relinquished her to her partner for the cotillion and made his way in search of Pelham, only to find that he too had just taken his place in one of the sets that were forming. If Dominic was up to some ploy of his own, there would be no talking him out of it, and it could be that they shouldn't even try. Dominic was not a fool, and if Drummond was not in it with him, he would be very much surprised. Dominic would still need to be watched, of course—but with the utmost discretion, and discretion was not one of Pelham's most dependable qualities. Better, perhaps, if he kept this matter to himself.

Minerva had been resigned to the fact that Lavinia Winterton would be at the ball—Lord Winterton and the earl were friends of long standing, and Lavinia and Georgie had grown up very much in each other's company although their friendship had grown less warm of late. She wished she might know in what degree

Dominic's attachment to Lavinia still lingered. He concealed his true feelings so well that she wasn't even sure of her own place in his affections. What she was now sure of, however, and must take what comfort she could from, was that he would never wittingly encourage Lavinia to hope, no matter how much she might continue to hang her heart on her sleeve.

But Lavinia's proved to be a fickle love for when the latest prize on the Marriage Mart had condescended to favor her with his attentions at Almacks's but a few days since, she had very quickly decided that lost causes were futile. Lord Flavian was not above thirty, as dark as she was fair, and had just the hint of a rake in his make-up; he was also said to be worth twenty-five thousand a year and, as if that were not enough, was heir to the ailing Duke of Bream. He had until very recently been touring the Continent.

"My dear, I didn't know a thing about it until today!" Georgiana whispered to Minerva behind her fan, when they managed to snatch a few moments together. "Apparently he took one look at her and was immediately enslaved. Well, I suppose you can't blame *him*, but really, after all her protestations that she would never marry if she could't have Dominic . . . Oh, forgive me, my love!"

"Pray don't apologize," Minerva said quickly. "It is the best news I have heard in ages!" But—*poor Dominic*, she thought, to be so summarily discarded.

"Of course, it is no more than I expected! I always said that she would snap up the first really eligible man who came on the scene, but trust her to land an absolute prize!"

Minerva made no reference to Miss Winterton's good fortune when next she saw Dominic, and he gave no indication of having heard the news. But as he still seemed in good spirits, she banished all thoughts of Lavinia Winterton from her mind, and instead gave herself over to enjoying the spectacular sight of the Duke of York dispensing affability to all those fortunate enough to be presented to him. He was immensely corpulent, with the beaklike nose and protuberant blue eyes, the puffed-out cheeks and full pouting mouth that proclaimed him a member of the Royal Family. She had not been fortunate enough as yet to see the Prince Regent, but Dominic told her that York resembled his father much more closely than any other of his sons.

"But how he wheezes, poor man," she murmured, totally fascinated by this genial giant. "I only hope he may not burst out of his pantaloons! They do seem to be stretched almost beyond what is possible!"

Dominic's lips twitched. "If they do, my dear, you may perhaps offer to mend them for him!" Her merry laugh drew more than one admiring glance her way, though she seemed unaware of attracting attention. "I am sent," he continued, "by Lady Maude who has complained to me that you have not yet made your compliments to her this evening."

"Oh dear, I am truly sorry! Where is she? I will go to her at once."

"Sitting with the dowagers," said Dominic dryly. "Which, I suspect, is what is making her so scratchy!"

Minerva spent some considerable time sitting with Lady Maude, who quizzed her at great length about Esmeralda and Sir Richard. "I cannot think," she protested, "why I was not informed of her intentions. I should naturally have attended the wedding, though to be getting married at all at her age seems frivolous in the extreme. I do not understand why she should feel it necessary!"

Minerva kept her countenance with difficulty. "I believe they have become very much attached over the last few months, and she was destined to find herself rather lonely, you know, following upon my own marriage. Uncle Richard came along at exactly the right time!"

"One need never be lonely, if only one will make a push to go about. However, that is neither here nor there. And how are you, my dear child?'' Lady Maude looked her up and down. ''Charming,'' she said, in her carrying voice, ''but it's high time you were breeding. It don't do to dally over these matters. Dominic will be needing an heir if that painted popinjay is not to succeed him!''

Minerva knew not where to look. She kept her head lowered to hide her blushes, and prayed that no one had heard; and in so doing she failed to notice the slim figure in the mulberry coat and green striped waistcoat who stood not two yards away, his own face the color of his coat. Unknowing, and to cover her embarrassment, she made some inconsequential remark which scarce made sense, but fortunately Lady Maude was already following some new train of thought. And then it was supper time and Dominic came to rescue her.

True to his promise, the Duke of Wellington arrived just prior to supper and made much of meeting Minerva again. He was in high good humor and his neighing laugh could be heard frequently above the excellent playing of the Scots Guard's band.

It was well after midnight when Minerva finally came face to face with Gervase Wilmington. He had already endured more than a little veiled innuendo from Dominic, enough to put him in a vicious temper, although his mood was not immediately obvious; only when one looked into his eyes did one become aware of a sudden chill. His manner was as ever scrupulously polite.

''Cousin Minerva,'' he greeted her in his finicky voice. ''I believe that congratulations are in order? You must forgive me for being so remiss.''

His eyes never left her face, marking its sudden wariness, quickly masked.

''Congratulations?'' she repeated, praying that her voice would not sound odd. ''I don't understand you, sir.''

His watchful smile reminded her irresistibly of a bird of prey marking out its victim. ''I'm sorry. I do not

19

"WELL, THAT settles it," Dominic said at last. "You wanted to go to Abbey Park, so go we will—and as soon as possible."

He hadn't spoken at all on the way home from the ball, and Minerva, sensing that he was working something out in his mind, had not attempted to break in on his thoughts with her own worries. She was not by nature given over to nervous apprehension, and put it down to her condition that tonight she had experienced fear of another person in a way that she never had before. She remembered what Dominic once said of Gervase—that he had been the kind of little boy who pulled the wings off flies—and tonight, for the first time, she understood what he had meant. It wasn't anything he had actually said, but rather a subtle feeling of malevolence.

When they arrived home Dominic had followed Minerva into her room. Mattie had already had instructions not to wait up, so they were able to talk undisturbed.

"Is it because of Gervase that you want us to go? Surely that won't do any good—you have already said that he knows the place as well as you do yourself."

"Perhaps so," he said, watching her fingers busying themselves among the confining pins until at last her hair came rippling down, shining like silk in the candle-glow. "But the situation has changed, and it will be easier to guard you on my own territory than here in London."

"Guard me?" Again she felt that involuntary shiver of apprehension. "Then I did not imagine it? You also think I am in danger from Gervase?" Through the mirror she could see him standing rigidly with one hand gripping the end of the bed until the knuckles showed white. She rose swiftly and went to him, putting her arms around him as if by doing so she could somehow make everything right.

She was surprised at the intensity with which he held her, his fingers pushing into her hair to draw her close until her head rested against him. "I should never have got you involved in this!" he groaned. "God knows, I never intended—never envisaged Gervase as the villain of the piece, or I'd have stopped him long ago!"

"It doesn't matter," she declared passionately. "We are in it together, and that's all I care about!"

He lifted her head so that he could read what was in her eyes. "You really mean that!"

"Well, of course I mean it! How else would you expect me to feel?"

It was as if he had never really looked at her before. Surely it hadn't always been there—that love shining out at him? There had been moments, of course, when things had been good between them, just as there had been moments of late when he had been happy simply to have her beside him. But from the beginning his love for Lavinia had lain between them like a specter, and somehow it had never quite been exorcized. What a fool! He realized suddenly how long it had been since that love had held any substance, and how, almost without knowing it, Minerva had become a part of him—of his heart, his soul, his conscience, even; he tried to visualize his life without her and found the prospect intolerable.

"Have I been very blind?" he asked with something akin to humility.

But there was no hint of reproach in her clear eyes. "No, of course not. We made a bargain in which love had no part; that somewhere along the way I fell in love with you was pure chance, and as such was beyond my control. But I never wished to foist it upon you."

"Oh, my dear and most special love," he murmured huskily, pulling her down on to the bed, his mouth crushing hers, his kiss telling her that all she had ever wanted was now hers in full measure. It was some time before either of them were coherent, but at last they sat up, disheveled but foolishly happy. "I don't want to be sensible, my lovely Minerva," he said, absently twining her hair about his finger, "but time is not on our side. I am almost certain that Gervase has guessed about the baby. He can't be one hundred percent certain, of course, but I doubt he will wait to find out. So I must have you somewhere where I can hold you safe."

She prised his finger free and sat away a little. "But that is ridiculous!" she declared. "I refuse to be hidden away like some prize possession. It goes against everything in my nature, just as it appalls me that Gervase can go around killing people, willy-nilly! And I don't think he should be allowed to get away with it!"

"Oh, Minerva, I do love you!" But his laughter held a touch of desperation as he attempted to pull her close again. She resisted.

"Now what have I said?"

"Nothing—except that most young ladies of my acquaintance would be swooning with fright and begging to be protected! They certainly wouldn't be arguing about whether or not someone should be allowed to get away with killing them!"

"Oh, that! Well, all I can say is that you must have been acquainted with some very poor-spirited women in your time! I certainly don't intend to sit around waiting while a creature like Gervase plans my demise." She chuckled suddenly. "Lady Maude called him a painted popinjay! Such an apt description, don't you agree?"

He smiled, but briefly. "Minerva, be serious, I beg of you. Listen to me." He took her hands in his as he explained how he and Drummond had been spending their nights of late.

"So that was it," she said. "I knew there was something! Was Charles in it too?"

"No. Just the two of us. I didn't want anyone else involved, but I was getting a little tired of being the passive prospective victim and decided to precipitate matters, in the hope that if Gervase got rattled, he might also grow careless." He grimaced. "Only I hadn't foreseen the extent to which I might be landing you in danger."

"Humgudgeon," Minerva retorted. "If it comes to *that*, then two heads will surely be better than one."

He was silent for a moment before saying a little unsteadily, "I appreciate your sentiments, my love, but if it should, as you so succinctly put it, come to that, you will do exactly as you are told."

"Tyrant," she said accusingly.

"Maybe," he said grimly, "but in this case I am adamant. There is far too much at stake to take chances, so you will, for once in your life, obey without question. And since we seem to be approaching a showdown, I mean to have the choice of battleground. So, Abbey Park it is."

"Dominic?" Her voice was suddenly urgent. "What about Lavinia?"

He looked quizzically at her. "Who pray, is Lavinia?"

"Oh, please—don't joke about it!" she cried. "It is terribly important to me! She is going to marry someone else, did you know? Do you mind?"

With a muffled exclamation he pulled her close again. "My darling girl, of course I knew! She has made sure that the whole world knows, but as for minding! Is that what you have been thinking? *Oh, Minerva*, don't you know, even now? Lavinia's beauty dazzled me for a while, but it is you who have taught me that love is something more than mere physical attraction—it's laughing together, quarrelling and making up—a meeting of minds as well as hearts. It's—oh, for pity's sake, beloved, kiss me and shut me up before I get lost in my own peroration!"

She did so, and with such a degree of ardor and enthusiasm that any lingering doubt was banished forever.

They were very circumspect when it came to making their arrangements for leaving Town, assembling only the minimum amount of luggage, and leaving Matthews and Moss and the butler to follow in a few days' time, thus creating the impression that they were not in fact leaving at all.

The servants caused the most trouble; unaware of the reasons for secrecy, they were all three in their own way outraged—Matthews, because she had never allowed Minerva to go anywhere without her; Moss, out of sheer pique that the marquess did not consider him indispensable, was even heard to murmur that he might well be obliged to look for another situation. But Dominic was by now used to such threats and took little account of them. In Marsham's case, he was merely distressed to think that Abbey Park would not be fit to receive them.

"There is only the caretaker, Larkin, and his wife, my lord, and neither of them is used to catering for company. If you was only to let me go on ahead, my lord," he implored, but Dominic would not hear of it.

"Lord Claireux and I have a fancy to . . . er, live life in the rough for a day or two," Minerva had put in blithely—a remark which conjured up such dire disasters in the old butler's mind that Dominic had to reassure him all over again.

The only other people who knew of their plans were Pelham and Charles, and they were strictly charged with the need for discretion.

Dominic was insistent that they should make an early start so that they might take their time on the road. This rather surprised Minerva, who recalled the very different method of travel at the start of their honeymoon. What a lot of changes there had been in just a few short months.

"Do you remember how we were—at the beginning?" she asked Dominic.

He smiled wryly at her. "I behaved like a boorish oaf."

"You were certainly moody, but with good cause!"

"That, my dearest one, comes dangerously close to heaping coals of fire! You were quite unlike any woman I had ever met, forthright to the point of painful honesty, sometimes—and you were forever quoting your father at me, which did little for my temper."

"Oh dear! How forbearing of you not to tell me so." Minerva chuckled. "It makes one wonder how we ever came to accept one another in the first place."

"I doubt we would have, if you had not pressed your case in the most unmaidenly way. In the end, I was left with little choice but to accept!"

Her laughter rang out, escaping through the windows which were open to the warmth of the day. Drummond, riding behind, thought that he would never understand some folk—laughing, for all the world as if they was going on a picnic!

It was quite late in the afternoon when they turned onto a private tree-lined road, and at last came within sight of Abbey Park. The house was clearly visible from the road, being on high ground, and the late afternoon sun warmed its mellow stonework. Minerva could hardly fail to notice that Dominic had become more and more preoccupied as they came closer to their destination, but she endeavored to lift him out of his mood.

"Why, it even looks like an abbey from here!" Minerva exclaimed, as she caught a glimpse of gothic arches.

"There are still some remains of the old cloisters, but

most of the house was rebuilt early in the last century by my great-grandfather."

He had hardly finished speaking when the coach stopped. He let down the window. "Not here, Joshua. The main gateway leading to the house is about half a mile further . . ." His voice trailed off as a man on horseback rode up, a pistol pointing directly at him. He half-turned and saw that the other window was similarly covered. Damn! This wasn't how he'd planned things. And where the devil was Drummond?

"What the hell do you think you're playing at?" he demanded.

"We are not playing at anything, coz," came an odiously familiar voice. "I fear this is all in deadly earnest."

Gervase rode up alongside the first man, whom Dominic now recognized as one of his would-be assailants from the other night. His cousin was as dapper as always and looked incongruous beside his rough companion. He leaned forward slightly in the saddle, the better to see them both.

"You thought you were being so clever, Dominic, creeping away at crack of dawn! But I have had you watched every minute of the day and night, and a little judicious questioning of one of your more insignificant servants yielded all the information I needed."

"You won't get away with it—not again." Dominic's voice was at its harshest.

Gervase seemed not in the least perturbed; if anything, he was amused. "You think not? I managed rather well last time, you must agree."

"Hagarth, you mean?"

"A greedy man," Gervase sighed. "I really couldn't let him bleed me dry."

"So you got the manservant to help you dispose of him. Then you stole all those incriminating documents, and hoped that I would get the blame."

"Yes. A pity about that. I really thought you would be arrested and charged. However," he smiled, "*nil desperandum*, as they say. I can be amazingly patient when I have to be. And looking on the bright side, I did succeed in making you decidedly unpopular for a while.''

Minerva's outrage threatened to explode, but Dominic laid a hand on her arm.

''And of course you had that document box. I suppose that later, when you had disposed of your accomplice, it became too much of a temptation not to make good use of it?''

''Quite so.'' Gervase sounded a trifle smug. ''You would be surprised at the wicked skeletons some people have tucked away in their innocent little lives. They deserved to be fleeced! And once again I was able to raise questions in certain quarters about you. That pleased me, though it was no longer enough. Once you were fortunate enough to find someone rich to marry you—'' he saw Dominic's hand clenched and smiled again— ''I knew you would both have to be disposed of.''

''Well, I hope your present henchmen are taking note,'' said Minerva, speaking for the first time. ''Because, of course, you'll need someone else to dispose of them once they've done their worst, and you will not wish to soil your own hands.'' She was scathing. ''But then, what is a body or two more among so many!''

Dominic put out a warning hand, but Gervase, though tight of mouth, made no effort to stem her accusations.

''Your wife does not want for spirit, Dominic. Such a pity she must share your fate. Perhaps,'' he said, ''you are wondering how I intend to dispose of you both? No? Well, I shall tell you anyway. It has afforded me a great deal of pleasure to plan your demise. I have, I think you will agree, devised the perfect murder.'' He saw the anger that leapt into Dominic's eyes. ''Don't,'' he said, ''attempt anything foolish, I beg of you. If you do, Jem has orders to bring his pistol down on dear Cousin

Minerva's head, and we wouldn't want that, would we?"

Minerva could feel Dominic's rage barely held in check. She knew exactly how he must be feeling; her own hackles were stretched to the limit. Unobtrusively, she reached out for his hand and closed her fingers around it, for her own comfort as much as his. His clasp was strong and warm, and made her feel she could face anything.

"Very touching!" Gervase sneered. "But I mustn't keep you in suspense any longer. Your driver has been taken care of—no, he isn't dead—yet."

"And Drummond?"

"Your man?" For a moment, Gervase looked less than happy. "He managed to elude us, but I have men looking for him. If necessary, he can be dealt with later. What we are going to do, you see, is create a tragic accident." He was himself again, odiously complacent. "You surely cannot have forgotten where this road leads, dear coz?"

"The old quarry!" Dominic exclaimed.

"Just so. The very place, don't you agree? The horses are spooked and bolt, and your driver, a less than competent old retainer, is unable to control them."

Until now, Dominic had been more angry than apprehensive, his mind calculating what his cousin was likely to do and how he could best foil him. But now, for the first time, he felt the cold hand of fear. He had forgotten the quarry. It hadn't been worked for years, not in fact since the stone it had yielded had been used up in rebuilding the house. How deep it was he could not remember, though as children it had drawn them like a magnet. Gervase in particular had always been fascinated by it, daring any village child who ventured near to climb down; once, he remembered with sickening clarity, a boy had been tempted by the promise of a penny from Gervase, and had slipped and fallen to his death. Even in summer, water lay sluggishly at the bottom, coated with a bilious slime.

"I see you have the picture, coz." His cousin's voice intruded upon his thoughts. "Clever, you must admit. If the fall doesn't kill you, the water most certainly will!"

For a moment there was a red mist in front of his eyes. "Oh, you devil! You haven't changed one bit from the evil little boy I remember!"

"Dominic, no! Don't provoke him!" Minerva's hand was on his arm, digging into him.

Dominic pulled himself together. She was right. He turned to look at her, tried to smile. If only Gervase hadn't sounded so sure of himself—as though he had everything worked out to the last detail. Drummond was free, of course, and he would know what to do. The soldier in Dominic refused to contemplate anything less than ultimate victory. He must not panic—Minerva's life and the future life of their child rested on his judgment, and if he should be proved wrong?

The mens' horses were growing restive, and much as he might wish to savor his moment of triumph, Gervase must act soon if he was not to give his cousin the slightest chance to seize the advantage.

"I suppose you are wondering about the finer details? They did, I must confess, give me particular pleasure. You have always despised me, coz—don't think I don't know it! But now we shall see who is the cleverest. I could have you rendered unconscious, but it pleases me much more to know that you will know exactly what is happening and be powerless to save yourself, or more poignant still, your wife and unborn child!"

"You are quite mad!" Minerva shouted at him, quite forgetting her own advice to Dominic.

"So you say, but I shall be alive when you are dead!" He spat the words at her. "One of my men has secured the doors by means of ropes, so you cannot open them. You may close the windows or not, as you please." He glanced at Dominic's breadth of shoulder and smiled. "There can be little hope of your trying to escape that way, I think! *If* anyone finds your bodies, there will be no sign of unnatural death—no bullet wounds, nothing in fact that would not be consistent with an accident. Your unconscious driver will be tied to his seat by his own belt, which should break long before the coach reaches the quarry, throwing him off. At his age, I doubt he will survive the fall, but one of my men will make sure he don't suffer." He heard Minerva's cry of protest with equanimity. "So, Cousin Dominic, what do you think of my little plan? Ingenious, you will agree?"

Dominic ignored the question. "You really want the title *that* badly?"

"I have always wanted it. *You*!" He spat the word out. "I really hated you because you never seemed to care—just accepted it as your right!"

"Which it was." Dominic suddenly seemed to tire of the argument. "Oh, get on with it, then. I would as soon be dead as listen any further to you."

"And so would I," Minerva agreed steadily.

Dominic covered her hand with his and squeezed it tight. They had the satisfaction of seeing Gervase's face suffused with rage, and then they leaned back, their heads turning toward one another against the squabs as though he did not exist. Vaguely, they heard him issuing orders, and then some thumps which Minerva assumed was Joshua being propped up on the driving seat. "Poor Joshua," she murmured. "At least he shouldn't suffer." She looked into her husband's eyes. "Are you afraid?"

"Apprehensive," he admitted. "But we aren't finished yet."

The banging grew more frantic and there was some shouting, above which Gervase could be heard screaming, "Now! Now, you fools!"

Then someone discharged a firearm and the horses whinnied and set off in a panic. "The devil!" Dominic swore under his breath. He sprang up and stumbled to the window on his side, while Minerva hung out of the other. The ground was rushing past at a frightening pace and they were being bucketed from side to side. In the distance there were several figures milling about and, a moment later she caught a glimpse of a horseman coming fast. But he still seemed a long way off.

"How far to the quarry?" she shouted.

"Not far enough, unless Drummond gets a move on!" Dominic was leaning out perilously in an effort to free the door, but they had made too good a job of it, and his size hampered him. "Oh, Minerva dearest, forgive me! I took too great a risk! I should never have . . ." As he spoke the horseman drew level, grinned up at him, and flashed past. "Charles! Thank God!"

"It's all right, Dominic!" Minerva cried, almost simultaneously, "Drummond is coming!"

It took the two men agonizing moments to bring the crazed horses under control, finally stopping them about five yards short of the rim of the quarry. Dominic helped Minerva down and turned to their saviors with the pale ghost of a grin.

"That, to paraphrase my erstwhile commander-in-chief, was the nearest run thing I ever saw in my life! What in the name of heaven went wrong?"

"Sorry, my dear fellow," Charles said wryly. "One of the Runners got jumpy and let off his piece! Damn near lost my own horse in the melée that followed!"

"Charles, I don't understand any of this, but I could kiss you!" Minerva cried, suiting the word to the deed. He accepted her salutation, smiling his sleepy smile.

Drummond was carefully lifting down Joshua, who was barely conscious and looked awfully gray. They laid him on the ground and Minerva knelt beside him. "Dominic—do you have any brandy?" she asked.

He reached for his flask, but Charles was before him, kneeling on the ground, quite heedless of his immaculate buff breeches, and lifting Joshua's head to hold it cradled against his arm while Minerva attempted to get him to swallow the brandy. "He's a tough old thing," she said, as much to convince herself as anyone. "He'll be all right."

Sounds of banging began again, fainter than before, but seeming to come from the coach. Dominic looked at Drummond and realization hit them both at the same time. "Oh, Lord'a mercy!" the groom exclaimed. "Blest if I gave him so much as a thought, what with all the excitement!"

They ran across to the coach, reaching up to the long, capacious baggage box that Hezekiah Braithwaite had had built beneath the driving seat. They unhooked the end and lifted it up. The young Runner who was helped down bore little resemblance to the zealous officer in the pristine coat who had so willingly climbed in there at the last change of horses some few miles short of Abbey Park. He was dusty, bruised, and battered, but the light of enthusiasm had not quite gone from his eyes.

"I heard it all, my lord. Every bloomin' word!"

20

"DO YOU mean to tell me that you arranged this whole thing? That you knew the Runners would be there, and didn't say a word to me?" Minerva's outrage was awesome to behold.

"Unforgiveable, I know, my love," he admitted, striving to look penitent and not quite succeeding. "But I wasn't altogether sure what would happen or when, and I didn't want to raise any false hopes."

"Humgudgeon! Don't my love me! It was infamous, allowing me to think that my last moments were upon me!" Minerva's indignation dissolved quite suddenly into unwilling laughter. "Oh, well, we aren't dead and your despicable cousin is in custody where he belongs, so in time I might forgive you!"

Charles and Pelham had exchanged alarmed glances during this exchange, but now they relaxed, knowing that all was well. The four friends were sitting in the shabby comfort of Abbey Park's drawing room awaiting the arrival of refreshment in the guise of a tray of tea and some of Mrs. Larkin's biscuits, and whatever Larkin could find in the cellars that was remotely drinkable.

The caretaker and his wife had been thrown into confusion by the unexpected arrival of Lord Claireux and his lady. Mrs. Larkin had sent down to the village on the instant for her sister's girl to help with airing the beds and preparing the good lord knew what for their lord and ladyship's dinner.

The Runners had departed with their prize prisoner, still hysterically protesting his innocence and cursing his cousin, and Dominic had watched him go, his face impassive. Most of Gervase's accomplices had also been rounded up and taken away, and Joshua had been put to bed, still looking decidedly frail but refusing with surprising volubility to let a doctor near him. "I baint had no doctor near me in more'n sixty year, and I en't starting now!" he had maintained against all Minerva's persuasion.

"It was a dreadful experience, but I think he'll be all right after a good rest," she said in some relief. "He was always a great complainer, but he really is very strong for his years." Her mind reverted to the matter uppermost in her mind. "Dominic, what I still don't understand is how you could possibly know what was in your cousin's mind?"

"I didn't—not entirely," he confessed ruefully. And then, seeing her expression, hurried on. "But I do have a pretty good idea of the way his mind works, and once I had gone onto the offensive, as it were, it was all down to guile—feeding him the information we wanted him to have—"

"We?" Minerva inquired with deceptive sweetness.

Dominic looked more than ever like a small boy caught out in a misdemeanor. "Drummond and myself, at first. I told you—"

"Not the half of it, by all accounts. Go on."

"An old army mate of Drummond's agreed to infiltrate the ranks of my cousin's band of thugs, pretending an overriding grievance against me from the days under my command." He grimaced wryly. "It was he who struck up the friendship with the young serving maid at Grosvenor Street which gave the information he passed on to Gervase under our instructions the ring of truth."

"Devious devil, ain't you?" Pelham exclaimed in awe. "I had no idea you could be so conniving."

There was a brief interruption in the form of Larkin, who tottered in with a tray and set it down on the settle near the fireplace at Minerva's request. In addition to the tea, there were two dusty bottles of Chambertin. "It was the best I could do, m'lord," he said apologetically. The young men exchanged glances and Dominic said gravely that it would do splendidly.

"Chambertin!" Pel exclaimed when he had gone. "I'd no idea you kept such a good cellar, dear old fellow!"

"Neither did I!" said Dominic with a grin.

"Should be decanted, of course, but never mind."

"You and your wine!" Minerva reproved them. "Do go on, Dominic."

"Charles guessed what was going on in the last day or two." Dominic poured the burgundy, sipped it and nodded approvingly as he continued obligingly, "Something you told him, my love, obviously alerted him to the fact that Drummond and I were running some kind of operation. But by then, I had decided to force Gervase's hand, so he and Pel were brought in to help to devise a trap into which, hopefully, he would fall."

"But you didn't think to tell me!" Minerva said. "I am deeply wounded, but go on."

"I was pretty sure Gervase would want to strike as quickly as possible, and I was equally sure that, with his intimate knowledge of the terrain, he would do so on that stretch of private road, as it offered all the advantages of surprise within a confined area." Dominic stopped, and then continued with sudden gravity, "What I had not allowed for in my calculations, however, was the existence of the quarry at the end of that road, or the fact that Gervase's mind had grown so twisted! And for that, my dearest Minerva, and for bringing you within inches of death, I shall never quite forgive myself."

"Oh, no—you must not blame yourself for that! I

won't allow it!" she cried, stretching out her hand to him.

He took it, crushing it in his own. "When the plans were complete, I sent a message to Mr. Abel Nugent at Bow Street, and arranged to meet him at a place where I could be fairly sure we would not be watched, and together we devised the finer details of the trap. You see, it was no use simply stopping Gervase—I also needed to have him caught in the act, and if possible, confess to Hagarth's murder in the presence of a law officer—hence the enterprising young Mr. Lockley, who volunteered to conceal himself in the baggage boot of the coach. The rest you know. Charles and Pel came down ahead of us and put up at the local hostelry so as to be on the spot to meet the Runners. Looking back, I suppose it was a dangerous gamble, but it seemed worth taking when one viewed the alternative." He looked almost pleadingly into her eyes. "Perhaps I should have told you, but I beg you to believe that it was not from lack of trust."

"I know *that*," she exclaimed. "I just wish I hadn't missed all the fun!"

Later, much later, when they were alone—Charles and Pelham having left for their comfortable inn in the village where the landlord had promised them a poached salmon, fresh from the nearby river, and a couple of braised chickens with a special mushroom garnish—Dominic and Minerva wandered hand in hand through the house.

Dominic talked about his childhood here and Minerva, seeing it as it had been through his eyes, was enchanted with all she saw. It would take but a little effort, she declared, to turn it once more into a perfect home in which to bring up children. "And they will be able to have long holidays in Yorkshire," she said enthusiastically, carried away by the prospect.

Dominic's eyebrow quirked. "Are there to be many children, then?"

"Of course," she said decidedly. "Shall you mind?"

"I'm not sure. It rather depends on what part you expect me to play in this grand design—other than to father them, that is." He watched with delight as she blushed. "And what, pray, is to become of this grand social life you were planning for us in London?"

"Oh, that," she said. "Well, I daresay there will be time for that, too. I still think we should have a house in London—and as for the rest, well, all I ever wanted was that *you* should be accorded your proper place in society, and thanks to the few good friends we had, that has largely been achieved. Now your name will be officially cleared, and I hope the skeptics will be thoroughly ashamed of themselves! But as for the rest, I never had pretensions to become another Lady Maude."

"Thank God for that!" Dominic said on a shout of laughter that reverberated through the echoing room. He pulled her close. "I couldn't do this to a Lady Maude, or this . . ."

"Dominic!" Minerva was overcome with delight as his lips trailed dangerously close to places which, if Larkin should walk in on them, all unsuspecting . . . "Not here!" she pleaded, in a peal of joyous laughter that joined with his own.

"You are right," he said, sweeping her up willy-nilly. "I know of a much better place!"